The Difference Between Right and Wrong

A Novel

By Lindsey Brunette

To my 8th grade journalism teacher who told me I would absolutely be a novelist one day. It only took 25 years.

Content Warning

Hi Reader,

Thanks for being here! Just a quick heads up about some potentially triggering content you'll find inside:
- emotional manipulation by a potential romantic partner
- fragile male ego
- male on male physical violence (attempted)
- heavy drinking (circumstantial)
Or as one of my early readers told me to say: "This book contains men."

But I promise, everyone ends up happy in the end! (well, almost everyone...)

Happy reading!
Lindsey

1.

I never had a mantra. I have known women who swear by them: *'Today is the first day of the rest of your life!' 'Inhale the good shit, exhale the bullshit.' 'Live, laugh, love.'* But I was never into that kind of thing. I have never believed that positive thinking was enough to get me through any situation in life. I worked hard to get to where I am today: university, law school, long hours at the firm to pay my dues ... and now I am really wishing that I had one of those cheesy mantras to fall back on: *'Everything is going to be okay!' 'What doesn't kill you makes you stronger!' 'I am worthy, I am strong, I am enough.'*

"Ms. Graves, do you understand what we're saying?" asks Mr. Cruz, one of the law firm's top partners. I must be wearing the blankness of my thoughts on my face.

I whisper my understanding: "You're letting me go." No matter how hard I try, I cannot find the strength to *live, laugh, love* my way out of this situation.

"You're a phenomenal lawyer, Kenley," says Ms. Jackson, another of the partners. "The firm just hasn't bounced back the way we expected after the pandemic, and we have to look at ways to stay afloat. Unfortunately, that means that we can no longer afford the salaries of some of our more junior attorneys. We're letting some incredible lawyers go today."

All of the partners are here, which should have been my first clue. They never gather together for meetings with individuals unless it's for something big. Foolishly, I had thought that I'd finally put in the time and was going to get the recognition I thought I deserved. The last thing I expected when I walked into this meeting was to lose my job.

Looking out at the Downtown Los Angeles skyline, I try to muster the courage to speak; to thank them for the opportunity; to maintain my dignity and hold my head up high. Some of the windows in this building look west, and on a clear day you can see the Pacific Ocean, but the offices at Sullivan, Dunkirk, Jackson, Cruz, and Karjanian look east toward the smoggy, congested quagmire of Southern California, and the view doesn't do anything to evoke thoughts of *Today is the first day of the rest of your life!* Except that it is. Today is the eighteenth of August 2022 and it is the first day of the rest of my life. Where do I go from here?

They're still talking. About severance packages and reference letters and whatever else people talk about when firing someone from their dream job. I'm sure they'll give it to me in writing—they're lawyers after all—they know better than to rely solely on a verbal contract. There is nothing else that I need to hear right now; what they've said already has been more than enough. All I can think about is leaving. I've never felt so claustrophobic at forty stories up.

I have wanted to be a lawyer since I was nine years old. That was the year my family adopted my brother, EJ, out of foster care. My parents took my sister and me along with them to the adoption hearing, and when the judge declared that EJ was ours, I felt a kind of excitement and exhilaration that I had never experienced before or since. I knew right then that I was going to be a lawyer who helped families with adoptions, and I had been pursuing that dream ever since. Right up to a few minutes ago, when the partners at Sullivan and Dunkirk yanked the rug out from under me.

"Marie will give you a packet on the way out," someone says finally, indicating that they are done talking and that I will, in fact, receive everything in writing. I do my best to smile and nod politely as the partners each stand to shake my hand. The truth is, I have no idea what expression I am wearing. My face is completely numb, and

I know that what I am feeling is the opposite of *what doesn't kill you makes you stronger*. I don't want to be made stronger. I am plenty strong enough. If this is what makes me stronger, then I would rather that it kill me.

"Thank you all for the opportunity," I say. The power in my voice is striking and startles me a bit. I don't know where that poise is coming from.

I leave the conference room and head straight back to my office to begin the task of packing up the last seven years of my life into a twelve-by-fifteen-inch banker's box, and I do it with my head held high, which seems like a surprising choice. I can't seem to turn it off. Maybe my mantra is the slogan printed on the side of my favorite coffee mug: *I don't want feelings. I want tacos.*

"Drinks?" Luke asks as he comes through the door of my office carrying his own banker's box full of personal belongings. I can see his favorite USC pennant sticking up from the back, nearly hitting him in the chin as he walks, and reminding me of our hours spent cramming in law school to get us to this moment.

"No! You too?" I can't believe they'd fire Luke. He's the best lawyer I know, and I'm not just saying that because he's my best friend.

Luke and I met on our first day of law school just down the road at the University of Southern California. He was back in his hometown after completing his undergrad at the University of Oregon, fulfilling his family's legacy of producing only top-tier Beverly Hills entertainment lawyers, and I was doe-eyed and completely unprepared for my arrival in the big city from the town in the Midwest where I had spent my entire life. There was nothing about us that should have clicked, but I soon found myself spending every waking moment with Luke and our small group of friends. When Luke broke from his family tradition and chose to specialize in family law instead, we had both ended up as interns at Sullivan and Dunkirk, and our bond had only grown.

"And Marlena," he says, setting his box down on one of the chairs opposite my desk.

Just yesterday, a distraught foster mother had sat in that same chair, pleading for help in keeping the child she had raised since infancy. I had told her I would do everything I could. Now I wonder what will happen to her case.

"Damn." Marlena had started around the same time as us, though she was older and had already raised a family. She had decided to go to law school once her children were in high school, with a goal to work in immigration law. When her husband left her partway through her studies, she switched her focus to family law and served as her own lawyer in their divorce settlement. She had left him with nothing.

"It's bullshit," Luke says. I'm reminded to *inhale the good shit, exhale the bullshit*. "The three of us made this firm so much money in the last year."

That might be true, but it doesn't matter; decisions have been made.

———

"One white wine, one scotch on the rocks, and one vodka soda with lemon," Luke orders. My drink of choice is actually a vodka soda with lime, but Luke always orders lemon—insisting that it's the better citrus for the cocktail. These are the two people at Sullivan and Dunkirk that I had been closest to, so there is no one from work with whom I'd rather be drowning my sorrows, but it is still bullshit that we've all been fired.

"This is bullshit!" I echo Luke's earlier sentiments as we huddle around our high-top table. "It's a cop-out so that they don't have to keep paying us!"

A waitress sets our drinks on the table and I drink my vodka in one swallow, ordering another before she can walk away. The bubbles from the club soda burn my throat on the way down.

"Easy there, cowboy," Luke says as he, too, downs his drink. Marlena is more conservative with her glass of white wine, taking a small sip and setting it back down on the table.

"I don't know what I'm going to do," she says in a hushed voice. I wish I could offer Marlena a word of encouragement, but I don't know what I am going to do either.

"Did they say it the same way to you guys? That they can't justify your salary longer term?" Luke asks.

Marlena and I nod. When my second drink arrives, I know that I could down it just as quickly as the first, but I decide to take a play from Marlena's book and sip it softly instead. Like a normal person who hasn't just been fired from her job.

"I don't know what any of us are going to do. I mean, what firm is going to want to hire a lawyer who got fired?" I ask.

It is strange to think that I won't get up in the morning and drive into Downtown Los Angeles, that I won't buy coffee at my usual corner coffee shop before the sun has even fully ascended. The problem is that I don't have a plan B. I'd never had a plan B. This was plan A, and it had been working out until now. I didn't have a backup plan because I had never considered that I might need one.

"Fired ... I got fired," I repeat softly under my breath. The words themselves haven't exactly sunk in yet. I figure the more often I repeat them, the sooner I'll have to accept them. I have never been fired before. I'd never even been harshly punished for anything in my life. I had a five-year plan, a ten-year plan, a lifetime plan. Girls like me, with our life plans and our laser-focused drive, we don't get fired. But I got fired today. So, what kind of girl does that make me, really?

—————

"I'll get the next round!" I exclaim drunkenly. Marlena is gone—she'd left after her first glass—but Luke and I are still going strong. The plates of chicken wings and fries that we had shared has done little to sop up the liquor.

I should probably stop, we both should, but while I am clearly inebriated, I am also still able to tell you so, which means that I am not yet drunk enough to forget about losing my dream job. There is still a functioning logic center in my brain that needs more alcohol to drown it out. This is not usually like me, but it is the only solution that I can think of. Going home would be admitting my defeat, and that is not something that I am ready to do just yet.

"What I don't get," Luke says after I've ordered our drinks, "is why they'd give us each four months' worth of pay. That's a year's salary. They should have kept you at least, you were the best of us."

"If I was so good," I start loudly, and I am not sure how coherently, "then I wouldn't have gotten fired. But I got fired. You got fired. We got fired."

I step off my barstool and turn to face the room. "We got fired today!" I shout. A few people turn and look, but no one seems like they can be bothered with my life-altering news. I know then who would care and reach for my purse to find my phone.

"What are you doing?" Luke asks, putting his hand over the screen of my phone before I can unlock it with facial recognition.

"I have to call my mom, I have to tell her we got fired today," I slur.

"No, no, no, you can't call your mom now. You're drunk," he replies.

I stare at him hard as my drunk brain contemplates what he has so emphatically said. He is right, I can't call my mom tonight. Besides, in Illinois it has already passed the hour that my parents consider to be the acceptable cutoff for a phone call. Even once I've decided, though, I keep staring hard at Luke. He has been a good friend, with me through all of the ups and downs of law school and Sullivan and Dunkirk. I can't even begin to count the number of times we've eaten delivery sushi at our desks after hours, taking small, forbidden sips of the bourbon he kept in his bottom drawer. It is fitting, really, that I would spend my last Sullivan and Dunkirk night out drinking with Luke, since he had been my drinking buddy all along.

"I think I might have to call my dad," Luke says, breaking the silence of my intense stare. His dad is a well-known lawyer, but Luke has always refused to use his father's credentials to get work.

"I think ..." I begin, leaning in toward him across the table as if I have a secret, "I think we need shots." I don't want to talk about work anymore. I don't have a job, so there isn't any work left to talk about.

I get up before he can protest. Getting drunk had been his idea in the first place, and I know that if I go home, I am going to sit and dwell. Drunk Kenley is even more of a doer than sober Kenley, so it is likely that I will wake up to find that I have applied for seventy-five new jobs in places like Nairobi and Istanbul if I leave now.

Upon returning to the table with four tequila shots, limes, and salt,

Luke gives me a look. He doesn't hesitate though when I sprinkle salt on his left hand and put a shot in his right. I feel the room spinning as I take the second shot and sit back hard in my chair.

"Come here," Luke motions for me to lean back across the table. I have to grip the sides as I do and am surprised to hear him whisper, "You have a piece of lime on your cheek," before he leans in and kisses me just next to the mouth.

I haven't been kissed in ... I don't know how long. Two years maybe? I haven't had time to be kissed with the demands of my job. I haven't had time to go out. I used to try to see friends on weekends, but that was always structured around how much work I had brought home before those relationships had fizzled out altogether. Now I can't remember when I had last made time for a social life. Men don't exactly want to kiss workaholics.

I turn my head and smile coyly. Luke smiles back and then says something about how we should close our tabs, snapping me back to reality. Reality is, of course, the place where I feel the most comfortable, and so I am grateful to him for bringing me back.

As we walk outside, I notice how quickly the night has turned cool. The air offers a refreshment that allows me to steady myself on the sidewalk. I don't know where I am going to go. My car is still in the garage at Sullivan and Dunkirk, but I am in absolutely no condition to drive it. That's when Luke offers for me to come back to his place. It is only two blocks away and it is just nine o'clock. I'd been to his place before, of course, and always lamented that I stayed in my rent-controlled studio in Silver Lake when he had upgraded to a one-bedroom downtown. While at Sullivan and Dunkirk, you couldn't beat the commute.

We are standing on the corner, waiting for the walking man, when Luke leans over and kisses me again. For real this time, without any lime-pulp pretenses. He cups my face in his hands and gently lets his tongue explore my mouth. I let him because I am drunk, and also because he is Luke, my friend with whom I feel safe. But kissing him feels weird. It doesn't feel like anything ... shouldn't kissing feel like something?

Luke grabs my hand as we cross the street and holds it all the way to his front door, and he makes it clear that he thinks we need coffee. I had enjoyed the companionship of being kissed and having my hand held on what has otherwise been a lonely day, and it feels confusing when he lets go suddenly. Even if Luke is just my friend, it is nice to have my friend for comfort on a night like this.

Inside, he sets about making coffee while I find my way to the restroom. The neatness of Luke's place has always surprised me. I know him to be a tidy and organized person, but because he is a guy and this is his "bachelor pad," I always expect it to be in a bit more disarray. Of course, like me, Luke is almost never home, so there really isn't time to make an apartment feel truly lived in. I wonder how that is going to change now?

When I come out of the bathroom, Luke is sitting on the couch, scrolling through the list of streaming platforms on his television. I sit on the opposite end of the couch, still a little woozy, and semi-hug the arm. He settles on something and ever so slightly scoots closer to my end of the couch, where he puts his hand on my knee.

It's weird when you have known someone for as long as I've known Luke, and things have always been a certain way, and then one day they're not that certain way anymore. Has Luke always wanted this? Has he never made a move because we worked together? There still seems to be so much hesitation on his part—the kissing me in the bar and then pulling back and saying we needed to close our tabs, the holding my hand on the walk to his place and then being focused on making coffee. I don't move his hand because I don't mind it being there, but it comes with so many questions that I'm not sure I'm prepared to answer.

I notice him staring at me then. I look back and smile just before he leans in and kisses me again—and again and again and again. As we kiss, we reposition so that I am laying on my back against the couch and he is on top of me. He seems to want to explore every part of me, moving his hands, his mouth, everywhere in his quest.

If it has been two years since I've been kissed, it's been even longer since I've had sex. I had a boyfriend during my first year of law school, but we broke up because I couldn't handle him and my schedule both. But there haven't been many guys since. I could count them on one hand. That makes me wonder when was the last time Luke had sex, and how many women he's been with over the years. He's a good-looking guy, and though we'd worked the same hours, I know he had managed to date here and there—better than I had done.

"What's wrong?" he asks suddenly, pulling back from me.

"Nothing, tequila shots are making my mind wander," I say, gently pulling his lips back down to meet mine.

This is going to happen and I am going to be a willing participant, even if I'm not entirely sure what I feel.

This is the first day of the rest of my life.

2.

I wake up the next morning in Luke's bed with a serious headache and a huge desire to flee. I have made worse drunken decisions in my lifetime certainly, but I hadn't intended to muddy the waters with Luke by sleeping with him. I look at the clock: 8:35, which should be just late enough to get my car out of the garage under Sullivan and Dunkirk without running into too many former co-workers, as I am clearly wearing yesterday's clothes. Or I will be ... as soon as I find them. As I move to push back the covers, Luke stirs.

"Mmm, good morning," he says. In the morning light he has a sexy layer of scruff on his face, and it's hard not to look at him. Why have I never paid attention to how attractive he is?

The problem is that it would be easy to fall into a relationship with Luke. We've been friends for years. He's cute, smart, funny; he's everything I would think I'd be looking for in a man. And last night was ... exciting. The timing is wrong, though—my life has just been thrown completely out of orbit. Turning to Luke now would be no different than rebounding after a breakup, and I am not looking for a distraction right now.

"Hey," I say awkwardly, pulling the comforter up higher toward my neck. Even though he'd seen it all last night, I suddenly feel incredibly self-conscious about my nakedness. When he leans in to kiss me, I recoil. He seems taken aback.

"I should probably get going. I have a whole life to redesign," I lie.

"Okay ..." he nods very slowly. He seems confused, a little hurt even, as if our drunken tryst had meant something more to him than the comfort from another person that I'd been seeking. Had this been something Luke had wanted since before last night? No, I can't allow myself to go there. Not today. I have too much else to think about without complicating things with Luke, even if it is all just in my head.

"Last night was fun, but I just think that I need to regroup right now," I say as I find my clothes. My head pounds with every step. As if he knows, Luke gets up and hands me a glass of water and some aspirin, which I eagerly swallow.

As I walk toward the front door, Luke asks if he can call me later, and I'm pretty sure I say yes before darting out of the apartment and running for my life.

I don't stop running until I make it all the way to the street outside his building. Once I hit the sidewalk, I have to stop and catch my breath. Both because I've been running and because I need to make sense of what I've done. This is not me, losing control like this. As I stand on the street, hunched over with my hands on my knees, I realize I am crying. It is the first time I've cried since I received yesterday's news, and though these aren't the hard sobs I probably need to cry, it feels good to release that emotion.

Okay Kenley, I say rationally to myself, *let's start with the most recent thing and work backward. You slept with Luke, one of your best friends. Why did you sleep with Luke? A) You were wasted. But he didn't take advantage of you; even while you were wasted, you wanted it. So, B) do you actually like Luke as more than one of your best friends? You've never considered it, I know, because you couldn't—because you see him every day at the office. Though, now you won't see him every day. Does that change things? Would he be someone you would date? Maybe, on paper, but you can't go there right now. But C) if you make it clear to Luke that you can't go there right now, will that ruin everything? Can your friendship survive this? Because you need Luke's friendship, he's been with you through so much. So, what now?*

That is the question, of course: what now? I straighten myself up and reach into the inner pocket of my purse to find my phone, which is down to fifteen percent battery. Before I can talk myself out of it, I open up my messages and type one out to Luke:

Kenley: Sorry for running off. Last night was crazy. With everything that happened yesterday, I just need some time to think. Can we talk later?

Luke: Yes! Looking forward to it!

I am one of those people who says what they mean. I don't speak in metaphor or hyperbole, and when I don't know what to say, I panic and I run. Which is what I have done to Luke. In being one of these people, I expect the same from others. Do not beat around the bush, do not be coy, say what you mean. I don't have time to figure out whatever implications come along with your words. It would seem to me that it would be easy for Luke to just come out and say if he likes me. After all, he had initiated everything, from the invitation to get drunk to going back to his apartment. But then again, if I don't know how I feel, how can I expect him to know either? Life is never as black and white as I want it to be.

Coffee would help. I practically can't function without coffee, and here I am, almost two hours late for my first cup. Since I am still in the area of the office, I make a beeline for my usual spot. As I wait in line, I never consider my appearance. I had been concerned about the timing of getting back to the garage for my car, but never thought about the barista who had served me yesterday seeing me in the same clothes.

"Dang girl, running late today?" she asks. I smile politely as she writes my order and name on the cup without my having to say a word. "Wait ... I know that look. Good for you, girl!"

"Oh, haha, thanks. Yeah, crazy night!" I reply. I try to keep it nice while implying it is none of her business. But, in a way it sort of is her business. I had seen Shannon, the barista, almost every morning for the last three and a half years. I know that she is currently in school for fashion design and that she has a dog named Monique Lhullier. For Shannon to celebrate my alleged conquest is not outside the realm of possibility. Still though, I feel embarrassed that someone would see me like this.

Shannon gazes at me expectantly. Her look seems to say, *What is the story? Who is the guy?*

She has seen Luke in the store with me a few times before, and I know that this will be my last visit to this particular location, so I am honest.

Shannon is more excited than I expect her to be at the news. She'd been waiting for us to hook up. We make a totally adorable couple, she claims. I smile big and return her "totally." What does it hurt? I am never going to see her again.

Of course, the reaction of my barista gives me something else to think about that I haven't considered. What will people think if Luke and I somehow end up together? We'd taken pictures together before, during law school and at company events. I'd never paid much attention to what my friends or family had thought of those, because thoughts of Luke as anything but my friend had never crossed my mind.

With drink in hand, I finally head back to the garage, choosing to walk down the ramp rather than go inside the lobby to catch the elevator. If I am going to try this hard to avoid my former co-workers, I have to fully commit. So down the ramp I go, then to the stairs that lead down to the P2 level. I walk to my usual spot, except my car isn't there. Which is when I notice the posted sign for the very first time in all of my years of parking in this garage: NO OVERNIGHT PARKING.

I stumble, groping for the nearest wall and when I find it, I proceed to sit. Tears are coming again. My desire to remain inconspicuous in this garage is about to fly out the window.

Seriously, could there be one more thing?

I am sure I've seen the sign before, but I'd never paid attention because even though I worked long hours, I was out of the garage by no later than eleven p.m. Has my car really been towed? I can't find out here of course, there is no signal below ground to call the phone number listed on the NO OVERNIGHT PARKING sign. For that, I have to trek back up the stairs and climb all the way back up the ramp.

"Excuse me?" I tap on the glass of the manned pay station. A small Latina woman slides open the window, barely looking up from whatever she has been watching on her smartphone. "Hi, um, can

13

you tell me where they take the cars that get towed from this garage?"

"No. Call the number," she says, pointing to the sign on the window that shows the same number I'd seen downstairs. I thank her and step to the side to let a car, one with its driver still inside, come into the garage. I type the number into my phone and wait as it rings and rings.

"Hi, hello, I am trying to find where my car would have been towed to from the garage at 500 Hope Street in Downtown?"

It is an hour before someone can call me back about the location of my car. In the meantime, I sit in the back corner of a different coffee shop, next to an outlet where I am able to charge my phone, making lists on a notepad that I found at the bottom of my purse.

Lists help to calm me, and these particular lists are all related to my new five-year plan: firms I can apply to; other types of organizations that hire family lawyers; how to pay my bills; how to tell my parents I've been fired; things that make Luke dateable; things that make Luke undateable. The last two lists are the longest, because I can think of almost nothing else besides what happened between us last night. None of these lists have helped me reach any sort of clarity, either.

I am beyond exhausted, and finally no longer drunk, by the time my Uber delivers me to the lot where my car had been towed. It is already almost eleven fifteen, and I just want to go home. Nevertheless, I drag myself up to the window to pay the fee to get my car back. "Ignored posted signs" cites the tow report. I sigh. When I arrived at work yesterday morning, I had no idea that I would need to ignore the posted signs and leave my car in the garage all night. I'd never even realized until now that those signs posted all over the garage actually meant something. It had been towed at 2:03 a.m. as I had drunkenly slept just blocks away.

I wait in front of the office for someone to bring my car up, and I notice the large scrape on the driver's side before it has even come to a complete stop. That was certainly not there when I'd left my car the morning before. I'm not normally one to dwell on the negative, but for actual fuck's sake. I'm not going to ask again if one more thing can happen because I'm beginning to think that I would just be tempting the universe.

"S'all yours," says the technician, a boy who can't be older than twenty-one, as he climbs out of the driver's seat. He leaves the door open as if daring me not to mention the giant scrape.

"Thanks. But, um, this was not here the last time I saw my car," I remark, making exaggerated motions with my arms to point out the large yellow stripe and slight dent that go down the length of the car's side.

"We cannot be held responsible for damage or loss done to the vehicle," he quotes robotically. "You signed off on it at the desk."

I am sure that is true, I had to sign a lengthy document in order to reclaim the car. *Kenley, you are a lawyer. You can get out of this.* I am too tired and too hungover, though, to put up a fight. Besides, I have signed it and my argument would never hold up against that in court.

I climb into the driver's seat and close the door. The boy has moved far enough away and no one else is around, so I feel safe to finally let it out.

"HOLY FUCKING COCK SHIT FUCKING DAMMIT FUCK!" I scream, banging my fists on the steering wheel. The horn honks once. My job, Luke, the car ... what next?

With that out of the way, I feel a little more put together. As I pull out of the impound lot, I think back to the lists tucked safely into my purse: "how to tell my parents I've been fired" seems to be the only one that has any current relevance. And I kind of just want to talk to my mom after the day and a half I've had. It takes a few minutes though before I can resolve myself to dial the number.

"Hello, counselor!" my father answers cheerfully.

"Hey, Dad!" I say, trying to sound upbeat. If it had been my mom, she would have been able to tell that something was wrong, and then I would have broken down immediately. It is better to be able to talk to my dad first, leave the emotion out of it.

"To what do we owe this pleasure?" he asks me, feigning a quasi-British accent. He's already home from work, as he goes in most mornings before six.

I take a deep breath and then sigh, blurting: "The Law Offices of Sullivan, Dunkirk, Jackson, Cruz, and Karjanian are doing some restructuring and letting go of some junior staff."

My father is silent on the other end.

Even though my parents have vocalized their dreams of me growing up to have a family of my own, they've always been incredibly proud and supportive of my career goals. I know that they love all of their kids equally, but they'd always taken particular pride in my success because it was different from the routes taken by my brother and sister. My sister is a high school English teacher, but now that she is expecting, she isn't sure if she is going to go back to that —our mother had stayed home with us kids, and Jess has always had the same dream for herself. My brother is a personal trainer, he lives in town near my parents and has dinner with them every Sunday. I am the lone wolf, out in the world doing my thing—which happens to be a thing my blue-collar parents couldn't personally understand. Through all of my education, though, they showed their pride. My dad took me out for an expensive dinner on the night I got into law school, just the two of us, and spared no expense. I hate to disappoint them.

"Are you there?" I ask finally. The few seconds of silence are more than I can bear.

"They just let you know today?" he questions, his jovial tone changing to one not of disappointment but concern.

I can't tell him that it was yesterday. I can't tell him that they hadn't been my first call, that I had needed to wait to collect my thoughts—and also get completely hammered and have sex with my former co-worker—before I could call to tell them. The older I get, the more I realize that the things you keep from your parents aren't lies, they're just little acts of protection.

"Yes, I'm driving home with my things now," I say finally. The second part is true.

"Well, Ken, I'm really sorry to hear that."

I am a total daddy's girl, and knowing he is sad for me breaks my heart. My dad is the hard-working type. He'd met my mother at Illinois State University. A farm boy on a track and field scholarship, he majored in agribusiness because he had never known anything different. He'd made a great living for us, working his way up to senior management at a major pork distributor in our town. Over the years, though, I'd often wondered if it hit him that he could have done something else; did he ever realize that he didn't have to stay in the agriculture business? What he might have done if he'd figured that out in enough time. When I chose law as my profession, the pride he displayed when he told people about me—that said it all, really.

"I don't know what to do now. I mean, I haven't had time to think and process any of it," I say.

"You know our door is always open," he replies.

"Thanks, Dad. I know," I say as I merge into traffic on the 710 and point the car in the direction of my apartment.

It is true, and I do know. But what almost thirty-three-year-old woman wants to run home to Bloomington, Illinois and live with her parents at the first sign of trouble? No, I can take care of myself—I have been for a while now. Still, I have to think of something. If not for finding another job, I have to think of something to keep my mind off of Luke. I can't stop thinking about his kiss, and his touch, and the way he made me feel a little like I was lying there watching it happen to someone else.

3.

Luke: Dinner?

Luke's text woke me up from a nap that was verging on three hours. There is a missed call from him, too. I forgot that I had given him permission to call me.

Okay Kenley, think about this. You want to see him. You've been thinking about him all day. You have to eat dinner, and Luke is your friend. How many dinners have you had with Luke? One hundred. Maybe more. This will be no different. Okay, yes, none of those hundred dinners occurred after you slept with him, but it's fine. If you don't let it go there, he won't let it go there. You are in control of this situation. But what will he think if you accept? Does he want you to be his girlfriend? And if you accept this dinner invitation, will he think that you want that, too? Pay for yourself. Go stag. Don't treat it like a date, and he can't treat it like a date. You've got this.

Kenley: Yawn. Just woke up from a nap. Is it possible to sleep one's sorrows away? Dinner sounds great. I just need to grab a quick shower.

Luke: Hmmm... wish I was there!

His response is almost immediate but I don't reply right away because I need to stay objective, especially if we are about to discuss what happened last night. Instead, he sends the location of a restaurant in my neighborhood and the time to meet him, saving me from having to say anything at all about where he wishes he was right now. I honestly have no idea what I *would* say. Since when does Luke think of me in the shower?

What does a girl wear to her first dinner out with her best friend with whom she's just had sex for the first time? Do I go sexy, maybe tease a little? Or conservative and keep it all tight and buttoned up? I finally settle on a floral print maxi dress with sandals. It's true to myself, offers good body coverage, is flattering, and makes me feel confident. I might as well cover all of my bases. My hair, which I typically wear clipped back at the nape of my neck in a way that I had decided long ago was professional but unassuming, is still wet from my shower, and I decide to let it air dry into something that somewhat resembles sandy blonde beach waves, and that I hope say that I am trying without trying too hard.

Luke is already standing outside the restaurant when I arrive. I haven't thought about how he might greet me tonight—over the course of our relationship we've shaken hands, high-fived, and in more social settings even gone for the occasional hug. Sure enough, though, tonight Luke leans in for a kiss. It isn't a full-on attack, just a tasteful peck on the lips, but the public display of affection makes me blush and pull back a little anyway. I might have guessed that Luke would kiss me tonight, but I still wasn't prepared for it. This is not who we are together—the "us" that is Luke and Kenley are just friends.

"Shall we?" he asks, leading me inside. The restaurant he's chosen is a quiet neighborhood place where I used to meet up with my girlfriends for dinner and drinks back when I was still putting effort into my friendships. Each time we'd comment on how perfect this place would be for a date. The more time passes, the more convinced I become that that is exactly what this is—I am on my first official date with Luke.

"So, about last night," Luke begins after we've made appropriate small talk and ordered our meals, both declining the wine list for obvious reasons.

I can't help the guffaw that escapes my lips. I take a sip of my water and wait for him to continue but he doesn't. He looks at me with the same expectation, and I am suddenly grateful for the cliche he's used to break the ice.

"There's a lot of change coming at me all at once. You know that is not my strong suit," I say finally. "It's just … a lot to process."

Luke keeps his eyes on me as I speak, those piercing gray irises staring right into my dull brown ones in the way I know he always makes eye contact with everyone.

He had been one of the shining stars at the firm, known for his warmth and the kindness he showed even as he helped former couples through the complications of divorce. He made each client feel like the most important person in the world, which was different from my facts-based approach. "People underestimate the value of eye contact," he had told me once back in law school. He meant it, too—he looked into the soul of a person when he looked into their eyes. "I think he's lying," he had said more than once in meetings after a quick consultation with a client. Luke's eyes were part of what made him such a good lawyer.

"I could say something smooth about how I've wanted this for a while, but I don't know if that's true," he answers.

It is a relief, actually, to hear him say that. It answers some of my own questions, and having fewer things to puzzle over puts me one step closer to that feeling of clarity.

"I wish I had a plan," I say, changing the subject. I know it isn't the last of the conversation about what had happened between us, but I need to take that off the table for now. "I made some lists of my options this morning while I waited to find out where my car was being impounded."

He looks at me quizzically and I remember that there is a huge chunk of my day about which Luke doesn't know, so I regale him with the story of my morning: the barista, the parking garage, the list-making, the impound lot, the scrape on my car, talking to my parents … and in those minutes, it feels like I have my friend Luke back, like nothing has changed. In those minutes, I can almost forget that anything else has happened.

He doesn't mention our night together again during dinner, so I don't either, and it feels normal and good and right. I still don't know if I want to try to have Luke as more than my best friend, or if I think that could ever even work, but for a few minutes it is nice to think that it could.

In movies and on television, you see a woman wake up one day and suddenly look at her best male friend differently. It's like all of the sudden she just knows that she's been a fool and he's been right in front of her the whole time. I was hoping to find that same sensation here, that feeling of knowing with absolute certainty that moving forward like this with Luke was right—but I don't. I am still so unsure.

"I feel like I'm spinning round and round on a merry-go-round, just waiting for it to stop," I say as the check arrives. Luke reaches for it, but I'd made a promise to myself and reach for my purse anyway.

"No, I've got it," he assures me. Fine, let this be a date. Maybe that will help me to decide.

"Where'd you park?" I ask him. The night is young, but I don't want to be the one to imply that I'd like to spend more time with him, though I think that I would. After all, maybe spending more time with Luke on this real, actual date will help me to decide where I want things to go between us.

"I called a ride, but I'm not quite ready to go home yet. Want to take a walk?"

Relieved, I agree, and we head down the street. Luke holds my hand as we stroll through the familiar neighborhood. Tonight I let him because it is comforting, and because his hands are warm. We walk in silence for a while before he finally speaks.

"You know, they say alcohol is the serum of truth," he says.

I acknowledge his statement with an airy laugh through my nose, but I don't respond. I want to see what else he is going to say first.

"I think what happened last night, with the help of a little truth juice, was my heart's way of telling me what I want."

So that's it. He wants this. He wants me. I don't know how to respond. Truth serum or not, I still feel so confused. Luke is my best friend; he's smart and funny and yeah ... he's pretty easy on the eyes. But, there has only ever been one thing in my life that I had been certain I wanted, and I'm still reeling from having it ripped away. Had that only been yesterday? It feels like so much has happened since then. Adding my feelings of uncertainty about whatever is happening here with Luke makes everything feel even heavier.

"How can you be so sure of what you want?" I ask. I stop walking, unsure of how I could comprehend taking another step let alone contemplate anything else.

"Nothing is ever certain," Luke begins, "but I know that last night I finally got a chance with a woman I have admired and respected for years, and it felt good. And I do think that there is a chance that, yeah, this is what I want."

But why isn't anything certain, though? That is what I need. Absolute certainty.

Kenley, breathe. Do you like Luke? ... He's my best friend ... THAT is not the question. The question is: Do you like Luke? Here you are on a date with him, enjoying his company, even wishing the night wouldn't end, and yet you want finite answers that no one can give you. Take a breath. Do you like Luke in this moment? Take a breath. What about in this one?

By the time we reach my apartment, my breathing exercise has helped to squelch my panic, and I am certain that I know what I am doing when I invite Luke in. He has been to my apartment a few times before, but this time is different because as soon as our lips touch, I know that this is the first time he's been here like this.

It's sometime after two in the morning and I am wide awake. Luke is sound asleep in my bed, which is probably the reason I can't get my mind to rest. He seems so at ease here, and I feel so completely out of sorts. I've been drinking chamomile tea on the sofa for thirty minutes, willing it to usher in drowsiness. Instead, it seems to be having the opposite effect, sending adrenaline through my veins as I review the two lists scrawled out hastily on the notebook in my lap:

The pros and cons of Luke:

Pros:
- It's Luke
- You get along
- You're already best friends
- He respects and admires you
- He seems to know what he wants

Cons:
- It's Luke
- It could ruin your friendship
- So many unknowns
- There's so much I haven't done yet

There isn't much to put into the cons list that I can think of, and yet that is where my mind is fixated. I keep thinking about the last bullet point, the idea that there is so much I haven't done yet. I don't even know how that one got there, but it felt right as I wrote it down and it feels right now as I ponder the lists. If my pros list and the way Luke has been talking over the last forty-eight hours are any indication, then this thing with Luke is more than a fling, so what does that mean for the things I thought I'd do someday before I settled down?

I don't know what time I fall asleep, but when I wake up it's to Luke standing over me on the couch, holding my notebook in his hand.

"What are some of the things you want to do?" he asks. I would have expected him to be upset at finding that I had reduced him to a pro/con list, but I guess his calm demeanor is a testament to the fact that we have worked together for so long that he understands my process.

"Get a tattoo, go skydiving, to name a few," I say, almost without thinking. I didn't realize that they were already on the tip of my tongue. These were the kinds of things that lived in the back of my mind, but that I never thought I would do. I had always told myself that there would be time for those things later, after I had established my career. There were other things, too, things like getting married and having a family. I'd devoted my life as a lawyer to helping other families, but that hadn't meant I didn't one day want one of my own. It was because of family that I had gotten into this line of work in the first place. Just like with hurling my body out of a moving aircraft, I had always been waiting for the timing to be right.

"Do you think that being with me would stop you from doing those things?"

Did I think that? I don't think that was why I had written that on the cons side, but now I don't feel so sure.

"I think that what I meant by that was that giving into this feels like it would be giving into more than just right now, and I always thought that before I … gave into more than right now … there would be certain things I would have done," I say. It's vague, but I have a feeling that Luke understands.

"So do them," Luke says.

I am taken aback. I can't believe I'm having this conversation before caffeine.

"What do you mean?" I know what he means, of course. This is the most literal thing he has said to me in two days.

"Do them. If anyone is capable of doing the things they've always wanted to do, it's you."

Really? Is that how other people see me, too? Strong. Capable. Those are not words I typically used to describe myself. Driven, sure. Motivated, absolutely. Could I channel that drive into something else? Would pursuing these unspoken dreams be enough to sustain me? And what does that pursuit mean about Luke? If he's encouraging me to do these things, does that mean I've been wrong about his feelings and expectations?

"I'm not going anywhere, by the way," he says then. It's as if he can read my mind. "I'll help you if you want. My sister has a friend who is a tattoo artist, we could make an appointment this weekend. Or I don't have to help you. You just tell me what you want."

That has been the issue, hasn't it? My being able to tell him what I want? Instead of answering, though, I kiss him because it's the sweetest offer I've ever received.

"Do you have a condom?" he asks then, bringing me back to reality —still my favorite place, in spite of all of this recent confusion.

I don't. Of course I don't. I haven't had sex in years.

Luke curses. He'd only had the one and we'd used it last night.

I've had exactly four partners in my life, which is either a lot or very few given one's personal opinions. I am not a prude by any means, I just don't have time for dating, and I don't believe in one-night stands. I am fine with my number, and I've never been ashamed of any of my experiences … still though, I am very out of practice, and this whole idea of asking about prophylactics isn't in my vernacular.

"Sorry, I'll get some," I vow, as if I plan to have infinite amounts of sex with my best friend. It does us no good now, but they don't hurt to have on hand no matter what the future holds.

"We'll just go to my place next time," he says. Against my will, my heart skips at the thought of there being a next time.

"Like maybe … tonight?" he continues.

My heart races and I wonder if he can feel it. I can feel the heat in my cheeks, too. I kiss him again to avoid having to use my words.

"I like you," says Luke. I feel my heart pound in my chest, warmth rising up inside of me. I know what I am supposed to say back. I am supposed to say that I like him, too, and then we'll smile and kiss some more and probably end up having condom-less sex. But I know that I can't say what I am supposed to, not yet.

"What's going to happen?" I ask instead. He doesn't seem at all surprised by my question. Luke has known me for years, he knows how my mind works, and that even through all of the kissing, and the sex, my mind has been processing all of it.

"I don't know," he says. "But sometimes that's okay. We don't always have to know everything."

He's right, but even so, that doesn't make the idea of the unknown hurt any less.

4.

Think happy, be happy.

I can't remember the last time I was happy. I am afraid to admit it but it's true. I'd been so busy climbing the corporate ladder and chasing my goals that I had forgotten to work happiness into the equation. Well, that's not exactly true. I had made plans for happiness, but it was supposed to be the reward at the end of my journey. I figured that if I kept doing the next right thing and checking all of the boxes on my way to the top, that happiness would undoubtedly fall into place. Now I have no job, and no happiness.

I know that they say happiness is a choice, but that wasn't an idea that had ever made sense to me. It was far easier for me to swallow the idea of happiness if it was something I had to earn, if it was something after which I was chasing. Choosing happiness always felt a little bit selfish, to me. How dare I be happy without merit? And so, I can't remember the last time I was.

"Are you happy?" I ask Luke over dinner, our fourth in a row.

"In this moment? Or in general?" he replies.

"In general."

"Yes, I try to find something to be happy about every day."

"What about on days when there isn't anything to be happy about? Like, the day we got fired."

"Even on that day I was able to find something to be happy about," he says.

"You were?! What could possibly have made you happy about that

26

day?!"

"You," he says earnestly.

It's sweet, but it's not the answer I am looking for. I want someone to tell me exactly what steps I need to follow to be happy. I don't want to beat around the bush with any kind of allusive tips about an individual's personal happiness. I want the actual path to true happiness spelled out for me … or better yet, made into a list.

"Do you remember that day in law school when we drove to the beach and sat there saying nothing for three hours, until the sun had completely disappeared beneath the ocean?" I ask.

"I do. Torts was making us insane, and you said you wanted to run away," he answers.

"That was it, I think."

"What was?"

"That was the last time I can remember being happy," I say.

I don't know what it was about that night. There wasn't anything particularly special about that trip to the beach, but I can't remember a time since then that I have felt as happy as I did watching that sunset.

"That was a long time ago," Luke says. His face looks sad, but I don't detect an ounce of pity in his voice. It was a long time ago, but I think I had been too busy to notice. Everything had been going according to my plan ever since that night, and so I hadn't stopped to consider whether I was happy or not. I hadn't needed to check in because I figured I was chasing the reward, and that by the time I finally felt that feeling again, I would have earned it.

"I was happy that night, too," he continues after I don't answer.

"If I remember correctly, you were more than eager to run away that day, too," I say. "What did you choose to be happy about that day?"

"You," he says again.

Does that mean that he has been thinking about this for a while? He's right that that trip to the beach was a long time ago, and even back then he chose to find happiness in me. I don't want to read between the lines of this admission, but it is hard not to. If I made him happy at the beach all of those years ago, why hasn't he ever said anything? Why has he waited until now, a particularly bad moment for me, to finally express that I make him happy?

Every time Luke and I have a conversation lately, I am left with even more questions, when what I am looking for are answers. I don't know how I feel about being the cause of his happiness. He has been my friend for a long time, and our friendship has provided moments of joy, but I don't know if I would attribute those moments solely to Luke. It feels like a lot of pressure to carry the weight of someone else's happiness on my shoulders. I can't remember the last time I was happy myself, and yet I am expected to provide Luke with happiness, too? I don't know if I can do that.

The thought that I could choose something in every day to be happy about keeps me up all night as I try to think about the things that have made me happy over the last few days. When I start with the day I lost my job, it feels hard to look at my life in a positive light.

Okay, Kenley, think it through. Luke said that even on days when bad things happen, he can find one thing to be happy about. So, start at the top: what is one thing that happened on the day you were let go that made you happy? Go. ... Finding comfort and companionship in my friend. Okay, the next day you found out your car had been towed and it had a huge dent in the door. What is one thing that happened that day that made you happy? Go. ... My dad's support. Okay, the next day... My internal dialogue continues throughout the night.

Every single thing I can come up with over the last several days that has made me happy is something that I didn't have to earn. Finding comfort in Luke just happened, my dad's support was implied ... there wasn't anything that I had to do to earn those moments of happiness, and yet I still feel the need to convince myself that those weren't moments of *real* happiness. *Real* happiness is something that I have not yet completed enough life points to attain. Period.

Since I am awake anyway, I pull out my notebook, turn to a fresh page, and begin my next list. This notebook is full of lists, but somehow "Steps to Happiness" feels like the most important one that I have ever made:

1. Find something in every day that makes me happy
2. Do some of the things I never thought I'd do
   2a. Get a tattoo
   2b. Go skydiving
3. Find a job that makes me FEEL FULFILLED
4. Find "the one"
5. BE HAPPY

The key to being an effective list maker is to add things that you know you can easily check off. Since I had already begun trying to think of something from every day that makes me happy, I added it to the list so that I can already cross it off. It's a tactic that makes me feel more accomplished, even if slightly dishonest. Everything else on the list, though, feels daunting. But, at least with a list, I feel more equipped to begin.

5.

For every description you could come up with for Luke, his sister Lauren would be the exact opposite. Where Luke is solid and bookish, Lauren is edgy and waif-like. While Luke followed the traditional family career path of becoming a lawyer, Lauren had dropped out of college and now works as a model while playing gigs with her rock band, *The Smoke Alarms*, on weekends. Though the two couldn't be more different from one another, they have remained incredibly close. So, it's a no-brainer that Luke would call his sister to help me get my first tattoo.

"Yo!" Lauren calls out to us in an exaggerated, drawn-out way as we approach her on the Melrose Avenue sidewalk. It almost seems like a question, which is what makes me realize that Luke is guiding me gently with his hand on the small of my back. I immediately step away from him, but it doesn't do any good, Lauren has already seen it.

"Hey, Laur," Luke says, giving her a hug.

"Don't 'Hey, Laur' me, you fucking liar. 'Splain yourself!" she responds playfully, pulling away from their hug to look at me.

"Things have ... uh ... changed?" Luke offers with a sheepish grin.

"I'd say!" Lauren replies. "That's so rad!"

She's only a few years younger than Luke, but her language and lifestyle make it seem like there are decades between them sometimes.

"Hi Lauren, long time no see!" I chime in.

Lauren isn't exactly a stranger to me. I've interacted with her a few times over the years, particularly at the family holiday party that Luke has invited me to every year. That detail makes it sound like an intimate affair, but that is far from the case. It is the kind of party where everyone the family has ever met is invited, professional bartenders and caterers are hired, and I am pretty sure I have seen more than one celebrity roaming around the grounds of the estate. (Yes, estate. Luke's world is so different from my own.)

"Kenley! Oh my god, girl!" she exclaims, bringing me in for my own hug. "I have been waiting so fucking long for this."

"To hug me? Or?" I ask, playing dumb.

"Oh my god, you two are fucking made for each other. Ugh, I can't even stand it," she says.

The tattoo parlor is unsuspecting from the street. It has a simple colored awning over the door and a window that features a silver emblem and the word "Tattoo." I wonder if I've driven right past it before without even realizing it was here. There are a lot of places like that in L.A., I have found. You sometimes don't notice something is there until you start looking for it ... not unlike what has started to develop recently between Luke and me.

"Tony has owned this shop for years," Lauren is saying as she holds the door open for us. "He's such a fucking badass, he did both of my sleeves."

"Lauren, language!" Luke warns, though I know he's mostly joking.

"Oh god, prude!" Lauren laughs.

"TOOOONNNNYYY!" she bellows through the shop. I worry at first that she might startle someone, and I picture a tattoo needle slipping and making a permanent error on someone's skin. The lobby is decorated with images of tattoos, and samples of work. Lauren hands me a binder to browse while we wait.

I had tried to put some thought into what my first tattoo might be, but nothing had felt important enough. I want it to mean something, so that every time I look at it, I will be reminded of its very special significance to me. I have no ideas. Part of the reason I had never taken the plunge into getting a tattoo, though I had said that I wanted one for years, was because the very idea of being here terrifies me. It's not the tattoo parlor itself that is scary, but the idea of making a quick decision that is so permanent. I know that, ultimately, it's my fear of making decisions that has trapped me into my life plan for so long. If I just followed the plan I made for myself, then I would never have to make any decisions and risk finding out what would happen if I was wrong.

Tony isn't what I am expecting, though I am not sure what my expectation was exactly. He's a thin Latino man in his early thirties wearing a solid-colored t-shirt and jeans. He has a few tattoos on his arms, but nothing that screams "tattoo artist" to me ... not that I know what would scream that exactly. He asks me what I am thinking of, and when I admit that I don't know, he changes his approach.

"Do you have a mantra or a life motto?" he asks.

I can't help the laugh that escapes my lips.

"I've been trying to figure that out lately," I admit.

"Okay, well, I don't like to tattoo anyone who isn't sure ..." he starts.

"No! I'm sure I want a tattoo, I just need to think about what I want," I reply.

"How about: why are you getting a tattoo? Who is it for?" Luke prods.

"I am getting it for me, as a reminder that I am in control of my own life and destiny," I respond quickly. It is one of those answers that I couldn't have given if I had time to think about it, but in the spur of the moment, the truth comes out. As soon as I've finished speaking, Tony starts drawing. It only takes him a minute or so to show me a simple black bird. It's beautifully drawn and looks like it has been created by some fancy font system rather than by hand.

"I like that," I tell him, and he smiles.

"I'm thinking it means that you're finally ready to fly, like a little bird," he says. My eyes immediately fill with tears, and I know that it's right, and that I will have it placed on the inside of my right wrist for the rest of my life.

———

I can't stop looking at it. My wrist is all red and swollen, covered in plastic wrap and petroleum jelly, but even through the gore I still can't stop looking at it. Luke and I stop to get a drink at patio restaurant on Fairfax and I can't help but think that if I had time to do social media, this would be the perfect shot: my fingers wrapped around the stem of a wine glass filled with soft yellow liquid, and the little bird beneath it with a faded view of Luke in the background. It would be a snapshot of time, but not at all a picture of what my life looks like right now.

"What's wrong?" Luke asks. "You just started frowning. You don't hate it already, do you?"

"No, I love it. I'm just thinking about ... how this moment would be perfect, except for the fact that my life is falling apart," I say.

"Your whole life?" Luke asks, picking up my fingers and intertwining them with his. I feel my cheeks flush immediately, pulling my hand back. I am still not one for public displays of affection, even if we're in relative privacy at our own table on a nearly deserted sidewalk. I am still trying to wrap my head around the idea of the relationship I have had with Luke for so long changing behind closed doors, and so the idea of having that on public display is unfathomable. I still don't know how I feel or what I want to see happen between us. Maybe it's my fear of making decisions rearing its ugly head. Maybe I am so afraid of making the wrong decision that I am not allowing myself to live. But this feels different, this doesn't feel like I am being cautious for caution's sake. With Luke, there is something in my gut that is telling me that I just don't know.

"Well, you did one thing today that you've always wanted to do, so that's got to count for something, right?" he says after I don't respond.

I look down at my wrist again and smile. That's the thing I love most about my tattoo: that I finally got it.

6.

You are the author of your own story!

Or something. Am I? Really? I wrote my story when I was nine. The joy and excitement that I got out of the adoption hearing for my brother, EJ, changed my life. The way I saw it, my family's lawyer and the judge who made the adoption official were heroes. To top it off, that year my fourth-grade class was learning about Illinois state history, which would be nothing without mention of President Abraham Lincoln, a lawyer. I had figured out my life before I even hit double digits, and I'd never questioned that decision until now.

I don't know what it would look like to be the author of my own story. But getting my tattoo has gotten me energized. For the first time in the days since I was fired from my job, I feel like I can breathe. Feeling like I have control over my immediate future is helping more than I could have anticipated.

Becoming the author of my own story feels especially daunting when I've never applied for a job before. I had submitted internship applications back in law school, and that's how I had ended up at Sullivan and Dunkirk, but I've never conducted a real job search in my life. I need a new job, but when it comes to finding work, I don't know where to start. I've submitted a few applications online, including one at a nonprofit supporting foster kids that kind of sounds like it was made for me. They had reached out almost immediately to schedule a phone interview, and I've been dying to tell someone about it.

"I called my dad," Luke says before I get the chance. We are sitting in his kitchen eating Indian food from one of my favorite restaurants near our former office.

"How did that go?" I ask, already knowing the answer. Luke is going to get a job at his father's high-profile firm, and that will be the end of the discussion. It had been written in the stars all along; it's a wonder he has managed to evade it for so long until now.

"I can start whenever I want," he says. I can sense there is something else he wants to say but has stopped himself. I am not at all surprised to hear about his quick job offer. He has it much easier than I do in that regard.

"And so can you," he finally finishes.

I set down my fork and looked at him. We hadn't discussed this possibility. It doesn't feel much like being the author of my own story to have Luke working to get me a new job, especially without my consent. But then again, getting a job at another law firm after termination is almost impossible. It's a development that I had not seen coming, and it sits wrong with me.

"I know we hadn't talked about it, but my dad knows that you're important to me and he offered. I told him I would mention it, that's all," Luke says, defensively. He is trying to recover, though I'm sure he doesn't know what he did wrong exactly.

I push back from the table and stand. Luke's apartment is in an old bank building that had been converted into apartments after years of disuse. I find a spot on the industrial brick wall to focus my attention, turning my back toward Luke and the table. I'm not mad exactly. This would solve a lot of my problems, and Luke has to know that, too. It solves a lot of my problems, except for two. One being Luke himself. If I were to go to work at his dad's firm, we would be colleagues again, just as we're starting to figure out whatever it is that we've become. Two, now that my list consists of the task of finding a job that leaves me feeling fulfilled, I'm not sure I want to work at a law firm anymore at all.

"I didn't think it was such a bad idea," Luke says then, coming up behind me and placing his hand on my hip. I shudder at the contact, like my body is physically repulsed at the idea of Luke touching me, but he doesn't seem to notice. "We already know we work really well together."

He leaves a trail of kisses down my neck as he says this, and an involuntary giggle leaves my lips. Despite my body's initial reaction to his touch, I am tempted to melt into him even though there is so much I still need to figure out. These conflicting feelings are part of the problem in all of this for me. I just want to feel sure one way or the other. Instead of melting, I turn to face him, so that my face is pressed close to his, and I can feel his breath on my skin.

"It's not a bad idea," I concede. "I just ... don't know."

Admitting I don't know something is the most vulnerable I can be. I pride myself on what I know, I often use knowledge as a crutch. Luke must know this about me, too, we've known each other for so long.

"So, when are you going to start?" I ask, changing the subject. He releases me from his arms and turns away before he answers.

"I don't know..." he says with the same kind of uncertainty that I have been feeling, and it catches me off guard.

I have known for years that Luke didn't want to work for his dad. He doesn't like his way of doing business and wants to feel like he is making a difference in the world. But, when he had decided to call, I figured he had finally made peace with it.

"I thought you'd be relieved to have an offer," I say.

Luke sighs. "It feels like I am taking the easy way out. Running to Daddy because I don't want to do the work on my own."

It *is* a little bit like that, but I don't say that to Luke. Instead, I reach for his hand and hold it in my own to try to offer some of the same comfort he has provided to me in my uncertainty.

"What are you going to do then?"

"First I want to take a break. I have been working straight since law school. It's not like his offer is going to go away," he says. "What are you thinking?"

"I'm thinking that I don't know if being a lawyer is everything I thought it would be," I pause, returning to my spot at his small dining table. "I thought that helping people with adoptions would give me so much joy, like I had felt when we adopted EJ. But instead of feeling joyful, I just feel tired all the time."

"What about that British television host and his American wife who you helped? I thought you loved getting to help them start their family," he says. He's referring to Sam and Molly Collins, some of my favorite clients. Sam had several potentially hereditary illnesses in his family and was afraid of fathering his own children, and so the couple had decided to adopt.

"Yeah, they were great," I say. "But they moved back to England, they weren't in L.A. for very long."

"There must be others," Luke prompts.

I sigh. I have worked with some amazing people and have helped build some awesome families, but so much more of my job was about paperwork and bureaucracy than it was about the people.

"Are you telling me that helping people end their marriages has made you happy every day since you passed the bar exam?" I ask him instead of continuing with his line of questioning.

"Well, no," he says. "But that doesn't mean that I don't find my job fulfilling."

"I'm happy to hear that, truly. I just don't know if I can say the same."

Even with all of my doubts, it's comforting to know that I have a job offer on the table. Knowing that I have a firm that will take me on gives me some time to figure things out before I start to feel stressed. Maybe, like Luke, I just need a break and will find that I miss being a lawyer. And if that happens, then I know that I have a job that is waiting for me whenever I want to take it. It's just not a job that excites me as much as the one at the nonprofit had.

"I had an interview today," I say after a moment of silence.

"What? That's amazing! Why didn't you say anything?" he asks.

"I didn't get a chance," I answer, trying not to sound bitter.

"Well tell me more. What firm?" he asks.

The excitement in his voice is a thousand times bigger than when he'd been talking about his job opportunity. As I tell Luke about the nonprofit and my phone interview, though, his excitement visibly wanes. It catches me off guard, because I had been so happy about it that I hadn't imagined anyone feeling differently.

"Is there money in that?" he asks.

"Well, they're not looking to hire a pro bono lawyer. It's a general counsel position and I would earn a salary," I say. "But I kind of like the idea of having a job where I can actually do some good with my law degree instead of thinking about money."

"Kenley, you need money. Have you even given it that much thought?" he continues with his questioning in a way that makes me feel uncomfortable.

I am not a stupid person. I placed near the top of my class in both high school and college. I'm educated and well-read and I don't appreciate having the concept of earning a living mansplained to me by anyone—let alone by my best friend turned lover.

"Luke, chill," I admonish him. "It was a preliminary phone interview, it's not like I have signed a contract. I am just feeling really burnt out and I am intrigued by the idea of doing something different. And if the way you talk about working with your dad is any indication, then maybe I am onto something after all."

Luke sighs and runs his hands down his face. "Come on, Baby, I don't want to fight," he says.

I am too annoyed at his prior insinuations to nitpick the pet name. If I had been less annoyed by the situation, then I might have given him a lecture on the infantilization implied through the use of the term "baby"—it's so condescending. I don't need him to take care of me because I am *not* a baby. I am a grown woman who can do what I want with my own life.

"I don't want to fight, either. I would just like for you to be a little bit supportive that I am exploring my options," I reply.

"I am supportive. I am just thinking of your plan, and I don't want you to sideline your dreams because of one bad experience," he says.

I could let this make me angry, but I know that deep down, Luke believes he's being helpful. For our entire friendship, I have been obsessed with my plan. I have been on an upward trajectory in pursuit of my goals, and to the casual observer, it could, indeed, seem like I am giving up everything that I have worked for.

But honestly, what kind of person follows the life plan that they made when they were nine? I don't know why no one ever stopped to question me or ask if I was sure that becoming a lawyer was still what I wanted to do with my life. However, I know that if they had, I would have been adamant in my reply that yes, I was going to be a lawyer and there was nothing anyone could do to stop me.

What else would I have done with my life? I did mock trial in high school, majored in political science in undergrad, got a 170 on my LSAT, and went straight into law school after my college graduation. Law is my only polished skill, and I am good at it. But losing the job I had dreamed of having might be a blessing in disguise. Without that jolt to my system, I might have never stopped to consider what I want for my life, and I can't let Luke, my nine-year-old self, or anyone else stand in my way.

7.

When I had first moved to California for law school, there had been nothing that I wanted more than to return to Illinois. It was ironic because I had been so desperate to leave the Midwest, and so I often kept my feelings of homesickness to myself. As time passed, though, I made friends and became acclimated to my life here. Eventually I became so busy that I typically only made it home once a year, around the holidays, and rarely had time to think about the town I had lived in from birth.

Looking back on it now, Bloomington, Illinois was a great town in which to grow up. While I lived there, though, I couldn't wait to leave. To hear my parents tell it, I *did* leave home for college ... to attend Illinois State University in the neighboring town of Normal. But, until I started applying for law schools, I had pretty much been in the same place all of my life. None of the law schools to which I applied were even in the state of Illinois, and I had ranked my desire to attend them by their distance from home. That's how I ended up in Los Angeles.

Now that I am suddenly not as busy as I was when I was working, the pull of home has been attracting me like a magnet. It would be so nice to sit in my parents' kitchen, sipping my mom's coffee. I long for the ease of popping into a chain restaurant for a quick dinner with my brother or sitting with my dad while we read the newspaper together (he's one of the only people I know who still gets the physical paper). All of a sudden, the nearly two-thousand miles between my original hometown and my current one feels a lot farther than it has in a long time.

"What if I came home for a week?" I hear myself asking my mother before I can give it a second thought. My sister's baby shower is coming up, and I hadn't thought I'd be able to attend because of work, but without that obstacle, there is no excuse. With the newfound revelation that I have nothing but time on my hands, going home to attend the shower seems like the perfect opportunity to get my head back on straight.

"We would love to have you," she says. "I'm glad to hear that you're taking a little bit of time to regroup."

I imagine that while her words remain calm, she's doing her happy dance at the mere mention that I might come home. My mom has always been a big proponent of letting us kids do our own thing, after feeling like she struggled with autonomy in her own upbringing. She never puts pressure on us to do what she wants us to do, but there's this way that she shuffles her feet when she is excited about something that always gives away when we've made a choice that pleases her.

"Is that how Dad feels, too? I feel like I'm letting him down by not getting another job right away," I confess. I get my workaholism from my dad. In our family working oneself to the point of exhaustion is what has been modeled for us, and it is hard to imagine living my life any differently.

"Actually, Kenley, you'll be surprised to know that your dad is very proud of you no matter what you do. He's worried over the years that you were too careful, too cautious, maybe because of the things you saw us go through when you were a child. He's been worried that you'd never take a step outside your comfort zone," she tells me.

"Well, he's not wrong," I reply. It's true, except for that one thing with Luke ...

"Perhaps not," she says diplomatically. "Anyway, he'll be delighted to have you, and I think he would agree that the break will do you some good."

My mom is a straight-shooting, lifelong farm girl. She grew up in Southern Indiana and met my dad in school at Illinois State. Her dream for getting out of town was to be a teacher, and she was for a while, until I was born, and she decided to stay home. Once I was in kindergarten and my sister was in preschool, she had gone to work as a tutor at a children's home in a nearby town. That's how she met EJ. He was four when he became ours, and I still don't think I've seen a more adorable four-year-old, with his tiny mop of black curls.

"Ken, you know I just want you to be happy," she adds for good measure.

The first question I am always asked about my name is what it is short for—my answer over the years has become: "Oh, nothing, it's just my name!" My Memaw, my maternal grandmother, had grown up Emmaline Kenley. She was an only child, and her father was the only son in his family, which means that the Kenley line ended with her. So, the name was passed down to me as a way to carry it on in at least some way. Because it is unique, I have always liked it. I've never met another Kenley in my life. And I always thought it was silly that my parents turned around and named my sister Jessica.

"It will be good to be home, it's been a while," I admit.

"We're excited to have you, I just wish it was for a bit longer," she replies.

"I'm coming for a week!" I laugh out loud.

"Kenley, someday when you have children of your own, you'll understand that there is never enough time in the world to spend with them," she says.

I am surprised by the knot that forms in my throat immediately.

Though I've been trying not to think too hard about what a future with Luke might look like, last night I dreamed that we had a baby: a little girl with brown pigtails and rubber-band arms. I woke up from the dream in a cold sweat, wondering what message I was meant to glean from it. My mom's comments put her little face right back into my mind.

She has dropped these kinds of hints often over the years, subtle digs that let me know that she wants me to have a family of my own. I had hoped that these gentle nudges might cease, or at the very least relax, when Jessica announced that she was finally giving my parents a long-awaited grandchild, but I can see now that my hope

42

had been in vain.

"I'm sure I will," is all I say in reply.

I want that for myself, too—I always have. I just figured there would be more time. I am only thirty-two, and the promise of being made partner had lingered over my career for so long that I thought if I could just wait until then, the timing would finally be right to meet someone and start a family. That was my plan, as silly and half-baked as it seems now.

"Well, it will be so nice to have you visit!" my mom says then, pulling me out of my thoughts. "Are you going to tell Jess about the shower, or are you hoping to surprise her?"   I hadn't given it much thought. "Is it wise to surprise a pregnant woman?"

My mom laughs and says she was sure that this surprise would be a good one. So, before I hang up, I tell her I will think about it and let her know. In the meantime, I have a lot of other things to think about, too.

Knowing that my parents have my back does wonders to put my mind at ease. Although I haven't lived near them for a decade, something inside of me still desperately wants to make them happy. Maybe that's because I am the oldest child, and also a woman, but my people-pleasing tendencies definitely started with my parents, whether they intended it or not. Hearing that I don't need to do anything to have their love and support lifts a weight off my shoulders that I didn't know I'd been carrying.

8.

A house is made of bricks and beams, a home is made of hopes and dreams.

I can't remember where I heard that quote, but it's all I can think about as I open the letter from my landlord letting me know that I have sixty days to vacate the apartment where I have lived for seven years because they are intending to sell to a developer. As a lawyer, I know that the legal jargon hidden between the lines is that the building will be torn down so that a luxury building can be installed on the site. These structures are going up across Los Angeles and are doing nothing to help the rising costs of rent or to aid the growing homeless population.

"You have got to be fucking kidding me," I say to myself, slamming the letter down on the counter.

As if there was one more thing that I needed to deal with at the moment. First my job, then Luke, my car, and now this. I feel like I cannot win, but I am determined not to spiral. I am trying this new thing where not everything that happens becomes the worst thing to ever happen. It's not good for my mental health to lose my mind over every little thing. And honestly, with everything I've experienced lately, it feels like I am somehow prepared for the universe to keep hurling shit at me like some cosmic chimpanzee in the sky.

Instead of spiraling, I take a deep breath and calmly fold the letter. All I can do is think about this latest mantra ... this apartment has been nice because my rent has hardly increased over the duration of my tenancy, but it really is just a bunch of bricks and beams. So often I have lamented that this tiny studio never felt like home, that it was just temporary until I had time to find something bigger. But until now, I hadn't had the time.

Even in the nearly two weeks since I had been let go, I have hardly spent any time at home. Until two days ago, I'd spent almost every night at Luke's, wondering what I was doing and why I was there. The best answer that I had been able to come up with was that it had been something to do, rather than sitting in my tiny apartment burrowing deeper and deeper into a hole of sadness. After the way Luke made me feel when I told him about my job interview, though, I had decided that being in my tiny apartment was infinitely better than whatever that was ... until I checked the mail. It's almost enough to make me want to change my mind. But I quickly shake off the thought. The whole reason I am having doubts about Luke in the first place is because he doesn't seem to want me to solve anything for myself, and this latest situation of needing to find a new place to live gives me the opportunity to do just that.

Kenley, think about your list. This could be an opportunity to change your circumstances by changing your surroundings. You haven't been happy in this apartment for a while. Now is the time to make a change and finally start living like a grown-up. Just think: a bedroom that isn't also your living room! A kitchen where there is room for a table! This could be perfect!

It could also be very not perfect, but I don't have time to think about that. Instead, I reach for my notepad and start making a list of my housing options, which basically boils down to where I want to live and my must-haves in my new home. Lists generally help keep me from spiraling because they are something over which it feels like I have control—they help me to feel like I have a plan.

When I was a kid, my mom would always throw around this expression: "You have to make a plan and work the plan." It is, undoubtedly, the reason I am a planner as an adult. But it's also probably the reason that I made a plan for my life when I was a mere child that I have continued to abide by until recently. I know my mom meant well … and what it does help me to do is to figure out in less than an hour how I am going to fulfill the request to vacate my apartment in sixty days.

By the time I go to bed, I am feeling pretty good about my prospects.

———

I don't tell Luke about my plans. I have long referred to him as my best friend, and yet it doesn't feel like something I can tell him, which I know should tell me everything that I need to know about the decision I have to make. I haven't seen him since the night he disparaged my job interview, though we have exchanged messages and kept up a friendly banter. Every time I respond to one of his messages, though, my stomach ties itself into a bigger knot of anxiety because it just feels wrong. So, when he calls me the night after I've made my game plan, I hesitate to answer.

"Hey," he says once I finally click the green button to accept his call. I can hear relief in his voice. "I thought you might have been avoiding me."

He's not wrong. Still, I say, "I'm not avoiding you."

"So, how are you?" he asks, as if it has been longer than a couple of days.

I am so used to Luke being my friend and to not having to think twice before I tell him something that I immediately tell the truth … or at least part of it. "Well, I just found out that I have to move out of my apartment within sixty days," I say.

It's not until he starts trying to offer solutions to my situation that I regret sharing it with him.

"Thanks, but I've got a plan," I say.

"Yeah, but it's been a while since you've looked for a new place. I just don't want you to end up being taken advantage of because you're a woman," he replies.

When I first moved to California, I was admittedly a bit naive to life in the big city. Since Luke had grown up here, I leaned into him a lot to show me the ropes and help me find my own footing. I accepted his advice throughout law school because I was so busy learning how to be a lawyer that I didn't feel like I also had time to learn how to be an Angeleno. As time went on, though, I had settled into L.A. and built somewhat of a life for myself … but Luke's advice hadn't stopped. I think I had mostly tuned it out because I don't remember noticing it until recently. If I think hard enough, though, I remember other times when he doled out his life tips whether I wanted to hear them or not. Like when I decided to take this studio instead of looking for a one bedroom, or when I was shopping for my current car. Luke, it seemed, was somehow an expert on everything just as I found myself in need. Suddenly I am recognizing how damn annoying it is.

"Did you need something?" I ask then. He had called me after all.

"Oh, I, um," he stammers. "No, I … do I need an excuse to call you?"

"Well, you've never really called me before, so…"

"That's because we saw each other every day at the office. It's weird not seeing you every day. I miss you," he says. This would be the perfect time for me to say that I miss him, too, but that would be a lie, at least in the way that he means it. So I don't say anything.

"When can I see you again?" he asks after I don't take the bait. I know he means when can we have another date, or more accurately, when can he take me back to bed. But I do need a favor.

"Well, on Saturday I have to take my car in for repairs on the door and I have to leave it with them in Glendale, so maybe you can meet me at the shop and then give me a ride back home?" I offer.

I hate asking for help, even from my best friend. If there is something that I can do on my own, then I am going to try to do that thing. I had planned to take an Uber so as not to be an inconvenience to anyone, but if Luke agrees then it could help us both: he'd get a chance to see me again and I would save money on getting home. Still, I am surprised that I found it in me to be so forthright in asking him. Normally this would be the kind of request that I would have to rehearse for days in order to cover all of the possible ways in which rejection could come. I am equally surprised by how quickly he agrees.

"Of course!" he replies. "That's no problem at all! Maybe we can go to the Galleria after, I haven't been there in ages!"

It's not that I ever expect anyone to tell me no when I do need to ask for help, it's just that I pride myself on being self-sufficient and not needing anyone else. To be honest, even though I'm not necessarily expecting people to say no, I am always a little bit surprised when they say yes. Luke saying yes, though, gives me two days to prepare for seeing him again. That preparation is honestly what I need right now more than anything. I don't think that's how it is supposed to be ...

9.

Bringing Luke to the auto shop was a mistake. The mechanics won't even look at me, preferring to direct all of their recommendations about *my* car to him. As if I am not the one who set up the appointment, confirmed the appointment, and arrived by driving the vehicle to their shop. My dad had raised his girls to know a thing or two about cars, which I could almost guarantee is a thing or two more than Luke from Beverly Hills knows. All I can do is roll my eyes. The misogyny of the world doesn't surprise me, but it never ceases to make me angry.

"So, we're going to need to replace the door," the mechanic tells Luke.

"How long is that going to take?" I ask.

"I have a few cars ahead of you, so I should be able to get it done in a couple of days," he says, addressing his "you" to Luke.

"Okay, and what will that cost?" I ask.

He runs some numbers on a calculator and turns back to Luke, who puts his hand up and speaks before the man has a chance to. "Look, buddy, you need to talk to my girlfriend. This is her car and her money," he says. Although I appreciate the chivalry, his offhand use of the word girlfriend makes my blood run cold.

It takes a few minutes to finalize the transaction with the mechanic, and by the time I climb into the passenger's seat of Luke's car, I am feeling a mixture of anger and frustration and confusion. Suddenly the sexism of the mechanic is the last thing on my mind.

"So, do you want to go to the mall? Or back home? Or ... what?" Luke asks when he sees how intently I am staring at him.

"Are you serious right now?" I ask.

"I feel like that's a trick question," he says after a short pause.

"Are you really going to call me your girlfriend to a random mechanic and then pretend like it is nothing?"

He doesn't respond right away, suddenly becoming intensely focused on the road. We drive in silence for several minutes, to the point where I almost want to scream before Luke finally speaks up.

"It's not nothing," he says softly. "It's ... something."

"Something?" I ask. Maybe Luke knows me too well. He is choosing his words carefully so that I can't misconstrue anything he says.

"It's something that I've been thinking about," he says. "It's something that I want."

"And you didn't think that maybe you should run it by me first before you tell some stranger?"

As if I wasn't already confused enough about Luke and his sudden interest in planning my life without consulting me, this adds a whole new layer to my dilemma. Getting me a job at his dad's firm is one thing, because I need a job, but telling people I'm his girlfriend without even talking to me about it first is something else entirely. How am I supposed to be the author of my own story if Luke is trying to write it for me?

"Can you take me home, please?" I ask. I don't want to let Luke decide how I'm going to spend my afternoon on top of everything else. Maybe it's petty of me, but I want this one small thing.

I am grateful that the distance between our stops is short because I don't want to have to spend time trying to think of small talk. Really, I don't want to talk at all. I want to sit and seethe in silence until I am safely inside my private abode where I can at least attempt to figure some things out.

"I'm sorry," he says, pulling to a stop in front of my apartment building. He looks like he wants to say more but stops himself when I don't respond to his apology.

"I just ... need some time to think about things," I say.

"Can I call you later?"

"How about I call you when I'm ready to talk," I say instead. I need the control here. That is what this is all about in the first place.

"Um, yeah, whatever you need," he says, hopefully.

I don't offer a hug or kiss goodbye. I don't want to add any levels of confusion for either one of us. Instead, I gather my belongings and climb out of his car, giving a small wave before climbing the steps to my building.

Am I overreacting? I ask myself once I am safely inside my apartment. It's stuffy and dark. I'd left the curtains closed, hoping to block out some of the sunlight which is known to heat up the apartment like a furnace. As I flip the window air-conditioning unit to the on position, I can't help but long for the comfort of Luke's high-rise apartment with its central HVAC system.

No. You're not overreacting. Since you first started sleeping with Luke, has he let you make any choices for yourself? No. Where to eat dinner, whose apartment to sleep at, where you should work, even where you got your tattoo. Those are all things that Luke has decided for you, my inner voice tells me. *What do YOU want?*

Truth be told, I have never considered being Luke's girlfriend. Maybe that makes me seem like a little bit of a whore, but I was never looking that far into the future. For the first time in my life, I had been living in the present moment, and the present moment included hooking up with Luke for instant gratification without expecting anything out of it. I know that's not fair to him, but until today I genuinely didn't realize he was even thinking that way about me. It's just that Luke was there at a moment when I was seeking comfort, and I used the convenience of having him close to my advantage.

When it comes down to it, though, I want to be the one who decides my future. I don't want to go with whatever seems easiest and most convenient. I want to work for it. I want to find my own job, and I want to decide who I will call my boyfriend. I know I can't control everything. Lord knows that recent events have shown me that is true, but I want to be able to have some control over my future.

"Do you think I am a control freak?" I ask my sister that night on the phone. We are less than a year and a half apart in age, and we have often butted heads over the years. I was always the goodie-two-shoes perfectionist, while Jessica toed the line of rebellion a bit more than I did. As we grew into adults, though, we have grown into a mutual love and respect for one another that some might not have seen coming when we were younger.

"Do you want me to answer that honestly?" Jess laughs. I can't help but chuckle, too; I already know the answer.

"I'm doing a little bit better with that," I say. "Things are pretty much out of control right now, and I'm not spiraling. Well, maybe I'm spiraling, but it's like … spiraling off the backyard pool diving board instead of the Olympic high dive."

"What's going on?" she asks earnestly. It is unlike me to call my sister without having it one hundred percent together.

"I kind of started seeing my friend Luke …" I begin, regaling her with the whole ordeal of the firing, the drinking, the sex, and everything that has followed. As I listen to myself talk, it sounds like I am telling someone else's story. These words sound so unlike me, and I wonder how old you have to be to have a midlife crisis.

"Oh my god, I love that you are coming to me for advice about a boy!" Jessica is giddy. It's a true reversal of roles. I can't even remember the number of times before she got married that Jess vented to me about this guy or that one. She's right that this is the first time I have ever come to her for one of these conversations.

Everything is different for Jessica now. She was wild in high school and college, but after she graduated, she'd gotten her teaching job and met her husband at work, where he coaches the school's baseball team. I had thought she was crazy for getting married at twenty-six, with so much life ahead of her. When it came to her own circle, though, Jess had felt like she was behind. She was one of the last of her college friends to tie the knot and she had felt like the world was moving on without her. I was relieved, at least, that she decided to wait a few years before having kids. I think it's because she knew that it was likely she would become a stay-at-home mom and wanted the chance to teach for a few years longer. She got pregnant at thirty, and now, at thirty-one, she is about to become a mother for the first time. It is so bizarre to think that in a couple of months, I will be an aunt.

"I just … am I overreacting, do you think?" I ask.

"I don't know," Jessica says thoughtfully.

"Ugh, that's not helping, Jess!" I exclaim. We both laugh.

"You've been talking about Luke for years, and I'm honestly surprised that you just now got together," she says.

"Really? Why does everyone keep saying that?" I ask, thinking of Lauren's reaction to seeing us together for the first time.

"I've heard the way you talk about him," she says.

"What does that mean? He's been my best friend since law school, how else am I supposed to talk about him?"

"It sounds like even though you just started seeing him, he might have been thinking about it for a while. I mean, I can ask Tanner, if you want a man's opinion," she says, offering her husband's listening ear.

"I just think that maybe he's ready for it to be serious because it's already something he's been thinking about, whereas it is completely new to you," she continues.

"So, what am I supposed to do?" I ask her, hoping that she'll have the exact right answer.

The answer she gives, though, is wildly unsatisfying. "Figure out what you want, I guess."

"Yeah, that's the problem," I say quickly.

Jessica is quiet for a minute on the other end and I wonder if she's still there.

"Honestly, Ken, if this has been going on for a few weeks and you're still not sure, then maybe it's not right," she says.

I can hear in her voice that she is almost afraid to be honest with me. Knowing that she has more that she wants to say, I don't respond.

"If this was just some guy that you met on an app or at a bar, you wouldn't give him this much of your time if you weren't sure. If you don't know at this point if you can see yourself with him, then it might be because you can't," she continues. "And that's okay, but you need to decide soon for both of your sakes."

My sister is right. I should feel more confident about Luke by now, but my head is still full of so many questions. I wish that giving an answer about what I want came a little more easily. It's not something I've ever had to articulate before in anything—I had made my plan so clear as a child that I just did the next right thing and the next that I never had to express my desires. Now I am an adult and finding out that I don't know how to say what I want. When it comes to Luke, I am even more lost. I wish I knew exactly what the next right thing to do was in this case. Instead, I pull out my notebook and flip to the lists I made when I couldn't sleep the night after my first date with Luke. The pros and cons. I quickly fill the cons column with additional items:

- Wants to plan my life for me
- I still don't feel sure

and throw my notebook back down on the couch before placing my head in my hands.

Why does being the author of my own story feel so difficult?

10.

You only live once.

That's the mantra I repeat to myself as I get into my car early that Saturday morning. The drive north of Los Angeles to the town of Camarillo is much shorter than it would have been at any other hour. I'm up even before the sun. I had taken a rideshare to get my car when the repairs were finished, partially because I didn't want to feel like I owed anyone and partially because I wanted the workers at the body shop to actually speak to me instead of to any man that I might have brought along. That was yesterday. I didn't even call Luke to tell him it was ready. I haven't spoken to him since the day I dropped it off.

Today is special because today I am about to check another item off of my list. Today I am going skydiving. I haven't told many people I'm here because I don't want them to worry. My mother would be beside herself all day until she knew that I was back on the ground safely. Luke would have tried to come along under some guise of support ... so I had only told EJ, my younger brother.

"Dang, really?" he had said when I'd told him my plans.

"I'm trying to use this time off of work to step outside of my comfort zone," I replied.

"Well, I would say you're doing that for sure," he said.

EJ and I have always had an interesting relationship. Since he had joined our family by adoption when he was four, I had missed out on the part of being his older sister where I was jealous of him or treated him like my human doll. At five years older, I had always looked out for him and confided in him all at the same time. He had been a quiet kid, the kind who was always listening and observing, so I had always loved sharing my world with him. It's been a long time since I've made a call like this one, though.

"Don't tell Mom and Dad until I tell you that I'm down, okay? I don't want them to worry," I said.

"Sounds good," EJ said. Then, "I can't believe you're doing this, Ken."

"Me neither. I'll text you when I'm done, okay?"

"Love you, Kenny. Good luck!"

The inside of the skydiving facility is small, made up only of a waiting room with a back office, a few benches, lockers, and diving equipment. I arrive early, as I am wont to do, and that gives me the chance to listen to the diving instructors give their spiel to all of the adventure-seekers before me. As I watch group after group go out to the small single engine plane, I can feel my heartbeat getting stronger and stronger in my chest. *I am really doing this.*

By the time it's my turn, I am a pro on how to harness up and what to do when it is my turn to free-fall from a moving airplane. My instructor, Gabe, tells me he makes about twelve jumps a day and that we're going to have a great time. As scary as it is to think about hurling myself toward the Earth at a high rate of speed, knowing I am doing it with a professional strapped to my back, who would also prefer to live, puts my mind at ease.

"Nobody knows I'm here today … except my little brother in Illinois. I didn't want to get talked out of it," I admit.

Gabe laughs. "Well, let's go show the world how brave you really are!"

The plane ride is short, and I am told I will be diving second, so I get to watch as the diver before me moves into position, leans forward, and disappears from the airplane. Gabe nudges me to move into the jumping position and he activates a hand-held digital camera attached to his wrist. Before I have time to know what is happening, Gabe gives me the signal and we are falling.

I expected the free-fall portion of the dive to be a little bit more terrifying. I'm surprised that the emotion fueling me is exhilaration, not fear. The one thing I notice is that it's loud. The sound of the wind at that altitude is deafening, and I feel like I am gasping for air. I want to smile, but the force of the fall is literally keeping my mouth open. The instructions had been to keep my chin tucked, but I have to fight against the velocity to keep it that way. And then, by the time I am finally able to control my body, Gabe pulls the ripcord, and the parachute deploys. Suddenly everything is quiet, our speed slows to a gentle glide, and Gabe steers the chute to coast us in the direction of our landing spot.

"Wow!" I exclaim.

"Pretty rad, isn't it?" Gabe asks. He turns the camera on his wrist toward my face, interview style.

"So, Kenley, you're doing your first skydive. How do you feel?" he asks in mock interview style.

"Amazing!" I say.

"I can't hear you!"

"I FEEL FREAKING AMAZING!" I shriek. It's true, I have never known a feeling like this. My wrist catches my eye as we fall, the little bird literally flying through the air. It feels like the perfect metaphor for this moment.

There is a car waiting near the landing spot to pick us up and drive us back to the airport. The nerves I had felt on my drive this morning are gone, replaced by a feeling of pride and accomplishment like I have never known.

As soon as I am reunited with my belongings, I fire off a text to EJ to let him know that I have landed safely. But there's only one person that I can think of who I want to tell all about my day ... and I need to figure out how I really feel about that thought.

———

Kenley: Look what I did today!

I have included a photo that Gabe took during the dive of me smiling and giving a thumbs up to the camera. I had had the whole drive back home to contemplate whether I wanted to say anything to Luke at all. And I decided that sending a text to my best friend about such a huge thing in my life was a perfectly normal thing to do.

Luke: No way! That's amazing!

The reply is so immediate it is as if Luke was sitting and waiting to hear from me.

I convince myself that that is silly, because how many times a day do I sit with my phone in my hand doing all kinds of things and enabling myself to respond to someone immediately?

Kenley: It was incredible. I've never experienced anything like it.

Luke: How are you?

Luke changes the subject. It's a loaded question.

Kenley: I'm okay. How are you?

I finally text a few minutes later.

Luke: I'm okay...

Luke: I miss you...

He sends back-to-back texts ending in ellipses. I'm not surprised that he misses me. I miss him, too, I haven't spent this much time apart from Luke since I met him in law school. I just don't know if we miss each other in the same way.

Kenley: Can we talk?

I hit send before I can overthink it. Talking to Luke shouldn't feel like a big deal. But when my phone starts ringing a few seconds later, I have to do some quick breathing exercises to prepare myself to answer.

"That was quick," I say, instead of the traditional "hello."

"Sorry. I figured, why wait?" he says.

"So ... how are things?"

"Lonely and boring. I'm getting closer and closer to just biting the bullet and starting with my dad," he replies.

"Would that be so terrible?" I ask. We all know he's going to work with his dad; putting off the start date isn't going to change that.

"No, I would just rather not be working at all and spend time with you, instead," he says.

I take a deep breath. There is nothing intrinsically wrong with his statement. "Luke ..." I warn.

"What, Kenley? Am I not even allowed to say that I miss spending time with you? We haven't spoken in days, which is not like us. I miss you, I miss my best friend," he says.

"I miss my best friend, too," I admit. "But can we ever go back to that? Will our friendship ever be the same?"

"Do you want to go back to that?" he asks.

This is, essentially, the question I have been wrestling with all along. The one that I am afraid to answer because even though I think it might be true, I am afraid that if I say that is what I want, then I'll lose Luke altogether.

"I don't know," I lie. I think I do know, but I am afraid of what will happen if I say so.

"Because you seemed really repulsed by the idea of being my girlfriend," he adds. There is a bite in his tone that I haven't heard before. I had never considered before this moment that my shock in hearing him call me his girlfriend might have hurt him.

"I wasn't repulsed," I say. "I just ... this has all happened so fast. You went from being my best friend, to the person I was sleeping with, to suddenly calling me your girlfriend in just two weeks. It doesn't feel like enough time." I leave out the part about him making all of my life decisions for me because, to date, I haven't accepted any of those decisions. The offers of being Luke's girlfriend and working at his dad's firm are on the table, but I haven't done anything with them yet.

"And while you're taking some time, does that mean I don't get to see or talk to you at all? Because that's a really shitty deal for me," he says.

"No, of course not. I'm sorry," I say.

"Thanks," he replies.

I mean my apology. I hadn't been repulsed by the notion of being Luke's girlfriend the way he had perceived it. I had been caught off guard and it freaked me out, but I didn't mean to hurt him, and for that I am truly sorry.

"What are you doing later? Do you want to hang out?" I ask as a way of making amends. There are plenty of ways that two best friends can spend time together that don't involve ripping each other's clothes off.

I hope Luke sees it that way, too, because he accepts my offer before I even have a chance to fully think through the question. Before I know it, he is standing on the steps of my building, holding a pizza and a six pack. I know immediately that the pizza is from one of my favorite spots in Downtown that we used to order from while working through dinner in the office.

"I brought a peace offering: pepperoni, our favorite," he says by way of greeting. Pepperoni is not my favorite, it's Luke's. I eat it because I don't dislike it and it's definitely easier to find than my own preferred toppings of sausage and black olive, but if the choice was up to me, we wouldn't be eating pepperoni pizza again. Still, I try to offer a smile at his attempt to smooth things over because I hope that it means we can be friends.

Even though it hasn't even been a week since I last saw Luke, having him in my apartment feels strange. I can't help flashing back to the last time he was here with me, the night I chose to sleep with him without any alcohol involved. Everything had felt different then, the idea of having lost my job was still so new, and I was looking for anything I could find to fill the void it had left in me. I try to put the thought out of my mind as I busy myself with getting plates and napkins from the kitchen and bringing them out to the sitting area, where Luke is finding a movie on my TV.

"Cheers," I say, clinking my beer bottle against his as I take a seat beside him on the couch.

It feels normal to sit here with Luke, eating pizza and watching a summer blockbuster. So much so that I could almost forget everything that has transpired between us. This is exactly what I had missed about our relationship, and it makes me wonder if it is something that we could go back to. That is, until Luke catches sight of the tattoo on the inside of my wrist and brushes his fingertips over it. His touch sends a shiver down my spine, but it's not the good kind. I'd describe it more as being the sensation of nails on a chalkboard.

"Does it still hurt?" he asks me, not lifting his fingers from my skin, deciding for me, as is his habit now, that I want this.

"Not really," I say. My voice catches in my throat, making it sound like I have just run a marathon. It does nothing to steady my breathing when Luke picks up my arm and places a soft, delicate kiss on the little bird. From my wrist, his lips trail up my arm, just brushing the skin and sending those jolts of electricity to all of my nerve endings. It is almost like I am having an out-of-body experience when his lips finally reach my neck and he plants several open-mouth kisses there before continuing the exploration to my earlobe, which he nibbles and sucks with just the right amount of pressure.

"Kenley, do you want me to stop?" he whispers.

Alarm bells are going off in my brain, but my body feels like it weighs ten thousand pounds and I can't move a muscle. I can already see his arousal through the bulge in his jeans, but whatever I feel is the opposite. What is the opposite of aroused? Repulsed? ... Just like Luke had accused me of being.

"Yes," I manage to say. It's what I wanted to say, what I had hoped would come out when he asked, but I am surprised at myself that I found the courage. This night is not supposed to be about sex. We're supposed to be hanging out like friends and figuring out if that is something we can ever be again. Luke backs away instantly, a stunned look on his face.

"Oo-kay," he says. I know he's wondering if he has misread things between us and the truth is that yeah, he probably has, but it's only because I let him. Two weeks of not feeling totally sure had encouraged me to lead him on. I kept thinking that maybe just one more date would help me decide. The look on Luke's face makes me feel like an asshole.

When Luke and I first hooked up, I was wasted, and I was consenting but also might have consented to do any number of wild things that night. I hadn't wanted dinner the night after to be a date, but I hadn't put up much of a fight when Luke had implied that it was, and when we hooked up again I guess I wanted to find out if I felt anything sober. After that, I had just kept waiting to feel sure that this is what I did or didn't want.

"I ... just ... this isn't why you're here tonight," I say.

Luke doesn't say anything. He has moved as far from me as possible on the tiny two-person couch.

I don't know what else to say. I have been telling him that I need space, but then as soon as we're together, he tries pulling this. Maybe I'm not the one who can't go back to being just friends.

When I had woken up this morning, it was with the mantra "you only live once" running through my head. I had meant it, of course, about the skydiving, but if I want to, I could apply it to everything that has happened with Luke since the day we got fired. What if I had never had sex with Luke, and I was left wondering if there ever could have been something between us? Would I have ever thought of him that way? It makes me wonder if I am wrong for not feeling anything for him ... but then I remember his micromanaging of my life, and it reminds me that all of this feels wrong.

"I guess you should go," I say, not sure of how else to end this night except by kicking him out.

"Wait. It's almost my birthday, and I wanted to ask you," he says before I have a chance to show him the door. "My parents are having a birthday dinner for me at their house, and I'd like for you to come."

He seems embarrassed to be asking the question, especially now that I have just rejected him. Honestly, it's kind of ballsy on his part to even ask. His family knows that our relationship changed. Lauren was the first person to see us together and his dad offered me a position at his firm because he knows I am "special" to Luke. But while I have attended all of their holiday parties for the last nine years, I have never been invited in such an intimate way. I feel like this invitation goes against everything I have just tried to express.

"Am I invited as your friend or ..." I start.

"As my friend, I swear. Please come, Kenley. I really want you to be there," he cuts me off defensively. Luke is my oldest friend in Los Angeles, and in theory there is nothing wrong with spending my friend's birthday with him.

"I just … I don't know Luke. It feels heavier than that. Lauren knows about us, and I know your dad didn't offer me a job at his firm as *just* your friend. I don't know if they will ever see me as your friend again," I tell him. I suddenly feel more naked in front of him now than if we had actually had sex.

"It's just a birthday dinner. I promise that they will only see you as my friend. I'll make sure of it," he pleads.

The sigh I let out doesn't do much to clear my head. "Okay, send me the details and I will be there," I say, wondering as soon as the words leave my mouth if I will regret this decision.

11.

Leo and Amanda Goldstein are the type of couple that you think of when you imagine life in Beverly Hills. His work as a high-powered celebrity attorney has paid for a life of luxury: a massive estate, a collection of high-end cars, art that belongs in a museum hanging on the walls, a staff to keep the house running ... the list goes on. I had met them a few times and been to their home for their annual holiday party, but my arrival to Luke's birthday dinner is the first time I have been invited to such an intimate affair. Although I arrive with Luke, I feel very much like an outsider.

"Kenley, it's good to see you, darling. You look lovely!" Amanda says as soon as we have stepped through the living area onto the open patio. Her words sound formal, yet she exudes an aura of warmth that makes her seem totally unpretentious.

"Thank you so much for having me," I reply, remembering my manners. I had been worried about what to wear because Luke's mother is always dressed in the latest styles. You'd never know she was a woman in her sixties based on appearance. My own mother is younger than Amanda by almost a decade, and yet she looks every bit of her mid-fifties. It's amazing what money will do for a person's aging process.

Small talk has never been my strength. I would choose to have a deep, passionate discussion over chatter about the weather and the newest film releases any day of the week. So as the small talk portion of the evening ensues, I mostly sit idly, twisting a cocktail glass around and around in my hand. Leo tells me that the housekeeper makes the best cocktails in Beverly Hills, which I am sure he means as a brag of some kind, though I still can't wrap my mind around the extravagance of having a full-time housekeeper in the first place. My aunt works as a house cleaner in her town, for one of those companies that sends a cleaner out to do the job in a couple of hours. Growing up, my sister and I used to marvel at the idea that people would pay her to come into their homes to clean for them, which seemed like such a luxury to us. Luke has always rebuffed the idea of having paid help at home, but I know that it's how he grew up, whether he wants it as an adult or not. Our childhoods were incredibly different; it's something we've talked a lot about over the course of our friendship.

"What's up, bitches!" Lauren calls from the entry. I can't imagine walking into my parents' home and calling them bitches, but that is Lauren.

"Out here, Kitty!" Amanda says in reply, before turning to me.

"Mom! Please, not the nickname in front of a guest!" Lauren says, making her way out to the patio.

One thing that I immediately fell in love with after moving to California is the ability to be outside nearly year-round. The patio at the Goldstein estate is reminiscent of a Tuscan villa: it sits in the middle of the opulent house with arches that surround it on all sides and lead to the living quarters. The courtyard is adorned with olive trees, and the soothing sounds of bubbling water rise from the four stone fountains around the perimeter. The seating area, a set of extravagant outdoor couches positioned around a built-in stone firepit, and the service from the house staff makes me feel like I am at a fancy hotel, not the home where my best friend was raised.

"It's not a guest, Kitty, it's family!" Amanda answers. At this, I bristle and scoot a little bit away from Luke on the couch. He had assured me that I was here as his friend, *not* as someone that his mother would consider family.

"Hi Kenley," Lauren says then. "How's your tat?"

"Oh, do you have a tattoo, Kenley?" Amanda asks then, surprised.

"Is that your only tattoo?" Leo asks then, inserting himself into the conversation before I have had a chance to answer the first question.

"It is. I had always wanted to get one, but I never found the time. I finally got it recently. Lauren helped get me an appointment," I tell them.

I still feel on edge, as if I am on trial, in ways I had not been mentally prepared for when I agreed to come to Luke's birthday dinner. I stand to show Amanda my wrist, which she touches softly and tells me it's very pretty and tasteful.

"Don't get any ideas, Mandy," Leo laughs. "If you had had a tattoo, I might have left you alone, and now you'd be the partner of your own firm somewhere instead of living comfortably with all of this." He motions around the patio and above to the rest of the gorgeous home.

"Come on, Dad," Luke warns.

"Yeah, Dad. Lighten up. Besides, what are you saying about me?" Lauren asks. I had been wondering the same thing, but she seems to be asking the question as a joke.

"Nothing, Princess. You're as beautiful today as on the day you were born," Leo says as Lauren sits down on the arm of his chair and leans in for a hug.

It's interesting to see Luke's family like this, relaxed and joking with one another. It is somehow not what I expect, even though I know they have always been close. I have a lot of preconceived ideas about people who live in houses like this one, and even though I know Luke's family, I can't seem to shake those ideas. The situation is heartwarming, and yet something else about the conversation has started to bother me.

"You were a lawyer, too?" I ask Amanda, returning to my seat.

"She was the best contract lawyer they had at the firm where I got my start," Leo interjects. "But when we got married, I knew I didn't want my wife to work, and I was blessed to be able to give her all of this."

I feel my brow furrow, though I try my best to keep a straight face.

"Do you ever miss it?" I ask her.

"Well, I had my kids to keep me busy, and now I have my committees and lunches," she says, avoiding the question.

This is immediately concerning to me. Like me, Amanda had once been a lawyer, but her career had been cut short by a man who planned the life he wanted, putting aside her hopes and dreams. It all feels a little too familiar, and a little too fishy.

"How's the apartment search going, son?" Leo changes the subject. It is news to me that Luke is looking for a new apartment. It would make sense, since he is no longer working Downtown, that the convenience of living there had disappeared, and I sincerely hope that is the only reason. The timing is suspicious.

"It's alright. I've seen a couple of places that I like in the Robertson area," Luke replies. There is an awkward gap between us on the couch, and while it's mostly my doing, it makes me feel uncomfortable, like I am on my own here against Luke's family.

"Well, make sure you consult Kenley," Leo says. "It's important that the woman of the house has input on where she'll live."

Before I can even fully process the statement, the crystal glass has fallen from my hand and shattered on the cement beneath my feet. It's a good distraction and gives everyone a chance to forget about what Leo has just said. Everyone except me.

"I'm so sorry," I say, kneeling to pick up the glass shards. I almost immediately cut my hand, but I don't even notice because I am too deep in my head, thinking about how Luke is looking for a new apartment because I am about to lose mine. He hasn't confirmed that suspicion himself, and my years of education tell me that I have to give him a chance to do that ... I also feel like I don't need to bother, because the pattern is exactly the same. I presented a problem and Luke has come to my rescue, whether I wanted him to or not.

"Oh, dear, you're bleeding," Amanda says, rushing to my side. "Esme! Please bring something to clean Kenley's hand."

"I'm so sorry," I repeat, unsure of what else to say and wondering where the hell my supposed best friend is right now, because the only people helping me are his mom, sister, and their maid.

"Come, Miss Kenley," Esme says before she leads me toward the kitchen.

The layout of this house has always been confusing to me, but it's even more so as I struggle to fight back the tears that are threatening to fall and have nothing to do with the blood that is spilling from the wound on my palm. Luke had promised me that I would be here as his friend and, perhaps stupidly, I had believed him. Why had I believed him when I should have known better?

You believed him because you wanted to. You believed him because you wanted it to be true that you could still be friends after everything that happened. But the truth is that only one of you is interested in just being friends, I tell myself as I follow Esme toward the kitchen sink.

"Are you okay?" Luke asks a moment later, the first time he has spoken to me since our arrival. It's a loaded question. On the surface he is, of course, asking about my hand. But we both know that his question means so much more than that.

I'm hovering over the sink, a towel wrapped around my wound, which gives me the perfect opportunity not to make eye contact with him when I answer: "I don't know." It comes out like a whisper, or like my voice is hoarse from crying, though crying about this is something I have tried not to do.

"Here, Miss Kenley," Esme says again, approaching me at the sink with disinfectant and bandages.

"Thanks, Esme, I can take it from here," Luke says, taking the items from her and dismissing her to clean up the glass on the patio.

The care with which Luke cleans and bandages my wound is unexpected, to say the least. The passion and compassion in the way Luke handles my hand is a reminder of the man I have spent so much time with over the last weeks, no longer trapped in the confusion of labels and what-ifs. His attentiveness to my wound is a reminder that above all, he does care for me. It's not until he is done, placing a soft kiss on top of the bandage on my palm, that I am able to look at him.

"I'm sorry," he says.

I'm surprised by the confession. If anything, I should be the one apologizing for causing a scene and embarrassing myself in front of his family, especially since it's his birthday. But instead of letting me respond, he takes my uninjured hand in his and pulls me behind him up a back staircase off of the kitchen.

After my first holiday party at the Goldstein house, I had spent what little free time I had researching it because I had been fascinated by a lifestyle so unlike the one I had known. I learned that the house had been constructed in the 1920s and features several outdated amenities, like this servant's staircase and a maid's quarters directly next to the kitchen and laundry room, which the current owners use as a home gym. In contrast to the staircase, the hallway upstairs has been through several renovations and looks bright and inviting. I have never been up here, and it feels a little scandalous to be here now, like I am sneaking around where I don't belong.

I remain silent, following Luke as he opens one of the pristine white doors and leads me through to his childhood bedroom. It is very much unchanged from how it must have looked when he had last lived in it. There are sports posters on the walls; the bookshelf above the desk contains several paperbacks of the literary classics we all read in high school; and the queen-sized bed is adorned with the type of plaid bedspread that I swear is only made with teenage boys in mind. The room screams "generic high school boy," and yet it somehow feels exactly like Luke.

"So, this is my room," he says sheepishly, dropping my hand.

"I like it!" I say. I am dying to explore, to open the drawers in the nightstand and desk to see what concert tickets and movie stubs I might find inside that give a glimpse into Luke's past. However, Luke brought me here for a reason, and as much as I want to explore, I want to hear his reason even more.

"I've never brought anyone up here before," he says.

"Ooo, no other girls?" I tease.

"No one. Boys or girls."

This makes me sad. To think that Luke might have lived his whole life without having friends come into his room feels impossible. Everyone has friends over ... or so I thought.

"Whenever my friends would come over, my mom would send us to the pool house, because we could make it as messy as we wanted and she didn't have to look at it," Luke says. Hearing the privilege in his explanation makes me feel a lot less sad for him.

69

"I never brought any girls there either, though," he says then. "At least not any that were more than friends."

I don't respond to this. We are more than friends, of course; that's what has muddied the line between us. But I don't answer because it feels like he is trying to make a point that I belong in the private and intimate parts of his life when no one before me ever has, and I don't know what to say to that. Instead, I turn out the desk chair and sit down in it. That feels safer than the bed if Luke is, in fact, trying to make that point.

"So, why bring me here?" I ask.

"Well, I wanted a chance to talk to you in private," he says. "This seemed like the most logical place."

I don't want to have this conversation today. Today is Luke's birthday, and the last thing I want is to ruin his special day. But I feel like I've been backed into a corner and if we don't have this conversation now, we might never figure things out between us. But, neither of us makes the first move to start the conversation. I think Luke is too afraid of upsetting me, and I still don't know what I want, which makes it hard to know what to say.

"I'm sorry about my family," Luke says finally. I haven't looked at the clock, but I am certain more than a minute has passed. "I don't really bring girls home, and when I said you were coming for dinner, my parents got a little excited. Plus, Lauren has already seen us together, and I know she's said something to my mom."

"It's okay. It's not them," I say. I'm still sitting in the desk chair, so it's easy to hide my gaze from Luke's. The cream-colored carpet is a lush Berber and I fix my gaze on an imagined pattern in its tight weave. As a lawyer, I am a powerhouse of confidence who can speak persuasively to every judge I have ever encountered. When it comes to personal matters, though, I avoid confrontation like the plague.

I wait for Luke to respond before I speak again, but when he doesn't, I already know the question: what is it then? I take a deep breath before I speak again, hoping that the inhale will help me to clear my mind.

"I'm scared," I say. It is a stupid answer to hear it spoken out loud, but it is honest.

"Of me?" Luke asks.

I shake my head quickly, still focused on the spot of carpet that looks a bit like a lion if you catch it at the right angle.

"Not exactly," I say. I'm unsure of my words even as I say them, because I still haven't been able to figure this all out for myself like I had wanted to.

"I am scared of losing myself in you," I say after a moment.

"Do you think I would let that happen? I know you better than anyone, and …" Luke starts but I put up a hand to stop him, finally looking up to meet his gaze.

"You know better than anyone that my entire life has changed recently. We lost our jobs, and then this happened between us, and I have been trying to think about what direction I want to go in next. But every time I feel like I am getting close, you seem to swoop in with a solution to my problems that I didn't ask for," I continue.

Luke doesn't say anything. He remains motionless from his perch on the edge of the bed. I had expected him to defend himself, at least, so I am surprised by his silence. He listens without a word as I recount everything that has happened between us and how helpless it has made me feel. I even tell him how freaked out I am about his mom having been a once great lawyer before giving it all up for his dad, and the latest revelation that he is looking for a new apartment just as I have been told I need to move.

"You say you know me better than anyone, and if that is true, then you know that I need some control over my own life. Lately it feels like you're taking that away from me. I know you're trying to help, but I feel like you're suffocating me," I conclude. I expect him to be mad, I hadn't meant to tell him that. It's something I have thought about, but I intended to keep the idea to myself, and it had slipped out in the heat of the moment.

Instead of being angry, Luke looks sullen.

"I'm sorry, Kenley," he says finally, sliding off the bed and coming to kneel before me. "I didn't realize that you felt that way. I don't blame you at all for being freaked out … I didn't even know I was doing it."

He looks so pitiful on his knees in front of me. The surroundings of his childhood bedroom just add to the aesthetic that he is a scared little boy. I guess that makes two of us who are afraid. I need some time to think, and now that I've finally told him how I feel, it seems like he does, too.

"I have been trying to figure this out, but it's hard because every time I say or do anything, you come in with an answer or solution like I am a damsel in distress," I say, placing my uninjured hand on top of the one of his that he has rested on my knee.

Luke lets out a breathy laugh in reply.

"And for you, maybe it's clear that this change in our relationship is written in the stars. But for me, I guess I thought it was just sex, until I realized that wasn't what you thought. All this time, I still haven't felt sure that I want more than friendship. Your friendship is so important to me, and I am afraid that it will be ruined now, no matter what I decide. I just need some time to figure things out," I continue. I am genuinely surprised that Luke has stayed quiet. He hasn't tried to interject or make me see his side once. I had been so afraid of bringing all of this up to him because I wanted to avoid a fight, but he hasn't given me one at all.

"How much time do you need?" is all he says when he does finally muster a response.

"Can you give me until I get back from Illinois?" I answer his question with one of my own. I'm only a few days away from my trip back home for Jessica's shower, and I want to use that time away from Los Angeles to get my head on right.

Luke nods, offering me a weak smile. He doesn't get a chance to say anything, though, because we're interrupted by a forceful knock on the door.

"Don't be naked, I'm coming in!" Lauren calls from the other side, turning the knob. Neither Luke nor I move from our positions, turning to look at the door and wait for her arrival.

"Mom sent me to get you, dinner is ready," she says before she is even fully inside the room. When she spots us, me still sitting on the desk chair and Luke kneeling before me, the smile drops from her face.

"This is … not what I expected to find up here," she says then. "Did

I interrupt something? Are you guys breaking up?"

Luke sighs heavily and rises off the ground, shifting his attention away from me and onto his sister. "You have to be together to break up, Laur," he says, putting his arm around her shoulder and steering her back toward the door.

I understand that I am supposed to follow, which is for the best since we are expected to use the main staircase at the other end of the hallway, and I don't know the first thing about this maze of a house.

12.

If you love something let it go. If it comes back, it's yours.

I remember my sister writing this in everybody's yearbook at the end of seventh grade. It was as if parting for the summer vacation was the worst separation a thirteen-year-old could endure. She had taken these words so seriously at the time, but I hadn't thought of them in years. Not until I told Luke to give me some time.

I get a man wanting to be a woman's savior. I hate it because I am my own damn savior, but I get it. There's something in it that validates a man's masculinity somehow. I know Luke was hoping that by helping me answer all of these questions I've been asking lately, I would find it easy to choose him. I know he certainly wasn't expecting my reaction of ... well, the exact opposite.

I'm not *not* choosing Luke. I just need some time to think, like I told him. And no time will be better to think than on my trip to Illinois. I think the change of scenery will help, and getting to talk to my parents and my siblings in person when nothing can get lost in translation. Still, picturing his sad face when I said goodbye to him at his parents' house on his birthday has left me filled with lingering feelings of shame and regret.

I kept picturing that face as I toured several apartments on the day after the birthday dinner. I kept reliving that goodbye the day after that as I went to an in-person interview at the nonprofit that has me so excited. I feel like I haven't had a second to process everything that has happened and decide what I want, but I can't stop thinking about that look of sadness and how bad it made me feel.

On the night before I am set to leave for my trip, I decide that I miss my best friend enough to reach out before I go. Even with that in mind, I hold my phone in my hands for a good thirty minutes before I can bring myself to send the text.

Kenley: Hey.

In true Luke fashion, the reply is almost instant. The more often it happens, the more it feels true that he is sitting there and waiting for me.

Luke: Hey.

Kenley: Leaving tomorrow. Want to be able to say goodbye.

This time the reply is not as immediate. I wait and wait, wondering what he must think and what I am really asking. I don't want to sleep with him, but I do want to see him. Because something in me needs to know that what I am doing is right, that I am making the best possible decision, following the best possible plan.

Luke: Be right over.

I haven't had a lot of stops and starts in my life. At least none that were out of the ordinary. There was the typical high school-to-college transition, the move to L.A. for law school, getting the job at Sullivan and Dunkirk. All of those had been according to my life plan and had been carefully orchestrated to go off without a hitch. They'd all been completely within the realm of my control. All of this stuff with Luke, though, has felt completely outside of my power. I consider giving myself a pep talk as a way to avoid sleeping with him. As soon as I have the thought, I decide against it, I know tonight will be different as soon as Luke says he will come.

He shows up about thirty minutes later. We are both wearing sweatpants, which is interesting because it shows both our level of comfort with each other and that neither of us is trying to impress the other. We don't hug or kiss hello, I simply open the door to him, and he accepts the invitation.

"I just ... wanted to see you before I leave," I say awkwardly. That seems obvious by my inviting him over to my place, and also feels like the only appropriate way to start the first conversation we've had since his birthday. It's only been three days, but it somehow feels a lot longer.

"Thanks, I'm glad you did," he says.

"Kenley I ..." he starts after a minute, at the same time that I say, "I wanted to apologize ..."

"What? No. You don't have anything to apologize for," he tells me. He's sitting sideways in one of my two dining chairs, facing where I am sitting on the couch. Part of me longs for him to be closer, but another part of me recognizes that this is as much distance as we can put between us without someone sitting on the bed.

"I told you that you were suffocating me," I remind him. "That feels like something worth apologizing for."

"I should be the one apologizing to you," he says. "I was being selfish and only thinking of ways to help you that would benefit me."

"They weren't unhelpful things, they just ... weren't my own thoughts. I have spent so much time following this path I laid out when I was nine that I really need some of my own thoughts right now," I say.

"I get it. I do, and I'm sorry." He looks sheepish, almost embarrassed.

"Thanks," I say, because his isn't the kind of comment that can pass without acknowledgement. "And I know we need to have a real conversation about all of this, but I just want some time to process everything when I am not being bombarded by putting my life back together. Can you at least give me until I get back from Illinois?"

"So, you are?" he asks then.

"Am what?"

"Coming back?" he continues with a hint of relief in his voice.

"Of course, I'm coming back!" I laugh. For the first time, though, a thought pops into my head that hadn't even been an inkling there before. What if I did go somewhere else? Could I?

"I should let you get ready for your flight tomorrow," Luke says then. His visit has been brief, but I don't know what else I expected exactly. What I definitely didn't expect is when he pulls me into his arms and says: "I am going to kiss you now, and then I'll let you go. I can't wait to hear all about it when you get back."

And it's the most intense kiss I have ever had in my life.

———

The first of my two flights to Illinois departs at 5:45am, but it's midnight and I still can't sleep. I had the best of intentions when I crawled into bed at 8pm, just after Luke left my apartment, and I haven't slept a wink. I keep thinking about that kiss. If I try hard enough, I can still feel the lingering sensation of Luke's mouth on mine.

I have been replaying it over and over in my mind. The way he had announced that he was going to kiss me hadn't even given me a chance to react, though I had felt my body respond immediately. His tongue had parted my lips in a way that was both forceful and gentle at the same time and had left me wanting more. The kiss was full of everything he didn't get to say in the room at his parents' house— it was a reminder of the passion we share, the care we have for one another, the anger he felt at being told that I feel suffocated, and the sadness he feels from missing me. His kiss said more in a few seconds than he could have said if we had talked for hours, and it's no wonder I have been left thinking about it.

Kenley, breathe, I tell myself. *You are looking forward to this time away from Luke, it will give you time to think. You are not a teenage girl who has never kissed a boy; snap out of this and get your head on straight. You are a grown woman with a once successful career, you do not need to give this man any more of your time. Go to sleep!*

I replay this pep talk again and again in my head, willing it to work like these talks have always done in the past. But it doesn't. As soon as I finish telling myself to go to sleep, I follow it up imagining Luke back in my apartment again, kissing me.

I wonder what Luke is doing. Is he thinking about our kiss, too? Is he lying awake and staring at the ceiling, imagining the feeling of my lips on his? I wish he wasn't affecting me this way. It's making it a lot harder for me to decide what it is that I want to do.

On paper, Luke is perfect. When I was in high school, I made a list of all of the things I was looking for in an ideal husband, though at the time many of the items on my list were designed so that Jordan Thomas, my high school's star quarterback and prom king, would be the only one to fit the bill. I don't remember what happened to the list, I am sure it eventually got thrown out when I moved to college or law school, but I still remember the gist of it, and Luke checks so many of the boxes. He's smart, good-looking, has a solid career, cares for his family, sees my intelligence, we have passion between us ... and yet, there is just something that isn't there. One thing I was adamant about when I was making that list in high school is that I would be allowed to be independent, that I would have my own mind and control over my own decisions. I don't know why that was so important to me back then; I think I noticed a change in my mother when she was strictly a stay-at-home-mom versus when she was teaching or volunteering. Because of that, it always felt important to me that I not be a subservient wife, even though my mom has had a happy life and says that she wouldn't change a thing.

If you love something let it go. If it comes back, it's yours, I remind myself again, as if I am going away for longer than a week and expect Luke to change that much in the meantime. I'm no better than my sister in seventh grade, applying so much weight to this cheesy mantra. I don't need to let Luke go, at least not completely. I just need a chance to get away and process everything that has been going on without reminders of him everywhere. Still, even knowing that truth, sleep doesn't come.

13.

Thank goodness for cross-country flights. Although my destination is in the middle of the country, the Central Illinois Regional Airport in my hometown is on the smaller side, and it's impossible to get a direct flight from Los Angeles. But that meant that I had four hours and fifteen minutes of flight time between L.A. and Atlanta to get a nap, and for that I am grateful. It's amazing what even a few hours of halfway-decent sleep will do to someone who is exhausted. It's equally amazing what a change of scenery will do for the mind. No sooner had the airplane begun to taxi down the LAX runway than the memory of Luke's kiss had begun to fade.

I'm sitting at the gate for my second flight, drinking a coffee because I am an anxious traveler and have convinced myself that if I so much as get up to use the restroom, my gate will disappear and my trip will be ruined. "Kenley Graves?!" I hear a man's voice call through the crowded airport terminal. Turning to find the voice, I spot a familiar face that I never imagined seeing again.

"It is you! Wow, long time!" he says, smiling. Approaching me across the airport terminal with quick strides is Jordan Thomas, the very high school superstar for whom my ideal husband list had been curated, all six feet and five inches of him. Until this moment, I had no idea he even knew my name. To say that we hadn't run in the same circle in high school would be the understatement of the century.

"Jordan! Good to see you!" I lie. I am wearing my travel clothes:

leggings and a sweatshirt with my feet shoved into the knockoff Uggs that my parents had given me for Christmas a decade ago. My hair is tied up on my head in a messy bun, and I didn't even bother to apply any makeup to the dark circles under my eyes. I am not dressed to be seen, and it's even more concerning that I have been recognized by someone I haven't seen in more than a decade while I am in this state.

"Yeah! How have you been?!" Jordan asks, taking the seat next to mine and spreading out his belongings. At first, I am taken aback by his comfort, until I remember that he, too, is from Bloomington and is likely taking the same flight to town.

"Um, good. Busy," I say. Small talk has never been my strong suit, especially not when I am caught off guard by it. More than that, though, I don't think that Jordan and I have ever had a conversation in our lives. I had imagined the moment of our first conversation a thousand times and a thousand different ways back in high school; having it at a gate in the Atlanta airport was never one of those ways.

"What are you up to these days?" he continues questioning me. I feel like I am being interviewed. But I am also a captive audience because there is no way I can get up from this seat that is near both the jetway door and a gate announcement speaker.

"Well, I've been out in L.A. for about ten years now," I start. I am struck by Jordan's smile. He seems genuinely happy to have run into me and even happier to be hearing about my life. It doesn't make any sense.

"Los Angeles, wow," he says, impressed. "What brought you out there?"

"Law school. I've been working as a lawyer out there since I graduated."

"Law was always your thing. I remember that about you. Glad to see it worked out!" he says. There is no way Jordan Thomas could possibly remember that about me. I mean, yes, I had been the captain of the mock trial team and president of the debate club. But he had been the quarterback of the football team. Our interactions were brief and entirely unnoteworthy.

Jordan looks much like I remember him, tall and muscular with

80

blond hair. The style of his hair has changed since high school, much less Justin Bieber, but aside from that, not much else has. Part of what got me through those years of my life were the reminders that so many members of the popular crowd were going to peak in high school while I was going to go on and flourish later in life. It's almost disappointing to find that Jordan has certainly not peaked yet.

"Husband? Kids?" he asks. The question stings in a way that I am not expecting. I had been doing so well not to think about my love life until he asked about it.

"No. Not yet. I've been married to my work, I guess they would say," I reply. Who would say that? I don't know. See also: bad at small talk.

"What about you? Where are you now?" I ask, desperate to get the spotlight off of myself.

"I'm here in Atlanta," he says. "Came down for college and never looked back. I'm a distribution executive at a major beverage company. Divorced, no kids." I appreciate that he answered all of his own questions in one fell swoop so that I don't have to ask them.

There is a lull in the conversation then, because what else do I have to talk about with Jordan Thomas? Even back in high school I couldn't think of anything to talk to him about, and then our worlds were much smaller. Aside from the fact that we both work in the corporate world, we still don't have much in common.

"Do you get back much?" he asks then, pointing toward the airport sign indicating our final destination. I tell him that I don't.

"Yeah, me neither. My folks are always on me about it, but life— you know?" he says. I chuckle, that sounds very familiar.

"They're mad because I'm not going back to see them this time, either. I mean, I will see them, but I got invited to my buddy's baby shower, and I already missed his wedding because I was on my honeymoon," he continues. My eyes widen. How many baby showers can there possibly be this weekend?

"Tanner and Jessica?" I ask.

"Yes, ma'am. You know them?"

"Jessica is my sister. I, too, am heading to town for the shower," I laugh.

Jordan smiles as if he has just received the best news of his life.

"Well, I guess we'll be seeing a lot of each other," he smirks.

I'm wracking my brain, trying to remember anything I can about Jordan besides the fact that he was our school's sports star. I remember that he had a reputation as a playboy because he was the best-looking guy in the school and all of the girls wanted to date him. I remember regularly scoffing at how he would try to get through school by throwing the teachers his award-winning smile. And I remember how I was secretly head over heels in love with him back then, just like everyone else. Until he called my name in the airport, I would have thought that this was more than he remembered about me. I don't consider myself someone who was all that memorable in high school. I was hyper-focused on my goals and didn't have time for the triviality that came with adolescence, or that is what I told myself and everyone around me. I had wanted desperately to be one of the cool kids, but I was unwilling to compromise my dreams to become one.

"Do you want to grab something to eat?" Jordan asks then. I hold up my coffee to indicate that I am all set, and Jordan settles deeper into his chair in response.

"Aren't you going to get food?" I ask.

"Nah, I'm not hungry. I was just looking for an excuse to talk to you some more," he smiles.

There is still an hour until our flight departs, but talking to Jordan makes the minutes fly by. He doesn't even flinch when I raise my finger to silence him when the gate agent makes an announcement. I didn't think that we could possibly have anything to talk about for so long, but somehow we find a way. We talk about what we love about our new hometowns and things we remember about high school, and I'm startled when the gate agent announces that it is time for boarding. Before I can stand to be the first person in Boarding Group Three, Jordan whips out his phone.

"Hey, let me get your number," he says nonchalantly. Sending an anxious glance toward the boarding line that is filling quickly, I rattle off my number and feel my phone vibrate in my pocket as he sends me a text.

As I take my seat on the plane, I half expect that Jordan will turn up in the seat beside me, and I can't tell whether what I feel is relief or sadness when he doesn't.

I have not thought about Jordan Thomas in years, and until he saw me in the airport today, I never imagined that I would think of him again. Our lives have taken us in different directions, but it had been more fun to catch up with him than I ever would have thought. It's not until I am settled into my seat with all of my electronics turned off, well before I have been asked to do so because heaven forbid that *I* should be the cause of a flight delay, that I think about Luke for the first time since leaving Los Angeles. It also hits me that this is the first time since we had sex all those weeks ago that I have gone any length of time without thinking about him in some capacity. As soon as we're airborne, though, I quickly nod off again, forgetting all of the problems, and all of the men, in my life altogether.

———

Jordan: Hi.

Is the first of several text messages that greets me when I turn on my phone after the impact of the plane's tires touching down on the runway awakened me from my dreamless slumber. I can feel a trail of drool caked onto my chin and wonder if anyone else had noticed how hard I was sleeping. It makes me glad that Jordan hadn't managed to trade for the seat beside me.

Jordan: How long will you be in town?

is the second text from the phone number I don't recognize. I don't even need to read the third message, which says,

Jordan: This is Jordan, by the way. You probably turned your phone off already.

to know who the texts are from. I catch myself smiling at his messages. It feels a little bit like I am back in high school again.

Being the nervous traveler that I am, though, I know that I can't respond until I am safely back on solid ground. For now, I have to closely monitor the deplaning situation to make sure that I don't miss my turn to exit the aircraft while simultaneously watching the overhead bin where I have stowed my carry-on to make sure that my bag is safe and remains in my possession. I can't be distracted by texting anyone, especially not someone as distracting as Jordan Thomas. Once I know that my airport travel experience is over, that is once I am safely inside of my father's vehicle, then I can respond to messages. Including one from Luke that says,

Luke: Hope you made it okay. Enjoy the time with your family.

I was never this distracted by Luke. Our relationship had come out of nowhere and had consumed many of my thoughts, but it hadn't distracted me from anything else in my life. I had just been terminated from my job, so it wasn't like I had anything to be distracted from, but Jordan is distracting in a way that I can't fully explain.

I am intrigued by his sudden reappearance in my life after all this time. It's like the icing on the cake to reconnect with someone like Jordan on the rare instance that I make it home for more than a few days, almost like a glimmer of what my life could have been like if things had been different.

"Hey you," Jordan's voice catches me off guard as I emerge from the boarding tunnel.

"Oh, hey!" I exclaim almost too enthusiastically. I wonder if he can tell I had just been thinking about him. "Were you waiting for me?"

Jordan looks sheepish then, rubbing his hand behind his head as if I have caught him doing something he shouldn't. "I was. I wanted a chance to see you again," he says.

"You're going to see me at the baby shower," I remind him.

"That's different, there will be people and games ... and you know those things always break off into factions. Men versus women. I'll hardly see you," he says.

It's true. I had been surprised to learn that Jessica had been okay with a coed shower, but it is just as much a celebration of Tanner becoming a father as it is of her becoming a mother.

"Well, here I am," I smile, shifting my duffle bag uncomfortably to my other shoulder.

"Allow me," Jordan says, taking the bag from me before I can protest. We walk through the airport together in comfortable silence, taking in the familiar sights that ease us back into life in Central Illinois. It's not a big airport, so it's not long before I spot my dad and say goodbye to Jordan.

"See you around, Kenley," he says before he turns on his heels and heads off in the other direction.

"Making friends already?" my dad teases as he picks up my bag.

"Whatever," I tell him, rolling my eyes and pushing him playfully. I had forgotten how good it could feel to be home.

14.

Home is where the heart is.

The painted wood sign that my mother swears looks vintage although she bought it at a commercial home decor store is the first thing that greets anyone who steps inside my parents' house. These days I don't know where my heart is, or if it is even tied to a place at all, but the sign is still a comforting reminder. The house looks the same as I remember it, which is another bit of comfort in the midst of everything else.

"We're here!" my father calls into the foyer as he sets my bags down and turns to close the door behind us. I am surprised by the silence of the house. Not that I think I deserve it, but I had sort of expected to be greeted with the fanfare of the prodigal daughter returned home after so many years. I suppose I should have expected the quiet; my mom has an entire celebration planned for later with my brother, sister, and brother-in-law. Although I had tried to explain that I would be tired from my day of travel, she had insisted that there should be a family dinner in my honor.

"Kenley!" my mother exclaims, rounding the corner and pulling me into a hug almost simultaneously. There is no judgment or concern in her hug, I am encapsulated by warmth, and I melt into her touch just a little bit more. My mother has never been the type to point out my flaws—if she thinks I am too thin, she'll offer me snacks; if she thinks I look tired, she'll offer me a melatonin gummy before bed.

Being the oldest child, my memories of being the one my parents doted upon are few. My sister came along when I was not quite two, so I settled into my role as the independent, oldest daughter when I was young. But Jessica and EJ won't be here for another hour and so, for now, I am the center of my parents' universe. I am quickly ushered into the kitchen, where my mom has been busy preparing enough food to feed seven families instead of our one, and seated on a bar stool before being offered every beverage that I have ever sampled in my life because she isn't sure what I am drinking these days. She seems disappointed when I choose water.

"So, how are you, Ken?" she asks earnestly once my dad has excused himself to take my bags down the hall to my childhood bedroom. It's a loaded question, which I think she can sense because she has specifically timed it for when my dad is out of the room. The thing is, only Jessica knows about Luke and only EJ knows about me trying to do some of the things on my list. I haven't told anyone about my apartment. So, when my mom asks this question, she is only asking about my job.

"Um, okay, all things considered," I say. It's true, though I could see the answer coming across as pacifying. If I really think about it, I am alright. While I lost my job, the termination comes with a severance package that is holding me over in the meantime, plus I am already interviewing for new work. I only have fifty days until I have to leave my apartment, but I have a plan and have already looked at several great places. And on top of that, there is a man back home who cares about me even though the feelings aren't entirely reciprocal. Things could be so much worse than me losing my job, being kicked out of my apartment, and not knowing what to do about Luke. So, in the grand scheme of things, I am okay.

"Well, we're glad you're here," my mom says when I don't give her an answer worth momming over. It's not that I don't want her to know all of the details of my life. I have always been incredibly close with my parents, it's just that even I don't know the details of my life as it stands right now, and I would rather come to them when I have something to report. I am a woman in my thirties; I don't need my parents figuring out my life for me.

"KENNY!" my brother's voice booms through the house before my mom has the chance to ask more questions. Even though EJ is now a tall, muscular twenty-seven-year-old man with a deep voice, I still expect the tiny four-year-old with a miniature afro that we adopted all those years ago to come around the corner to the kitchen and pull me into a tight embrace.

There are only five years between EJ and me, but growing up, I always regarded myself as his second mother and felt so much older and more mature than he was. It is always weird to me to be hugged by this massive man when I still think of the scrawny kid he used to be. I moved to college when EJ was thirteen, and even though I was still close by, I felt like I missed out on a lot of his teenage years, and I had missed his transition into manhood entirely. Still, EJ and I have always been close, which is why I trusted him with the secret of my adventures when I hadn't told anyone else.

"This looks dope!" he says, grabbing my wrist and examining my tattoo.

EJ is covered in tattoos across both arms and his torso, so the small bird on my wrist seems like nothing compared to the amount of time and money he has invested in his own body. Still, I can't help flushing with pride when he says it. I notice my mom looking, too, but she doesn't say anything. It's not like I was planning on keeping it a secret forever, it's just that "I lost my job, so I got a tattoo" didn't seem like the best thing to say to my parents when I am trying to prove that I am doing okay.

"Thanks! It's small but it's fun," I say.

"It's perfect for you," EJ says, letting go of my wrist just as my dad walks back into the room.

"What's perfect?" he asks.

"Kenley got a tattoo," my mom says matter-of-factly. It's hard to tell from her tone whether she is upset or disappointed or if it is something else.

"Kenley got a tattoo?" Jessica says then, rounding the corner into the kitchen. Her belly leads the way, and even seeing her, it is still hard to wrap my mind around the idea that in a few short weeks my sister will be a mother. Tanner, who has several tattoos of his own, follows closely behind her, like he's still unsure of how to behave in our parents' house even after five years of being married to my sister.

This is what I both love and hate about being home. In my family, everyone knows what is going on with everyone else all the time. There is something endearing about that: I know that I never have to go through anything alone because I now have five and three-quarters other people by my side. But sometimes I want to feel like my own person. That's part of why I only applied to law schools out of state.

"Oh my gosh. Yes, I got a tattoo. It's not a big deal," I say.

"Look at you! I can't believe it!" I continue, turning my focus to Jessica, who immediately responds to the attention. My mom's intention was for this dinner to be about me, but there is no way in hell that my middle-child sister is going to let that happen.

"Oh, thank you! He's definitely in there!" she says gleefully. It's good to see my sister so happy. There were some years when she was in college when it seemed like she might never settle down. And I like Tanner. He's a perfect match for her, which is something I feel like not everyone can say about their in-laws. Most of all, I am grateful to have the attention off of me and onto my sister, for however long it lasts.

I love my family. I really do. Yes, they're loud and all up in each other's business all the time, but to me, that's the definition of family. We are extensions of one another in so many ways, and that is something that I wanted to escape when I left Illinois all those years ago. It had been a shock to everyone that I would choose to go so far from home for law school, and even more of a shock that I had chosen to stay in California to practice instead of returning home, as had been expected of me. But even though they hadn't completely understood my desire to leave, they never made me feel like I wasn't as much a part of this unit as ever. Whenever I am here, I think about all of the things I am missing, like these dinners. Then as soon as I touch down back in Los Angeles, being there seems right. My heart is split between these two homes, so it always feels a little like I don't belong in either.

One thing I definitely miss are my mom's feasts. Whenever we're all at home and gathered around the table, there is enough food to feed an army, and tonight is no different. She has made an entire turkey dinner, as if it is Thanksgiving, complete with homemade apple pie. It's as ridiculous as it is delicious, and I hope that she never changes. The dinner is loud, with everyone talking at the same time as my mom talks to EJ about his work and my dad talks to Tanner about baseball and Jessica fills me in on the latest gossip with her friends. It's a beautiful cacophony that fills my heart with joy. For a fleeting moment, I think about my last encounter with a family at Luke's birthday dinner and it threatens to sour my mood. If Luke were here, he'd likely be telling my family all of the future plans he's made for me, as if they had already been decided.

"Will we be seeing any more of your gentleman friend?" my dad asks as if on cue. Everyone's attention quickly snaps to me.

"Dad. Oh my gosh," I say, my cheeks turning red.

"You told them about Luke?" Jessica asks innocently.

"I thought his name was Jordan?" my dad replies before I have a chance to answer. This piques everyone's interest even more. My mother even sets down her fork and clasps her hands in anticipation.

"I ran into Jordan Thomas in the Atlanta airport waiting for my flight, and he helped me with my bag. I'd hardly call him my gentleman friend," I say, hoping that this is enough to get them off my back. For a moment I think it worked, as Tanner talks about how Jordan is a childhood friend who is in town for the shower. But then ...

"Who is Luke?" my mom asks, far less innocently than Jessica had.

I lock eyes with my sister as she mouths *sorry.*

"A friend," I reply. It is true.

"A gentleman friend?" my dad asks jokingly.

"You guys know him, he's been my friend since law school," I say. My parents have only ever met Luke at graduation, but that is enough for me. Even though it hadn't been a happy thought to begin with, I can no longer imagine what would be happening if Luke were here.

"I know you've spoken of him for years, but why did Jessica mention him when your dad asked about your gentleman friend?" my mom asks. She still hasn't picked up her fork again.

"Oh my gosh. Can we stop saying *gentleman friend*? It's giving me the creeps," I reply. I have never felt this uncomfortable around my family before. We've never been the type to do merciless teasing or joke at one another's expense, and I know that deep down they just want me to be happy. And even though I have always rejected the idea that I need a significant other in order to be happy, they still desire that for me. Unfortunately, I am not going to get out of this conversation without providing a little bit of information.

Before I speak again, I try to carefully plan what I want to say, both to share my experience and preserve my innocence. As far as my parents are concerned, I would rather they assume I am a virgin until they die. "We've been spending more time together since we were both let go from the firm. It's just exploratory right now ... we're seeing where it goes. I didn't want you to, like, get your hopes up," I say.

This answer seems to satisfy them as my mom finally grabs her fork and continues her meal. It's weighing heavily on me, though. It's not entirely true. It is what had felt the safest to say to my parents, but I know that there is only one person who is doing any exploring: me. Luke already knows exactly what he wants.

Even with all of the secret sharing and the way I feel intensely uncomfortable about discussing my love life over a homemade meal, it is still amazing to be home. I've been so good at making excuses for staying away over the last several years, and now I can't remember any of them. Last night Luke had asked me if I was coming back to L.A. and I thought he sounded crazy, but now that I am sitting here at dinner with my family, feeling both wildly uncomfortable and full of love, I know exactly why he had to ask.

15.

When I head to my room that night, my heart is full. On my past trips home to visit my family, being here has felt more like an inconvenience and an obligation. I always felt like I had more important things to do, work to complete, family to help; this trip is different because, in Los Angeles, only life-altering decisions await me, but while I am here, I have nothing but time.

My childhood bedroom hasn't changed much in my absence. I had technically moved out of it at eighteen when I left for college, but I had only moved minutes away from home and came back to study and sleep in the quietude of my room fairly regularly. It wasn't until I left for law school that I had actually moved out, and in ten years not a lot has changed. The personal elements are gone. There are no longer photos of my high school friends and me on a bulletin board above the desk. Instead, my mother has hung a print of a painting that she probably got at the same mass retailer as her *Home Is Where the Heart Is* sign, the bedspread has been updated to something that is more appealing to guests than the turquoise monstrosity from my youth, and the closet is now used to store my parents' luggage. But the essence of the room remains unchanged and still feels very much like it always did. Especially the bed, which could have been made of stone and still would have felt comfortable to me after a day of traveling. I have so many memories in this bed. It was here where I was laid up for a week with chicken pox when I was seven. This bed is where I cried myself to sleep over an unrequited crush in seventh grade. It's where I sat in a nest made of my LSAT books while I crammed for the exam. More than anything else in this house, this bed is home to me, and it's where I am sitting when my phone pings with a new message.

Jordan: `I'm really glad that I ran into you today.`

I'm taken aback by Jordan's message, not because the statement is anything shocking but because I am surprised that I am hearing from him at all. The typing bubble appears and disappears three or four times on the chat before he sends another message.

Jordan: `I had the biggest crush on you in high school, you were always the unattainable girl who I thought would never like me. When I saw you today, it felt like maybe I was getting a second chance from the universe, and so I want to do this before I lose my nerve. Can I take you out tomorrow night?`

There are several things in this message about which I have questions. First of all, I am fifteen years late to learning that Jordan Thomas, the most popular boy at Bloomington High School, had a crush on me. How does that even make sense? Second, meeting me today was like a sign from the universe? Who says that? Third, what about Luke? I am supposed to be figuring out what I want to do about us ... not going on dates with other men.

Kenley, why is Luke even a factor here? He is 2,000 miles away and he doesn't have to know. Think of sixteen-year-old Kenley, staring into the mirror and admiring her new braces-less smile while imagining how it might make Jordan Thomas love her. Think of that girl who wanted so badly to be included by the popular kids and never thought a day like this would come. What would she want you to do? I say to myself. It has me responding

Kenley: `Okay`

faster than my brain can process what I've typed. None of this makes any sense.

———

When I wake up in the morning in the same bed I woke up in when I was in high school, I try my best not to freak out about the fact that

93

I have a date with Jordan Thomas tonight.

I remember back then, people would try to convince me that in the scheme of things, high school didn't matter. It didn't make a difference who was the most popular or who won the most football games or who gave the best speech that the Illinois High School Association Debate Competition had seen in a decade (okay, so that one was me ...). What mattered, they had tried to tell me, was what happened after graduation, when the world evened out in ways that most teenagers couldn't even fathom. I had remained unconvinced. Everything in high school had felt like the most important thing to ever happen, and I couldn't imagine how everything going on in my small little world at that time would just cease to matter. In retrospect, I see that they were right. As my world got bigger, the triviality of high school got smaller. But I still can't help thinking of that sixteen-year-old girl who would cross all of her fingers and toes and wish on every shooting star and birthday candle that Jordan Thomas might notice her. She would never be able to believe the events of the last twenty-four hours.

"Morning, Ken," my mom says from the kitchen island as I stumble into the room in search of coffee. Looking at the clock, I know that my father has already been at work for a while, which means my mom has been awake for hours so that she could have breakfast with him and pack his lunch before he headed off for the day. Still, she is in her pajamas and bathrobe, reading a magazine with her drugstore reading glasses slid halfway down her nose, while she sips from what is probably her third cup of coffee.

Over the years I have sometimes resented my mother's chosen role in life. She is the happiest woman that I know and loves her life beyond measure, but the times we have butted heads have always been about my feeling like she was fenced in by her role as a homemaker. Truthfully, it's part of the reason I am so ambitious about my career. But if my mom has ever regretted her decision to quit her teaching job in favor of raising her family, she has never shown it.

"Mmm, I missed your coffee," I say, inhaling the aroma from my steaming mug. My mom has used the same brand of coffee for years, the kind that comes in cans from the supermarket. Still, for some reason, it always tastes like the best coffee I have ever had. Maybe it's the nostalgia, but this cup of coffee tastes like home to me.

"So, I have a date tonight," I say, after I have swallowed my first sip. I know that there is nothing in the world that my mom wants for me more than to find love, so I might as well rip off the Band-Aid with my news. As expected, she squeals in excitement and takes off her glasses to show me that I have her full attention.

"Jordan Thomas? From Bloomington High? Oh, I remember how you loved him so much!" she says excitedly.

"I KNOW!" I laugh. "Apparently he had a crush on me, too? It doesn't make sense!"

"Well, of course it makes sense, Kenley. You are a wonderful girl!" she says.

I can't help but roll my eyes, not so much at the momness of it all, but more because that wasn't what I had meant. It's not something worth arguing though, and I go back to my coffee hoping that will be the end of the conversation. It's not.

"What about the other young man? The one your sister seems to know all about?" she asks. I don't miss the barb in her words; the fact that Jessica and I would share a secret, especially one about something my mom deems as so important, bothers her.

"What about him? We're not really together," I say, echoing what Luke had told his sister on that night at his parents' house. "And besides, I am not sure that it is going to work out."

This is the first time I have said the words that I have been thinking aloud. Luke and I have history and passion, but I don't know that we have a future. Even as I finally say the words, I feel guilty for stringing Luke along. He has been my closest friend for all these years, and up until two nights ago, I have let him believe that there is a chance for us to be more than friends when I think I always knew that it wasn't right. Really, it's just that I was thinking with my libido. I was wasted the first night that we hooked up, and it had been so long since I had had sex with anyone that it was easy to give into my suppressed desires. But the red flags are just too great to have me considering anything real with Luke. At the beginning, I think I was starting to ... and then he started micromanaging my life. I think what I needed time to think about was if that was something that I was willing to overlook, but I know deep down that I can't.

"Go get dressed, we're going shopping," she tells me then, as if it has already been decided.

"What? Why?"

"Are you telling me that you packed a date outfit in that beat-up duffel bag of yours?" she asks, looking down her nose at me in the way that only moms can do. I chuckle in defeat and spin on my heels back to my room because she is right, I don't have anything to wear on my date with Jordan.

———

Shopping with my mom is the kind of comforting experience that almost makes it feel like I never left Bloomington at all. Things have changed some in the decade that I've been in California—some of the stores I remember frequenting in high school and college have gone out of business. We have to make several stops before I find something that is suitable for my date, but the morning with my mom flies by, and I realize how much I had missed spending time with her.

"So, are you excited?" she asks me over sandwiches at a cafe that she told me she'd been dying for me to try.

"I guess so?" I reply, taking a sip of my iced tea. "It feels kind of surreal. Like, I come back home for the first time in forever and immediately get a date with my high school crush? I feel like I'm in that Gwyneth Paltrow movie ... the one about what would happen if one thing in your life happened differently. It's like ... what my life could have been if I'd stayed in Bloomington."

"*Sliding Doors*," my mother says.

"What?"

"The Gwyneth Paltrow movie is *Sliding Doors*, your father and I rented it from Blockbuster years ago. I can't believe I remember the name," she says.

The title of the movie is, of course, not relevant. It does describe a little bit how I feel about this date with Jordan, but I hadn't thought of it in years. My mom's remembrance of the title is irrelevant, too, except that it's all she says on the topic. There is nothing about how I could have come home after law school, how I could have been married with a family by now, or how the big city has made me a cynic. Instead, she simply offers the title of the movie. I don't know if it's a sign of growth or repressed emotions.

"Well, he doesn't live here either, so it's a chance for you to go out and have a little fun," she says then. That's the reason, then, that she isn't harping on me for leaving town. Jordan doesn't live here, either, so it's not like it gives her hope that I might stay.

"You have to sow your wild oats while you're still young. But don't give the whole farm away, you know … just a little taste of the milk," she continues, winking at me over her tuna salad croissant.

"Mother!" I gasp. "Who do you think I am?!"

"Kenley, please, you are a woman in your thirties. I know you're not still saving yourself for marriage."

"Oh my gosh! Can we not talk about this?!" My cheeks are the color of the tomatoes on my club sandwich. I do not want to be having this conversation about the history of my sex life right now. Like I said, I would be completely happy if my parents went to their graves believing I was a virgin, and maybe it's more for my blissful ignorance than theirs.

16.

I tried to convince Jordan that I could meet him somewhere for our date, but he insisted that he would pick me up. As horrified as that makes me, a thirty-two-year-old woman with overly involved parents, I had no choice but to accept because the gesture was sweet.

I'm just putting the finishing touches on my makeup when the doorbell rings. Of course Jordan Thomas, the god of Bloomington High, would be the kind of gentleman who rings the doorbell instead of texting or, worse, honking from the driveway. Trying to beat my parents to the door is futile, but I do put a little pep in my step to grab my purse and head for the foyer before they can embarrass me too much.

As I come down the hallway, I can already hear my dad's voice: "And what are your intentions with my daughter?"

Oh, gosh. I know my dad well enough to know that he is teasing, but I seriously hope that Jordan can tell it's a joke.

"You don't have to answer that," I say, emerging from the hallway just in the nick of time.

"Hey," Jordan smiles warmly in a way that makes my insides clench, a reaction that I was not expecting.

"Ready?" I ask, before immediately turning back to my parents. "Okay, we're leaving, I'll be back later!"

I know it's a little rude of me to physically pull this man, whom I have been waiting sixteen years to date, out of the foyer of my parents' home, but I am afraid that if we stay any longer my parents might say something truly horrifying, and I still desperately want Jordan to like me.

"Sorry about them," I say, once we're safely off the porch and down the front walk. I realize that I am still holding Jordan's hand, but neither of us makes any moves to let go.

"It's fine, really. It goes well with the theme I have in mind for tonight," he says. Jordan finally drops my hand when we reach the midsize SUV parked at the curb. A wooden cross hangs from the rearview mirror.

"What theme is that?" I ask as he holds the passenger-side door open for me. I have to wait for an answer until he comes around and climbs into the driver's seat, putting the key into the ignition.

"I wanted to plan the date I would have taken you on if I had had the courage to ask you out in high school," he says. "So far, I've borrowed my mom's car and been interrogated at the door by your parents, so things are working out perfectly."

Everyone who had attended Bloomington High knew about the kind of dates Jordan used to go on in high school. According to the stories, if you were lucky enough to get a date with Jordan Thomas, he would take you out to Evergreen Lake for a picnic, and if he liked you, the bed of his truck would be used for other activities sometimes performed in beds. Although I had been somewhat of a prude in high school, I would have died for the invitation.

"I heard about the kind of dates you used to go on in high school," I say. I want it out in the open that at my age, I am not interested in a truck bed tryst.

"The whole Evergreen Lake truck thing?" he laughs, shaking his head. "Never happened."

"You're kidding! You were a legend with that story!"

"Yeah ... I mean, I think I took a girl for a picnic at the lake when I was in eighth grade, but that was it. I don't know who actually started the rumor, but my teammates definitely ran with it, and I didn't stop them," he says.

"Wow, I feel like my life is a lie," I joke. "But seriously, why didn't you stop them?"

"I liked the clout, I guess. I didn't want anyone to know that I didn't lose my virginity until college," Jordan answers sheepishly. Gone is the confident jock from high school, replaced by this man about whom I know literally nothing.

"What about all the girls you went out with back then?" I ask. I can't let this go. I'd been joking when I had said my whole life was a lie, but it also feels a little bit true. I had built my fantasy about Jordan on this whole persona of his that has turned out to be fiction, and I think it makes my crush on him a little stronger. I had certainly faked my way through high school, and to know that Jordan had been faking it, too does something for me, as strange as that sounds.

"I dated a lot of girls, but I always kept it PG. When they told stories about our dates, I think they made things up because they all thought they were the only girl that I didn't go all the way with ... I know what you're thinking and, yes, I was a huge asshole for letting them think that," he says. He's staring straight at the road, like he's afraid to look at me.

"High school was such a charade," I say then, hoping to bring him back out. "We were all assholes. Do you know that I don't talk to a single person from high school? I was so preoccupied with getting out of school and becoming a lawyer that I didn't even bother to build relationships that lasted beyond graduation."

We drive in silence for a while, and I wonder if I have gotten through to him at all when he reaches a hand out and holds one of mine. "I can't believe you said yes."

"I have to admit, I am extremely confused. I didn't even think you knew I existed. But, my sixteen-year-old self would have killed me if I had turned you down. I had the biggest crush on you in high school, too," I say, squeezing his fingers gently.

"Oh, I knew you existed," he smirks. "I just didn't think you'd ever go out with me."

"What? Why?"

"I knew what the rumors said, and you weren't that kind of girl. You were smart and ambitious and beautiful. I always felt like if I were to ask you out, you would have laughed in my face, and I didn't want to deal with the embarrassment. When I saw you in the airport yesterday, my heart just about stopped."

I know what my own reputation was in high school about as well as I know what Jordan's had been. I wasn't exactly well liked, and I pretended not to care. I had a few friends that I'd been in class with since elementary school, but it always felt superficial. We'd go to the mall on weekends and rent movies to watch while we slept over at each other's houses, but it never felt like we were building anything real. It never helped that Jessica was only a year behind me all throughout school and had cared more about her social calendar than about her classes. Her whole life felt frivolous to me, like she wasn't working toward anything. You don't make a lot of friends by being a rigid rule follower, but it got me to where I am today ... which at the moment is nowhere.

"I'm surprised you never dated my sister," I say. "She was way more popular than I was."

"I think your definition of popular is not the same as mine."

"What do you mean?" I ask.

"Your sister might have been social, but I wouldn't call her the queen of the school. What? She was in drama? Wrote on the newspaper staff? She had a lot of friends, but I wouldn't have called those things cool," he says.

"Are you sure you weren't into my sister? Seems like you know a lot about her," I joke.

"You forget that she's married to one of my best friends, we've had a lot of time to chat about our lives at BHS. I didn't even know who she was, but I definitely kept track of you in high school," he says.

"Why? I was a nobody."

"Kenley, we've been over this. You're not a nobody. You're ambitious. You're smart. You're beautiful. Not much has changed. You were always the sister I had my eye on," he says.

"And how come you never asked me out?"

"Remember that whole thing about being an asshole?" he laughs.

The silence between us continues for a few minutes, but it's comfortable. It's not the kind of silence that feels awkward or makes me think I need to find a way to fill the void. We're just driving, holding hands, in the front seat of Jordan's mom's car. It feels like exactly where I am supposed to be.

"Okay, I feel stupid about this now, but we're here," Jordan says then, pulling into the parking lot at Applebee's. I can't help but smile. The idea is pretty cute. Not to mention I haven't been here in years, so I'm a little bit excited just to be back at the restaurant. One thing that it is hard to find in the city of Los Angeles is a suburban chain restaurant. Don't get me wrong, I love the variety of cuisines that are available to me within walking distance of my apartment. Sometimes you just want a big bowl of spinach artichoke dip.

"Oh my gosh, I love it!" I say, widening my smile, which in turn causes Jordan to widen his.

"What?" I ask self-consciously.

"Nothing," he says, sucking in his lips to hide his smile. "It's just that … I haven't heard anyone say 'oh my gosh' in years, and you are exactly everything I thought you were."

"Well, the night is still young. I have plenty of time to change your mind," I wink, unhooking my seatbelt.

———

It's been a while since I have had a true first date. Yes, I'd been on a few dates with Luke recently, but because of our circumstances we had skipped the whole "getting to know you" portion of things. So it could be that I am just out of practice when it comes to first dates, but it feels to me like this one with Jordan is going especially well.

The commitment to making it as if we had gone out in high school instead of sixteen years later is so cute. I even agree to participate in the same way, ordering a lemonade and an appetizer as my meal, just like I would have done back then. But what surprises me the most about this date with Jordan isn't the effort that he put into it to make it special, but the fact that he is so easy to talk to. I had so many preconceived notions in my head about who the legendary Jordan Thomas was, and I am happy to say that as obsessed as I was with those ideas back in high school, the real version is even better.

"Do you ever stop and wonder how they let us be adults? Do you ever feel like you are just pretending?" I ask, lifting a chip out of the cheesy pile of nachos on my plate. While I had ordered off the appetizer menu to be cute and stick with the theme, I'd be lying if I said I didn't choose nachos nine times out of ten anyway.

"I definitely thought things would be different by now," Jordan replies. He hasn't stopped smiling at me since we sat down, and it's more endearing than I would have expected.

"I was so ambitious in high school. I thought that if I just kept doing the next right thing and the next right thing and the next right thing then everything would work out, you know? And it didn't," I continue. I have a hard time not getting philosophical on dates if I'm honest. I'm not much for idle chitchat, I'd rather solve world hunger if I'm going to have a captive audience for two hours.

"Hey, I get that," Jordan says. It's the first time his smile has faltered. "Do you know why I was so into sports in high school?"

"Athletic ability and the sheer magnitude of your size?" I respond without thinking. But Jordan isn't fazed by my quick retort.

"I thought I was supposed to be. I mean, I guess I had skill, or it wouldn't have worked for me. But I wasn't in it for the love of the game. I had just watched too many teen movies about how football players ruled the school, and so I thought that if I wanted to be popular, I needed to play football. And a lot of good it did me, I didn't even get a scholarship to play in college. Now I am divorced, living alone in a two-bedroom condo. Best-laid plans, I guess."

I raise my lemonade in mock salute. "Unemployed in a studio apartment," I wink.

"We're killing it, girl," he laughs, lifting his soda to toast my raised glass.

"Absolutely slaying," I reply.

We talk about other things too, the usual first-date-type conversations, but the whole time all I can think about is how it feels so easy. Maybe by the time I had gotten around to finally dating Luke, it hadn't felt easy because our relationship had changed so suddenly. Being here with Jordan reminds me that being out on a date shouldn't fill me with anxiety like I had every time I was out with Luke. It should feel easy.

This actually is the first day of the rest of my life.

17.

The last thing that I want to do the morning after my date with Jordan is get the third degree from my mom. I don't feel like answering her questions about how we stayed at our table until the restaurant closed, and they had to ask us to leave. She'll ask too many questions if I tell her that after driving me back to my parents' house, Jordan asked politely if he could kiss me before placing a chaste peck on my lips, and it will remind me why I don't like to tell her when I'm dating someone to begin with. I love my mom, and we're close, but I've just never felt comfortable discussing my love life with her. I mean, this is the woman who told me that I should go ahead and let him have "a sip of the milk" since we live in different places, and he obviously won't be "buying the farm" ... so you can see my position.

Thankfully, it's the day of the baby shower and my mom has too many things to finish to waste her time meddling in my dating life. I am immediately put to work hanging crepe paper streamers and decorations that exclaim "Oh Boy!" from the railings of the back deck.

It's still hard for me to wrap my head around the idea of Jessica having a baby, and even more so that the baby is a boy. In all these years, I haven't known Jessica to have a nurturing bone in her body, and I have especially never seen her express any knowledge about caring for little boys. But I'd been away for the last ten years and hadn't seen her as a teacher or a new wife to know if or how these things had changed. It's one of the things that makes me feel the most disconnected from my family: the fact that everything I know about them is from ten years ago and, while we talk regularly, I have no idea who they are now. I know that it's my own fault for letting my work keep me away, but it has made me feel like an outsider in my family's home.

"Here let me help with that," comes EJ's deep, booming voice from behind me, causing me to jump. I had been enjoying the time with my thoughts, but if there is anyone I'm willing to share my solitude with, it's EJ.

"I'm excited to finally meet Kaylee today," I tell him. My brother has been dating the same girl for a while, but the last time I had been home was the holidays, and she went to visit her own family in Peoria. She had been working during our family dinner the other night, so I missed her then, too.

"Want to know a secret?" EJ asks, taking a piece of tape from the dispenser I am still holding. He doesn't wait for me to answer. "Kaylee's pregnant."

This is happy news, so I don't know why it feels like a punch to the gut. EJ is twenty-seven, has a stable job, and is in a loving relationship with his child's mother. There is nothing about this announcement that should fill me with dread, yet that's exactly how I feel. I can't let EJ see this reaction, though. He's told me this secret so that I can share his joy, and that's exactly what I intend to do.

"Oh my gosh! That's amazing! Congratulations!" I cheer, wrapping him in a tight hug. "I'm so happy for you guys!"

"Thanks! It's pretty new, I haven't told Mom and Dad yet, and I don't want to steal Jessi's thunder," he says. I can hear the happiness in his voice and know that I have responded correctly, even though my heart is aching for some reason I cannot identify.

Kenley, I tell myself. *This is happy news. You're going to be an aunt. Jessica's and EJ's kids will grow up together, everyone will be thrilled. Just be happy for them!*

These pep talks always used to work for me, but they always used to be logical. Lately I can't remember where I put the part of my brain that thinks logically. It seems to still be sitting at my old desk inside the offices of Sullivan, Dunkirk, Jackson, Cruz, and Karjanian, where I last had use for it. I didn't realize that I was supposed to pack it in the banker's box with my other belongings.

"Are you okay?" EJ asks. I realize that I've left tear marks on his shoulder, I hadn't even realized I'd been crying. I never cry.

"Yes, I'm just so happy for you!" I lie, plastering on a smile and hoping he believes me.

———

The shower for Baby Kauffman is nothing short of the event of the season. It looks like half of Bloomington is in my parents' backyard, nibbling on finger sandwiches and placing bets on the date of the baby's arrival. I'm not surprised there are so many people here. Jessica and Tanner both grew up in the area before settling here and getting jobs at Bloomington High. And Jessica, of course, looks right in her element as the center of attention as people happily greet her with hugs and place hands on her burgeoning belly. I can observe it all from a spot I found on the deck, leaning over the railing, that is ideal for watching the festivities without having to make small talk. It is the perfect vantage point, in my opinion.

"Hey you," Jordan says, approaching me as soon as he steps out onto the deck. He looks handsome in a light green polo shirt that shows off the size of his biceps. Even at five-foot-eight, which is usually considered fairly tall for a woman, I feel tiny standing next to him, clinging to my can of sparkling water like it is my lifeline.

"Hey! Long time no see!" I joke, immediately feeling embarrassed about it.

But Jordan doesn't react, he simply joins me in leaning over the railing and observing the crowd, neither of us saying a word. We had spent all of last night talking, which felt so easy, but standing next to him in silence like this feels easy, too.

"How many of these people do you know?" he asks after a comfortable amount of time has passed.

"Not many—my family, of course, a few of Jessica's friends who were in her wedding, but nobody that I am dying to see again. You?" I answer, not looking at him but sensing the closeness of his body.

Our arms are practically touching, and I have goosebumps just from the proximity.

"My parents, Tanner's parents, Tanner, Jessica, and you," he says, pointing to each person as he mentions them.

"How do you know Tanner, anyway?" I ask, turning my body slightly to look at him. The sixteen-year-old inside me still can't believe I get to look at him up close at all. Tanner had grown up nearby, but I'd learned early on in his relationship with my sister that he had gone to high school in Normal, which explains why I hadn't known him even though we had graduated the same year.

"Our moms have been best friends since elementary school," Jordan replies. "Even if we hadn't wanted to be friends, we were always together because they were always together. So, it worked out well that I actually like the guy."

Even though I don't respond, Jordan doesn't leave my side. I've always been more of the quiet observer in my family, but today feels different. Today I am not watching out of my deep introversion, but rather from a place of not understanding what the heck is going on in my life. I don't understand how I got here, to this place of being so disconnected from these people and this life. I have done nothing for the last ten years but pursue my dreams; I had thought that by now I would have something to show for it. Watching EJ and Kaylee greet Jessica and moon over her giant bump sends me over the edge.

"Are you okay?" Jordan whispers. I thought that I was doing a pretty good job of masking my emotions, it's something I had always prided myself on, yet somehow, he has seen right through me.

"Am I too young to be having a midlife crisis?" I ask. I expect him to shut me down, to tell me that not only am I too young but I am hardly in crisis, but Jordan Thomas, my high school dream boy, continues to surprise me.

"It's weird, isn't it? Watching life go on so perfectly around you when yours is nothing like you planned?"

The sarcastic laugh of acknowledgment that comes out of my nose must give him encouragement to continue, because he speaks again before I have the chance. "Sometimes I look at Tanner's life and I get jealous. I got married right before he did, but we didn't even make it two years. She cheated, said we wanted different things. I said that what I wanted was for there not to be another man's dick inside my wife. It got ugly. She got the house and a monthly spousal support payment. None of that was supposed to happen. I had planned this picture-perfect life, I did everything right, and it all went to crap. I still show up because Tanner is a good friend, but damn, events like these are hard for me."

Our circumstances are different, but it might as well have been me giving this monologue about my sister because the sentiment is exactly the same. I did everything like I thought I was supposed to, just like I always had for as long as I can remember. Now all I have to show for it is this sense that by doing everything right, I had done everything wrong. It's the reason I feel so confused.

"Do you ever wonder what would have happened if you never left Bloomington?" I ask, my voice barely above a whisper as I try to talk around the giant lump that has formed in my throat. "I mean, I look at Jessica and at EJ and how wonderful their lives seem, and I think about how maybe if I had just stayed instead of being so anxious to go somewhere else, then I might have that, too."

The party on the lawn below is loud and lively. Music blares from speakers and everyone in my family seems exactly in their element. Up here in this little corner of the deck, though, the vibe is completely different. It feels intimate. Even though Jordan and I haven't touched, heat is radiating between our bodies that even the most sharp-eyed outside observer could detect. Neither of us makes a move toward the other, though.

"Every time I come back, I try to imagine what life would be like if I had stayed. But honestly, I'm happy that I left. I have a life that I don't think I could have had here. I like living in a bigger city ... and not everything has been rosy, but that doesn't mean that the answer to those problems lies in Bloomington," he says, finally closing the gap between us and putting an arm loosely across my back.

"Maybe you're right. It's just hard to think objectively sometimes when you're surrounded by everyone's perfect, happy lives," I say, leaning slightly into his side.

"Think about the expectations of building your life here, though.

I know that my mom would expect me home every Saturday for dinner, and I would have to get my ass to her church every Sunday morning, even though I stopped believing in her god a long time ago. And there is all that high school-bigshot crap that we were talking about last night. When I'm here, I still run into people who expect me to be that guy. It's a lot of pressure. I like having my own life where those expectations aren't constantly in my face," he says.

As if on cue, my mom spots Jordan and me on the deck and throws me a double thumbs-up and a big smile.

"I have to move," I say, randomly.

"Not here, right? Not that there's anything wrong with here, but I don't think that's the answer," he says.

"No, not here. I love L.A., which is not something I imagined myself being able to say when I first moved there," I answer. Jordan is the first person I've told about my apartment since I got to Bloomington, and it feels good to say it out loud, especially without being met by the kind of judgmental response I would receive from my parents ... or Luke. Our private moment is quickly ended, though, when Tanner calls, "J-Money," from the yard.

"Don't let me keep you, J-Money," I wink, pulling away from him.

"Don't you dare," he laughs, kissing the top of my head before jumping over the side of the deck into the grass.

"T-Bone!" he calls, greeting his friend with some kind of elaborate handshake that they must have perfected as children.

Even though I know that Jordan and Tanner have always been close, the use of these nicknames surprises me. It's the kind of familiarity in friendship that I had never had. No one in my life has ever given me a nickname. In my family, we use shortened forms of each other's names: to them I am Ken, or to my brother (and only my brother) I am Kenny. My sister has always been Jess to us, except for the short period in elementary school when she was obsessed with *The Baby-Sitters Club* and insisted on being called Jessi, which EJ still uses. And EJ is short for Edwin Jamaal because the name had seemed like such a mouthful on a four-year-old, though my parents had insisted that, even after his adoption, he should keep it. No one in my life has ever called me K-Dawg or named me after our own private joke. I had never had any desire to be called Kenzo before today, and for some reason, that makes me sad.

With Jordan off mingling, I am left alone with my thoughts again. They're not bad thoughts, he had helped me with that, they're just … lingering. In my original life plan, thirty-two was still plenty young enough to fall in love and start a family, and all of the sudden I am wondering if I have been wasting time. It's not something I had ever paused to consider before I lost my job; I was perfectly content moving along, doing what I thought I was supposed to do, and waiting for all of that other stuff to come to me once the timing was right. Now I wonder if the timing is ever right for anything. I miss those days of being so sure that everything in my life was exactly as it should be.

"Having fun?" I ask Jessica, as she finally makes her way to the deck for a chair.

"I didn't expect seeing all these people to be so exhausting!" she laughs, propping her feet up on a second chair. I'm surprised by this admission. I never thought I would see the day when my social butterfly sister was tired out by a party, but I guess it took being eight-and-a-half-months pregnant for that to finally happen.

"Welcome to my world," I say, sitting down beside her. "Do you need anything?"

"No, I just need to rest for a second. My ankles are the size of grapefruits," she says. It's always hard to picture what someone might look like pregnant. Jessica had always been fit, and I imagined that she would have looked like she was smuggling a watermelon under her dress, but in reality, she's wearing pregnancy all over.

"It's a good look for you," I say, finishing my thought aloud.

"Cankles?" she asks.

"No, pregnancy. You look happy," I say. She squeezes my hand in reply, tilting her head back and closing her eyes.

"So … you and Jordan?" she asks then. Like EJ with his baby news, I was not looking to steal my sister's thunder today.

"Um, yeah … we went on a date last night. Apparently, he had a crush on me in high school? I am still not over that revelation," I say.

"Tanner said he used to carry on about this girl that he thought was too good for him, turns out it was you," Jessica replies. "He was wrong, though."

"I'm not good enough for him?" I ask. It's the opposite of being too good for him, and I'm not sure what else she could have meant.

"No, no, no," she says quickly. "You're actually, like, perfect for each other."

"We live on opposite sides of the country."

"Stranger things have happened," she says, closing her eyes again and letting me know that our conversation is over.

I'm not looking for a relationship. I had come to Illinois so that I could process everything that had happened with Luke and decide what I want to do about it going forward. I had not expected to meet someone else, and I especially had not expected for that someone else to be Jordan Thomas. Part of what brings me comfort in having a little fun while I am back here is knowing that we'll go back to our opposite coasts and that will be that. Whatever Jessica's "stranger things" are, that is absolutely not what I am doing here. Right?

18.

When my phone chimes at the breakfast table on Sunday morning, my parents both grin widely and wink at me as if we're all in on some secret together.

"It's Jessica, thank you very much," I tell them.

This doesn't wipe the grins off their faces like I had expected. The text is a message inviting me for a barbecue with my siblings at Jess's house, which of course I agree to. Since I got to town, I feel like I've spent most of my time with my parents because Jessica and EJ have their own lives.

After I had first moved away, every time I came home it was a big event. Everyone wanted to see me and spend time with me, and my entire schedule would be booked solid with family activities. As time went on, though, my visits started to seem like more of an imposition. Since I am the only member of the Graves family who doesn't live in town, everyone else had to interrupt their normal schedules and routines to accommodate me. My busyness at work started to serve as the perfect excuse not to come around more often, when the truth was, I had started to feel unwelcome.

"How's it going with Jordan?" my mom asks, as if I haven't just informed her that the message is from my sister. The truth is that the text from Jessica was kind of a fluke. Ever since the baby shower, Jordan and I have been texting nonstop. I was up until after midnight exchanging messages about everything and nothing. The only reason we had paused our ongoing conversation was because it was Sunday, and just like he had predicted, his mother expected him at church.

But to my mom's question, I shrug. "Fine, I guess, he's a nice guy," I say. Both true statements.

"Well, do you like him?" my dad asks, stabbing at his scrambled eggs like they have done something to personally offend him. I don't know why these conversations with my parents always make me so uncomfortable. They had always shown affection to one another in front of us kids and made it clear that there was nothing to be ashamed of in doing so, but something about telling them stories of my own love life sends shivers up and down my spine.

"Yeah, I like him. He's a nice guy," I say again.

"What your father is asking is, do you *like him* like him?" my mom asks, as if I haven't understood.

"Oh my gosh! I got it! I don't know what to say to that. I mean, it doesn't matter whether I do or not, nothing is going to happen between us. As soon as we leave town, we're going to go back to our lives and this will all be over," I say finally.

"And you'll go back to this Luke guy?" my dad asks.

"Oh, Bob, focus. It's not going to work out with Luke," my mom says.

I had almost forgotten that I had told her that over lunch the other day, since it was also the moment when I had finally admitted it to myself.

"It's raining men, hallelujah!" my father sings softly to himself as he continues to stab murderously at his breakfast. It brings a smile to my face even though the conversation at large is still uncomfortable.

"We just want you to be happy," my mom says. This is the sentiment that she has continued to echo ever since I moved out of the house for college, and I know that it's true. I just hate that in their minds, the only way that I can find happiness is to find love. To my parents, the two concepts seem synonymous, no matter what else I might do in my life that brings me joy.

"Thanks. I love you guys," I say instead, because there is no point in trying to argue to people who have been married for thirty-five years that I might be able to find happiness outside of a relationship.

I feel like a teenager when I ask my mom to give me a ride to Jessica's house later that day. It fits in perfectly with the vibe of this whole trip to Illinois, especially when we pull up out front and I spot a familiar SUV, complete with wooden cross mirror ornament. I am happy that I will get to see Jordan again, but also can't help feeling a bit like I'm being ambushed.

Jessica's house is modest but homey. I remember when they bought it a few years ago and she had wondered if it would have enough bedrooms to hold all of the children they hoped to have someday. The house itself reminds me of my parents, both inside and out. It's no secret that Jessica has a similar decorating style to our mother, and sometimes I wonder if she is trying to replicate my mom's whole life exactly. There are worse people to emulate, though, that's for sure.

I don't even bother ringing the doorbell because I can hear voices coming from the deck, so I let myself in through the gate, announcing my arrival as I come around the side of the house. Jordan's face lights up immediately when he sees me; so does Jessica's, because I know this was part of her plan all along. I wouldn't be surprised if she had conspired with our mother to put all of this together.

"Smells good!" I tell Tanner as I come up the two short steps to the deck. He's holding a pair of barbecue tongs in one hand and wearing an apron that says, "Mr. Good Lookin' is Cookin'." I make it a point to greet him first because I suddenly feel like I have something to prove to Jessica and to my mother.

Jordan is right beside Tanner, holding a can of soda as they make small talk over the grill, because that seems to be exactly what men do every time there is barbecue. I greet him with a small hug, aware of my sister clasping her hands in front of her heart and staring at us with an even bigger smile plastered on her face than the one she had when I walked into the yard. "I didn't know you'd be here, Tanner invited me over to catch up," he says into my ear.

"I wasn't expecting to see you, either. Jess told me it was a sibling barbecue," I say back. "That is exactly how an ambush works."

"How was church?" I ask when I have pulled away.

Jordan rolls his eyes.

"It was painful, and I'm glad it's over," he laughs, pulling me back toward him again.

"I'm happy to see you," he says into my ear with a kind of gruffness in his voice that activates something inside of me.

I had had a decent amount of sex recently, but it was never something I craved with Luke. While I had been consenting and enjoyed myself, I had never burned with desire for him the way that Jordan is able to make me do with just the sound of his voice—and we have hardly even kissed. I know my cheeks are red, but there is nothing I can do to hide the blush in them.

Thankfully I am saved by the sound of my brother coming through the gate and pull away from Jordan before EJ has a chance to notice and respond. It's not that I am embarrassed, it's just that clearly my family is already in my business about this and the last thing I need is to give them any more fodder. Even still, I think it is kind of cute when Jordan keeps two of his fingers wrapped around my pinky as I try to separate. He only finally releases them when EJ greets him with, "Hey man, good to see you again."

"Hey Kaylee, how are you?" I ask. When I met her yesterday at the shower, I liked her instantly. She's timid and sweet and looks so tiny standing next to my giant brother, but I learned quickly that she could bust his balls and give him a run for his money, so I knew that I didn't need to worry about either one of them.

"I'm tired, but good. I'm just always tired," she says. When I told her yesterday that EJ had shared their news with me, she seemed relieved that she didn't have to keep the secret from everyone anymore.

The little conversations flow freely amongst all of us. Though I'm usually bad at small talk, I feel comfortable with my siblings and that makes it a little easier. I like watching how Jordan interacts with everyone, even though we're so close to the end of our time together, because it almost makes it seem like he's not going back to Atlanta tomorrow and that I won't be going back to L.A. in just a few days.

"This feels very coupley," EJ says from over my shoulder then, as if reading my thoughts.

"I'm okay with that," Jordan says from over my other shoulder where I hadn't even known he'd been standing. For some reason, this makes me blush harder than when he had sent those feelings of desire shooting through my core not ten minutes ago.

"Hey, do you need anything?" he asks me, his hand finding mine again, as if he is physically unable to be near me without touching me.

"A water would be great, thanks," I smile.

As soon as he has gone on his quest, I turn toward my brother to talk to him face-to-face.

"So," he begins, "what's going on with that?"

"Nothing. I mean, it can't be anything. He's going back to Georgia tomorrow, and I go back to California on Wednesday," I say. I've been telling everyone this as a way to convince myself.

Even though it's only been a few days since I officially met Jordan, I would be an idiot to deny that something is happening between us. There is a chemistry between us that is undeniable. I find it so easy to be with him. He makes me feel like a giddy schoolgirl all over again. But ... he's going to be out of my life after tomorrow, and I need to get that into my head before I get hurt.

"Um, Tanner?!" Jessica calls suddenly from the open back door. "I'm pretty sure my water just broke."

I've never seen color drain from a grown man's face as quickly as it leaves my brother-in-law's. It's early—Jessica still has four weeks to go, but if I've learned anything lately, it's that we can only do so much with our plans. The barbecue tongs fall from Tanner's hand and make a loud noise as they hit the deck, causing Kaylee to jump.

EJ steps forward and turns off the grill, offering to stay and clean up while Tanner gets Jessica to the hospital. Everything happens so fast that it's hard to process all that is going on around me, except for that familiar feeling of fingers wrapped tightly around my own.

Kenley, it's time. Jessica is having her baby, and you'll actually be in town for it! Yes, it's early and she's probably scared, but everything will be fine. You're going to get to meet your nephew soon! Don't panic. Don't let Jessica see you panic. Take a deep breath ... take

116

another breath ... and another ... and another.

"Kenley, why don't you call your parents, and then I can drive you to the hospital?" Jordan asks, pulling me out of my thoughts. The touch of his hand keeps me grounded even after he is done talking, and I don't let go as I reach for my phone with my free hand and start to dial. Jordan calls his mother, too, as we watch Tanner and Jessica load into their car and reverse out of the driveway, leaving the house for the last time as a childless couple.

It feels strange to follow them to the hospital for what is one of the most intimate moments of their lives, but it also feels wrong not to stop by and make sure that everything is okay. The look in my sister's eyes when she had called to Tanner out of the back door had been one of pure terror. She's taken all of the classes and has done everything at home to prepare for the arrival of their son, but I wonder if it's hitting her now that you can never truly be ready. She thought she had four more weeks to wrap her mind around the idea of becoming a mother, but that was stripped away from her as quickly as my job had been.

"What are you thinking about?" Jordan asks as he steers me toward the car he has borrowed from his mother once again.

"Jess. She's panicking," I reply.

"She'll be okay," he answers quickly in an attempt to put my mind at ease.

"Are you panicking too?" he asks after a moment. We Graves women aren't exactly known for being the most cool, calm, and collected in high-stress situations, but I'm not panicking for the reason that Jordan may think. As I watched Jessica ride off in the front seat of Tanner's car, the feeling of wasted time hit me again like a ton of bricks. What if I worked so hard on my career that I never get the chance to stand in a puddle of my own amniotic fluid and be whisked away to the hospital? What if I have blown any chance I had of ever having a family of my own? Instinctively, I let go of Jordan's hand.

"Kenley?" he asks with concern.

"I'm okay," I say after taking a deep breath. "Let's follow them to the hospital, yeah?"

19.

Keep Calm and Push.

The slogan on the bottom of Jessica's socks is the first thing I see when I step into her hospital room. Though her water has broken, her labor hasn't actively started, and so she's sitting in bed, waiting for something to happen. Knowing Jess, her hospital bag had been packed for weeks, even though she wasn't mentally prepared for motherhood just yet.

"Hey Ken, sorry about the barbecue," she says when she sees me.

"No need to be sorry. How are you doing?" I ask.

"Well, I'm scared to death, but other than that I am just fine," she smiles.

"Mom and Dad are on their way," I tell her, looking around the room, trying to think of a conversation starter. Tanner had stepped out to call his parents, giving us a moment alone.

"Is Jordan here?" she asks me coyly. I feel the blush creep into my cheeks that means I don't have to answer if I don't want to.

"Yes. He drove me here," I say honestly.

"Kenley, I think this is a good thing for you," she says. "Even I can feel your chemistry."

"Chemistry isn't everything," I try to protest.

"No, but it's *a lot*," she interjects. "Don't mess this up."

"Why do you think I am going to mess it up?"

"You're already working to convince yourself that it isn't going to work out," she says.

"Well, that's because it probably isn't going to work out."

"Ken," she says, taking my hands in hers, "I think he could be the one."

"I thought Tanner was the one?" I joke, trying to make light of a situation that is making me uncomfortable. It's one of my go-to defense mechanisms.

"Ha. Ha. Very funny. You know what I mean," she says. Before I can respond, Tanner pushes back into the room and our moment is over. I give Jessica a kiss on the cheek before wishing them both congratulations and heading back out to the waiting room. I immediately spot my mother talking animatedly to Jordan, who sends me a pleading look.

"Hey, are you hungry?" I ask him, interrupting my mother mid-gesticulation. As much as it is an attempt to save him from my mother, it is also a genuine question—we were supposed to eat at Jessica's but her water had broken before anything was served. EJ had stayed to clean up, and presumably eat, but Jordan and I had chosen to follow her to the hospital instead.

"Starving," he says, looking at me gratefully.

"Hi Mom, we're going to go get something to eat. Please focus your attention on the daughter who is in the hospital giving birth," I say with a stern look, pulling Jordan away before she has a chance to protest or respond.

While there is a part of me that is happy to know that my family is putting their full support behind my relationship with Jordan (if it can even be called that), there is another part of me that hates it because I don't want to hear from them about how I am the one who screwed it up when it inevitably ends. I just don't see how it can possibly work out for us once we are no longer here in town, and I know that my family is going to be full of questions about what happened. It's the same reason I hadn't told them about Luke. I don't want them to get their hopes up over something that isn't real.

The problem is that sitting in the front seat of Jordan's mom's car feels real. It doesn't feel like we're just two former high school classmates who reconnected on this random trip back to our hometown. It feels like there is something happening here, and as much as I don't want my family to get their hopes up, I don't want to get mine up, either.

"This has been a surreal few days with you," I say. "I did not have 'date your high school crush' on my Bloomington Homecoming Bingo Card."

"Maybe it was fate," he says. "What are the chances we were on the same flight, headed to the same baby shower?"

"I don't believe in fate," I say, "but whatever it was, I can't believe it's over."

"Who said it's over?"

"You're going back to your life tomorrow. You'll forget all about me soon enough."

"Baby, I have never forgotten about you. I will never forget about you."

Baby? It sounds different when he says it, not at all condescending like I have always claimed. Somehow when Jordan calls me Baby, it makes me feel cherished. That revelation is like a punch in the gut because it is so different from how I felt the last time that someone called me Baby.

"Don't believe me?" he asks.

I shrug. It does all feel a little like lip service.

"If this was goodbye, I'd throw you into that backseat right now and fuck your brains out, because I would know that I had nothing to lose," he says.

My insides clench.

"And what does that prove?" I ask, my voice barely above a whisper.

"It proves that as much as I want you, I know we've got time," he says.

I wish that I didn't believe him. I had come back for this visit to try to get my life sorted out, not to complicate it further. But there is something about Jordan that is different. Maybe it's the fact that I had had such a big crush on him as a teenager, or the fact that I had based the entire list of qualities that I was looking for in a partner on him. If I am honest with myself, I know that I have already begun to feel something for Jordan that I never felt for Luke. I had hurt Luke

120

when I told him that what we had was just sex, but I realize now that, although hurtful, those words were true. The heartbreaking part, for me, is that in order to let Luke go, I am going to have to lose my friend. There is no way he is going to want to go back to the way things were before and I think that knowing that has held me back from ending this new relationship with him.

"Hey, you good?" Jordan asks, his fingers finding mine again as if they were lost without me.

"Is my poker face that bad? Maybe I *am* a terrible lawyer," I joke. Although I am kidding now, it's something I have thought about more than once since I was terminated by Sullivan and Dunkirk. Good lawyers don't get fired. That phrase has been running through my mind so much these last few weeks that it could easily be one of the mantras I'm trying out. The answer to Jordan's question, though, could be something else: Jessica had mentioned our chemistry, I have certainly felt it nonstop … maybe Jordan can already read me without me having to say anything.

"You just look contemplative," he says. The car comes to a stop at a red light, and Jordan pushes a strand of hair behind my ear.

"There's a lot going on," I reply.

"Kenley, I know this is new and wholly unexpected, but I can't believe that I'm finally getting this chance with you, and I don't intend to waste it," he says right as the light turns green.

———

Jessica's socks keep popping into my head even as Jordan and I spread our fast-food drive-thru feast out on my parent's kitchen table. Obviously *Keep Calm and Push* is meant to be taken literally as a mantra for her labor, but I can't stop thinking about how it applies to me, too. *Keep Calm and Push* through this period of unemployment. *Keep Calm and Push* past the drama that will surely come from ending my friendship with Luke. *Keep Calm and Push* ahead to the future that I see for myself without a plan.

The update from the hospital is that Jessica's doctor is starting Pitocin to help move her labor along, and she's resting comfortably, waiting for the contractions to start. I still can't believe I will be in town for the birth of my nephew. It wasn't what anyone had planned but I am glad that it is working out this way. With all of the events of this trip home, I can't imagine taking another one so soon, so I love knowing that I won't have to.

Jordan and I decided that it doesn't make sense to wait around at the hospital when nothing is happening, so we've chosen to hunker down at my parents' place instead. It's hard not to feel a little bit like high school Kenley all over again, finally having Jordan Thomas all to myself while everyone else is out.

"So, is this the room you grew up in?" Jordan asks at the conclusion of my house tour.

"My mom has redecorated, but yes, this is the room."

"It's nice to have a visual to put to all of the hours I spent thinking about you," he says, encircling me from behind and nuzzling his lips into the crook of my neck.

"I still find that hard to believe," I say.

"Why?"

"Because you were the most popular boy in our high school, and I was quite possibly the least popular girl," I retort.

"You weren't as unpopular as you think, and besides, I still had eyes," he says. "I was just too much of a chickenshit to do anything about it."

"Why?" It's my turn to ask.

"I knew even back then that you were too good for me," he says. This is the same thing that Jessica had passed along from Tanner yesterday at the baby shower. Was that only yesterday? It feels like so much has happened since then.

As hard as it was to accept that Jordan had a crush on me in high school, it's even harder to imagine him lying in his room at night thinking of me. I had been so unremarkable back then, or so I had thought. I didn't think I was the type of girl to garner anyone's attention, but maybe it's just that I was too focused on my future to notice.

Somehow we find ourselves lying side by side on the bed, staring at the ceiling. There is nothing sexual about it, but I have never felt more intimate with anyone in my life. I'm not even sure how much time passes before one of us speaks, and I am struck again by how easy it is to be with Jordan in silence.

"Want to play twenty questions?" Jordan breaks the silence first.

"Like, we just ask each other questions?" I ask.

"Yeah, anything you want to know. Are you game?" he replies.

"Okay. But I get to go first," I say.

I hear Jordan laugh beside me but he doesn't protest.

"Favorite color?" I ask.

"Blue. Same question," he says.

It goes on like this for several rounds while we name our favorite movies, television shows, bands, books, animals, and songs. It's a great way to get to know each other, and I am surprised by how much fun I am having just lying on the bed of my childhood bedroom with him.

"Why did your last relationship end?" he asks. I suck in breath, wondering if I should tell him about Luke and the complicated situation that awaits me when I get back to Los Angeles.

"My last official relationship was in law school. I couldn't handle the pressure of school full time and a boyfriend. So, I ended it," I say.

"I don't believe that you haven't dated anyone in that long," Jordan says, calling my bluff.

"It was my last official relationship. I've dated, but never anything serious. I came back here partially to escape this situationship thing I had gotten myself tied up in with a friend ..." I begin. It's not that I want Jordan to know all about my brush with sluttiness, but it also feels important for him to know that if he's serious about our relationship continuing after we both leave Bloomington, that there is someone waiting for me back in L.A. I can tell Luke not to wait for me until I am blue in the face, but that doesn't change what I have to do when I get back.

"So, I guess I have this guy to thank then," Jordan says when I have finished telling him the story.

"That's all you have to say?" I ask, surprised.

"Baby, I don't care about what happened in the past. And this thing between us, it came up fast and out of nowhere, so if you have loose ends you need to tie up when you get home, I get it," he says then, squeezing my hand.

"What about you? Any loose ends?" I ask.

"Is that your next question?" he asks. I tell him that it is and he laughs.

"Not at the moment, no. That hasn't always been true. My divorce kind of messed me up and I went a little crazy terrorizing the hearts of the good women of Atlanta. But right now, there is only one woman on my mind," he says, turning onto his side and kissing my cheek.

"Is the game over?" I ask him as his kisses move from my cheek to my jaw and slowly toward my lips.

20.

Waking up in Jordan's arms feels different than it did with Luke. Of course, there is the fact that we are still wearing yesterday's clothes because nothing happened between us, which makes a huge difference. We had kissed for a little while, talked for a little while more, and then fell asleep holding each other close. Waking up next to him makes me feel safe instead of making me feel like I want to run away. The contrast between the way Jordan makes me feel and the way that I had felt waking up with Luke is stark enough to drive home the point of what I need to do when I get back to L.A.

I also wake up to a text that the baby arrived at 5:43 a.m. Landon Robert Kauffman weighed six pounds, four ounces and was nineteen and a half inches long, and I know my dad must be over the moon to see that his grandson shares his name, at least in part.

I have always hated when someone sends a picture of a brand-new baby with a comment about how beautiful they are because I am yet to see a baby who is beautiful when they are first born, still I respond to the news and picture with multiple heart emojis.

"Is that him?" Jordan says groggily.

"Yeah, he was born a couple of hours ago," I say.

"Should we go meet him?"

"I need coffee first. That is something you're going to have to learn about me: I almost can't function without it," I tell him.

"How do you take it?"

"With just a splash of one percent milk," I say.

"I'll remember that," he says, kissing my shoulder.

"Good morning," I say. I realize it's the customary greeting, but on our first morning waking up together, Jordan and I had managed to skip it. That seems somehow fitting for our relationship, like we've skipped all of the normal pleasantries and just jumped right in.

One of the things that had terrified me about being with Luke was the idea of moving too fast. I had been afraid of our relationship progressing so quickly that I would forget who I was and what I wanted from life. With Jordan, though, I haven't had that same fear. Never once have I wondered if we are moving too fast or if I might face the same problem of losing myself. The biggest difference is, of course, that up until last night I saw us having a definitive end. But even waking up this morning with the knowledge that it might not be the end after all, that fear has not risen in me.

"Your brain is working already," Jordan says then, pulling me more tightly into the curve of his body so that he is spooning me from behind.

"Only a little," I reply, teasing him by grinding my butt against his clothed body and eliciting exactly the moan I was hoping for by doing so.

"Mmm, Baby, you're making this really hard for me," he says.

"Making what hard?" I ask innocently, wiggling against him once more. He lets out a breathy laugh at my joke, which makes me feel more satisfied than any sexual act could. I love that I can disarm a man like Jordan Thomas.

"God, I want you," he says, cupping my breasts over my shirt.

"But I want to be able to take my time," he says, massaging with his fingers as he places a soft kiss in the sensitive area just below my ear. A small moan escapes my lips as he nibbles gently on my earlobe. And then just as quickly as he started, he stops and pulls away.

"We should get up," he says, sitting up.

"Boo," I pout playfully. Jordan flashes me his megawatt smile.

"You're adorable," he says, leaning over and planting a kiss on my lips. "Man, I can't believe that this is finally real."

When we emerge from my bedroom, I am surprised to find my

dad sitting at the kitchen table. He looks up from his paper and eyes Jordan suspiciously but doesn't say anything.

"Uh, good morning Mr. Graves," Jordan says sheepishly.

By all accounts we haven't done anything wrong. We are two adults in our thirties who had truly only slept, fully clothed, next to each other in a queen-sized bed. But there is no guarantee my dad will see it that way, in many ways I am still his little girl, and this *is* his house.

"Hey, Dad," I say, hoping my nonchalance will make the whole thing a non-issue. "How come you're not at the hospital?"

"Your mother stayed. I wanted to give the new family some space," he says. "I called in sick to work. They must think I have come down with the plague."

It's true—my father has rarely, if ever, called in sick to his job at the meat processing plant where he works as a manager. I can remember countless school assemblies and events that my father missed because he was working. Rather than resenting him for it, I had adopted the same outlook about work for myself and look where that has gotten me.

"We were thinking of heading up there in a little while," I say.

"Yes, I see you have a guest," he says. I'm relieved because I can hear the laughter in his voice, but I am not certain that Jordan can tell.

"Yes, Jordan was at Jess and Tanner's yesterday when they had to go to the hospital, and I needed a ride, plus we hadn't eaten ... we fell asleep waiting for news about the baby," I explain.

"It's fine, Kenley, you don't owe your old man an explanation," he says. "Just don't tell your mother or she'll have your appointment at Country Lace booked before you leave town."

I know my secret is safe with my dad because he would feel too uncomfortable to bring it up anyway. He's right, though—if my mother found out, she would start planning the wedding tomorrow, and I only just found out that whatever this is won't be ending today, so I am going to need the time to breathe. As my dad and I have been talking, I hadn't noticed Jordan disappear and come back to me with a cup of coffee in hand.

"For you," he says, handing the mug to me. I can tell from the looks of the cup that he made the coffee to my exact specifications. I smile at him gratefully, but the simple action is much more meaningful to me than he could know.

Growing up, my PopPop, my maternal grandfather, had brought my MeMaw her coffee in bed every morning. She would sit and drink her cup while watching *Good Morning America* before eventually migrating to the bathroom, where she would place the mug on a warmer while she "put on her face." To me, it's the ultimate romantic gesture—the one that says that person is always thinking of you. It's the one thing I've always sought in a partner, the one thing from my ideal husband list that wasn't originally inspired by Jordan in the first place. Until now, I've never found someone who brought me coffee.

Well, that's not true—sometimes Luke would bring me coffee at the office, but he would always add vanilla syrup to it because he said he thought I'd like it better. I never did and would often go to the kitchen and dump the cup into the sink after he had left my office. I have never thought about how even back then he was trying to change me into who he wanted me to be instead of accepting me for who I am.

My face must sour at the thought because Jordan asks, "Is it not right?"

"It's perfect, thank you," I say, touching his hand gently.

He relaxes immediately, which I think has more to do with my touch than the answer. I still don't know what to make of the way Jordan reacts to me. No one has ever been so affected by my touch before, and it makes me feel powerful and terrified at the same time. Feeling placated by my touch, Jordan announces that he should call his mom to let her know that he's not dead in a ditch somewhere with her car, and he excuses himself out onto the deck.

"He brought you coffee," my dad says once Jordan is out of earshot. "That's a big one for you."

"Yeah," I smile. "Do you think we're moving too fast?"

"Because he handed you a cup of coffee?"

"No, because we technically just met."

"Your mother and I were engaged after our first date," he replies.

This is as close to family lore as the Graves family has. My parents, both small-town kids with limited dating experience, met in class at Illinois State, where they were assigned as partners for a presentation when they were both juniors. After their assignment was submitted, my dad asked my mom out for dinner and a movie, and by the end of the night they were engaged. They got married the weekend after their graduation in a ceremony officiated by the professor who had assigned them as partners.

"I know, I've heard the story a hundred times," I say. "It's just ... this isn't like me. I've always been a cautious person. I haven't even made a list about him, and I am a little worried that I don't feel like I need to."

"Well, maybe you've been too cautious?" my dad offers. It's impactful coming from him, and he knows it. I have always been cautious and carefully regimented because I learned it from him. Aside from the first-date engagement, my dad has never done anything crazy in his life.

"When you know, you know," he says then, as if this offers any clarity for my overly analytical brain.

"I am not sure that I know anything. That's what scares me," I say.

Before my dad can respond, Jordan comes back inside and announces that his mother has called off the search party, and just like that, my private moment with my father is over. But the conversation has certainly given me a lot to think about as I finish my coffee and announce that I am going to quickly freshen up before we head back up to the hospital. I am a little scared to leave my dad and Jordan alone together, but I don't have much choice. I can't go and meet my nephew in yesterday's clothes—people would talk. As if they're not talking enough already ...

21.

I never know how to hold a new baby. I know the technical form, of course, but I never know what to do with the rest of my body. It feels so rigid and unusual to be holding such a tiny person over whom you have complete power and control in that moment. It's a little frightening to think of Jessica handing her son over to me so willingly and yet as awkward as I feel, I am incredibly grateful that I am having the opportunity to hold my hours old nephew.

"Hi Landon," I say, looking down at the tiny babe in my arms. "I'm your Aunt Kenley."

In response, the baby's eyes flutter softly as he expresses a yawn. I know better than to think he is reacting to me, but it's a nice thought to think that we are forging our relationship out of this moment.

"I promise to be the fun aunt," I tell him. "I'll let you have as much ice cream as you want, and then I'll send you back home to your mother."

Jessica sticks her tongue out at me playfully before sinking back against the pillows. She is looking pretty good, considering it's been four hours since she had a baby and the endless parade of visitors through her room has given her no time to rest or recover. Jessica is too happy in her new baby bliss, and, because of the painkillers she's been given to help with the tearing, to tell anyone to leave, though.

"How are you?" I ask her, handing Landon off to Jordan, who looks even stiffer holding the baby than I felt. I know that the answer is "tired and sore, but happy" before she says the words, but I have heard it is important to check in on the mother and not only the baby. And I am nothing if not someone who does what they're supposed to do.

"How are you?" she asks, her tone dripping with insinuation.

"I'm good, just taking it one day at a time," I tell her. I can't help watching Jordan with the baby. His stiffness has subsided, and he gently bounces as he rocks the baby back and forth softly.

"Do you like him?" Jessica whispers.

"The baby?"

"No, stupid. Jordan. We heard he didn't go home last night," she says, raising her eyebrows up and down. Of course that piece of gossip would have come down the grapevine from Jordan's mother after he called her to check in this morning. News travels the fastest when it is perceived as scandalous.

"We fell asleep waiting for news about you," I whisper. I have nothing to be ashamed of about last night, so I don't mind admitting the truth.

Jessica seems a little disappointed though. "Oh. I was hoping it was more," she says, her face falling.

"We talked. About the future," I say. I hadn't wanted to tell anyone because I'm still not sure it's going to work out, and I don't want anyone, myself included, to get their hopes up. But I know how badly Jessica wants this to happen. She had apparently wanted this so badly that she put herself into labor trying to bring us together.

"We're going to try to make it work long distance," I tell her and watch her face perk back up again. She clasps her hands in front of her chest like she did at last night's barbecue.

Knowing that Tanner and Jordan are close means that Jessica has undoubtedly spent time with him over the years. It's funny to me that she has never mentioned him before, especially knowing how much of a crush I had on him when we were teenagers. Maybe she figured it didn't matter anymore now that we were adults, or she had simply forgotten. I do wonder, though, what kind of information I can get out of her about him when the timing is right. But now is not the time, because my poor sister can barely keep her eyes open, and I announce that we should go.

As we leave the hospital room, though, my heart sinks. I'll still have plenty of time to see my nephew before I leave on Wednesday night, but I have to say goodbye to Jordan in just a couple of hours.

Almost immediately, his fingers find mine in the way that I have come to expect, like he knows exactly what's on my mind and he doesn't want to let go, either. Sure, we've said that this isn't goodbye, but what if after we go back to our regular lives, the magic of these last few days together goes away?

"Want to help me pack?" Jordan asks.

We both know that this isn't really the question. The real question is: do you want to spend as much time as possible with me before I leave? And to that, the answer is yes.

———

The house where Jordan's parents live is not far from where I had grown up, but it feels like a world away. The two-story house sits back from the street behind a perfectly manicured lawn, and it is hard to believe that all of those years I had been dreaming about Jordan, he lived only a mile away from my parents' own modest single story with its front yard made more from dirt than grass.

"Hey, Mom!" Jordan calls when we enter. "Your car has returned. And don't worry, your son is okay, too!"

The petite waif who rounds the corner into the foyer is not who I would expect to be Jordan's mother. He is a giant compared to the woman who can't be more than five-foot-two. She's dressed in a pair of chino capris and a button-down; her dark blonde hair is cut into a neat pixie cut. She looks like she's ready to scold Jordan until she spots me.

"Oh, hello," she smiles warmly. "You must be Kenley."

I'm surprised that she knows me before I have a chance to introduce myself because it means that Jordan has spoken about me. It's not that I would expect him to keep me to himself—I had talked to my family about him, after all—it's just that everything between us had happened so quickly, and I wasn't sure that he would have found the time to mention me ... or that he would have wanted to.

"Yes. It's nice to meet you, Mrs. Thomas. I'm sorry I didn't get a chance at the baby shower," I tell her, extending my hand.

She shakes it firmly but eyes me up and down carefully. "Right, you're Jessica's sister," she says, acknowledging our missed connection. "We sure love her."

"Yeah, she's great," I say. I am so used to accepting compliments on Jessica's behalf that it's not even funny.

Such is the life of an introvert with an extroverted sibling, I suppose. Throughout my life, no sooner had a conversation begun with someone than they had something complimentary to say about my sister. When I was younger it used to bother me and make me feel like I would never measure up to my younger sister. Now that I'm an adult, though, I try my best to take the compliments in stride.

"And the baby? Carla said he is the most handsome little thing," she continues, speaking of Tanner's mother.

"We just came from there. He's perfect," I tell her.

"I am going to go up with Carla and meet him in a little while. I can't wait to have a little grandbaby of my own to love on," she says pointedly, shooting daggers at Jordan, who just shakes his head.

"Mom, you have grandchildren. Remember my sister, Elizabeth? Your firstborn? She has two children," he says.

"But they're not Thomases," she says. I can feel Jordan's tension increasing the longer we stand here talking to his mother.

"Did you need to pack?" I ask him and he shoots me a grateful look.

"It was nice meeting you, Mrs. Thomas," I tell her before I let Jordan pull me toward the stairs.

Jordan's room is a mix of the old and the new. Framed football team photos still decorate the walls, but the furnishings scream guest room. He doesn't seem nearly as comfortable in this space as I feel whenever I return to my room at my parents' house, which is something that I think I take for granted. Even though my mom has made some changes to my room in the years since I have not lived at home, at its essence, it still feels like mine. But I know that is a luxury that not everyone else has access to. Sometimes a room where you spent so many nights doesn't bring comfort at all.

"Are you okay?" I ask.

"I'm sorry about that," he says, reaching for my hips and pulling me toward him before wrapping his arms behind my back and caging me against him. I have to stand on my tiptoes to wrap my arms around his neck.

"Don't be sorry, I have parents too," I smile. We haven't talked much about our families yet, but I can tell from this interaction that Jordan faces a lot of the same pressure from his parents that I face from mine about settling down and having my own family. Maybe it's something about their generation that believes the only way to find true happiness and fulfillment in life is through procreation.

"Yeah? Do yours do that?" he asks, placing a soft kiss on my nose … just as my phone rings.

I groan when Jordan releases me but recognize the number as the nonprofit where I've been interviewing and tell him I need to take it. He quickly ushers me to an empty bedroom next door.

The room is another standard-issue guest room. The only clues that it might once have been the room that belonged to Jordan's sister are a series of dance trophies on a shelf above the dresser. Everything else about the room seems completely ordinary, and I can't help but wonder what her relationship might be like with this room and this family. Is it strained like Jordan's? His mother didn't even acknowledge her grandchildren, which doesn't seem like a particularly good sign.

"Ms. Graves, this is Mary from Family First. Is now a good time?" the HR rep on the other end of the line says. I assure her that now is perfect, though it's hard not to be a little bit distracted by the thought of the man in the room next door.

"Great! I want to first of all thank you for taking the opportunity to interview with us. We're fortunate that such a skilled attorney even submitted their resume," she begins.

My heart sinks, it sounds like a rejection, and until this moment I didn't realize how much I wanted this job. It's everything that I dreamed of when I imagined becoming a lawyer and working to help families with adoptions. I haven't gotten a single other interview, although I've applied at more than two dozen jobs, it all felt so predestined: finding this job, landing this interview … and now what? Now I'll have to go back to Los Angeles and call Luke's dad with my tail between my legs. And don't get me started on what will happen if I have to end my friendship with Luke and then see him every day at work. Ugh, this sucks.

"... and we would like to offer you the position," Mary concludes. I don't know what all she has said, because I was too busy analyzing what I would do when I didn't get the job. I almost can't believe that I've heard her correctly.

"I got the job?" I ask. I can't help the extremely unprofessional squeal that escapes my lips, both startling the woman on the other line and making her chuckle.

"So, I take it you accept?" she laughs.

"Oh my gosh! Yes! I am so excited to start working with you!" I exclaim.

The rest of the call consists of her explaining the salary and benefits and when I can start, but none of that matters to me, because I had boarded the flight to Bloomington completely unsure of what I was going to do with my life and now, I'll get to go back knowing that everything is falling into place. I wish I had a mantra for this, something that I could quote to myself as a reminder that things always work out the way they're supposed to—but I still come up short. Instead, all I can think of is how I can't wait to tell Jordan.

He's neatly folding t-shirts and tucking them into his rollaboard suitcase when I burst back through his bedroom door, causing him to jump. Watching a man like Jordan, who reminds me a little bit of Thor from the Marvel movies, jump out of his skin is somehow endearing. It's like there is still a little boy hidden somewhere inside of his giant man body.

"I got the job!" I shriek, doing a little happy dance because I can't help myself. It doesn't even cross my mind to be embarrassed of letting Jordan see me like this.

He's across the room to me in just a few strides, quickly picking me up and spinning me around. "WOOT!" he cheers so loudly that I am certain his mother is going to run upstairs to see what's going on. "I am so proud of you!"

I can feel the blush that creeps into my cheeks. I have spent many years accepting compliments on behalf of my sister, but I have never been great at accepting them for myself. No matter how hard I work or how much I might deserve something, it never feels like enough. More, I don't understand this feeling of simultaneously not feeling worthy of Jordan's pride while also relishing it. With the exception of my parents, I have never cared about making someone proud before, but now I suddenly want to do something every day to deserve Jordan's pride. For now, I'll settle for being in his arms.

22.

It's hard to believe that the last time I was sitting in a molded plastic airport chair with Jordan was just four days ago. So much has transpired between us in such a short amount of time and I don't know what's going to happen now that we have to say goodbye. That's the reason we're sitting here in the first place, in these chairs opposite the ticket counter—because Jordan asked me to stay until the last possible second. I don't know if that will make things easier or harder for me when he finally has to go through security to his gate.

The last four days with Jordan have been unexpected and unbelievable. Yes, the fact that he was my high school crush is one thing, but the connection I feel with him after such a brief time together is something else entirely. When I had been thinking about letting Luke go, I had pondered on the quote my sister wrote in everyone's seventh grade yearbook: *If you love something let it go. If it comes back, it's yours*, but it had never felt right. Even as I was trying to make it fit in my life, I knew that the second half of the phrase was untrue. It was never going to come back to me because deep down I knew I didn't want it to. But with Jordan, it doesn't even feel like I am letting him go—saying goodbye in the airport today is only the beginning. I have never been so sure of anything, and I am terrified.

"I can't believe I have to go," Jordan says. He's holding my hand, of course, rubbing his thumb across my skin in delicate strokes.

"I can't believe any of this has even happened," I reply.

Jordan raises my hand to his lips and kisses the knuckles. "Things have not been great for me the last few years," Jordan says. "After Erika cheated and our marriage ended, I was in a dark place. I feel like I've been trying to claw my way out of the flaming dumpster of my life ever since then, and I have just never been able to do it. I've tried everything. I tried drinking, sex, working out, throwing myself into my work, and nothing could ever get me out. I'm in therapy now, but it took me a while to get there. I lost touch with my mom's religion years ago. My faith has kind of become a hodgepodge of a bunch of different things, and I don't really have any one belief system that I subscribe to anymore. But right before I left for this trip, I did something I haven't done in … I don't know. Years? I prayed. I prayed for answers about why I have been so stuck, and I begged and pleaded to whoever was listening to please help me get unstuck. And the next day I walked into the airport, and there you were."

It's a heavy revelation, especially for someone like me who grew up only praying on Christmas and Easter, when my parents had felt obligated to take us to church. I've never relied on prayer for much of anything because I have always liked to take credit for my own accomplishments. I always struggled with the notion that someone would pray for a job, and then get a job on their own merits but feel like they owed the credit to whomever they had prayed. But I also know that there are a great many people who pray for things every single day.

"I like you because I've always liked you, I don't mean it to sound like I think we have to try because I prayed for it. I didn't even know what I was praying for exactly. I just think it's incredible that you came back into my life at the time that you did, and I don't want to waste this opportunity," Jordan says, backtracking in case I am weirded out by his admission.

"I'm scared," I say. I am choosing to see it as a sign of personal growth that I can say this to Jordan on day four instead of hiding behind my confusion for two weeks like I had with Luke. Jordan doesn't respond, he just squeezes my hand in acknowledgment.

"I'm scared that this feels so real so fast. I'm scared that when we go back to our lives, everything that has happened will be forgotten. I'm scared of going back to my life without you after I've just gotten to know what life with you can be like. Mostly I'm scared of my feelings, because I already feel more for you after a few days than I have for anyone in a while and I don't know what to make of that," I continue.

Being emotionally vulnerable gives me anxiety. I never feel like I can trust my own feelings, so I don't know how I am supposed to trust anyone else with those feelings. I am always worried that I am feeling the wrong thing or expressing it in the wrong way, or that I will be misunderstood because speaking of emotions is not the same thing as speaking of facts. The very thought that Jordan might misunderstand me somehow causes my palms to sweat, and I can't wipe them off because he's still clasping my hand tightly like if he doesn't, I might disappear.

"I'm scared, too," he whispers after a minute. We're just two scared people, sitting in the ticketing area of the Bloomington airport.

"Maybe I can park my flaming dumpster next to yours sometime?" I ask, making an attempt at a joke.

Thankfully Jordan lets out a soft, breathy laugh. "You'd better," he says.

Being the nervous traveler that I am, I have been watching the clock like a hawk, unable to comprehend that Jordan would rather sit here with me instead of being within eye and earshot of his gate. Watching the clock also means that I am acutely aware of how soon I am going to have to say goodbye to him. I cannot fathom how I can go back to my normal life without him, it seems impossible. But the clock says otherwise.

"You're going to miss your flight," I whisper. It's my secret hope that if he doesn't hear me then he won't have to leave.

"Yeah, I've got to go," he says, his voice barely louder than mine had been. As Jordan stands, not letting go of my hand, he pulls me up with him and straight into his embrace.

"Smooth," I say directly into his chest.

"Did you like that?" he laughs, placing a kiss on my forehead.

I am aware of people being all around us, and yet it somehow feels like we are the only two people in this entire airport, or maybe even the entire world. Jordan's arms are wrapped snugly around my shoulders, like he is afraid of letting me go, and I know he feels it, too.

"I'm going to figure out how I can see you again soon, okay?" he asks. I can hear the fear that he had admitted to in his voice, like he's afraid that I might say no and that when he walks away all of this might be over.

"Okay," I say, hoping that my voice sounds reassuring even as I try to talk around this huge lump in my throat. How is it that Jordan has had this effect on me so quickly?

"Paging passenger Thomas. Jordan Thomas. If you are in the airport terminal, please make your way to Gate Six for an on-time departure," an announcement that is my actual worst nightmare comes over the airport loudspeaker.

"You have to go," I tell him.

He nods reluctantly before leaning his head down and placing a long, lingering kiss on my lips that makes me wonder why I ever thought the kiss from Luke on the night before I left California was a big deal.

When Jordan finally walks away, I am struck by how he didn't say goodbye. It's not because he forgot, but because he is making a promise: this is not goodbye. This is just the beginning.

23.

Absence makes the heart grow fonder.

This is the only thing I can think of for the rest of my time in Bloomington, because as soon as I watch Jordan disappear through the security checkpoint, I miss him. I can't recall a time in my life where I have ever truly missed someone before. When I moved to California, I was homesick and missed the idea of being with my family, but there was never a moment that I had missed a single individual so much that it made my heart ache. All I can think about now is how Jordan has promised to find a way to see me again soon, and I can't wait until he does.

Kenley, take a deep breath. I tell myself. *This has been a whirlwind, but you still have a life to get back to. Remember the reason that you came home: to visit your family. Go back to your parents' house and have dinner with them. Go and visit Jessica and Landon tomorrow. Have lunch with EJ. You only have two days left with them, the reason you're here in the first place.*

And even though I do head back to my parents' house for dinner, just like I have tried to motivate myself to do, the pep talk feels futile because no matter what I do from here on out, Jordan Thomas has left his mark.

———

My parents are just as excited for me about the job as Jordan had been. It's been a while since I have had a supportive group of people behind me. I have friends back in Los Angeles, or at least I did once upon a time. Honestly, I'd been so busy building my career at the firm that it had become easy to lose touch without noticing. The reason it had been easy to build my friendship with Luke was because we were already working side by side anyway, but I hadn't made time for anyone else in longer than is a reasonable amount of time to still call them my friends.

"When do you start?" my mom asks. She's made a lasagna along with a loaf of bread from the grocery store that's been slathered with a thick layer of garlic butter and broiled until the edges turned brown. The side salad of crispy iceberg lettuce that clearly came from a bag, with a few tomatoes added on top has been drowned in store bought Italian dressing, and we're drinking glasses of iced tea. It's the most delicious meal I have eaten in ages.

"Monday," I tell them. "I can't wait to dive in and start making a real difference."

I'm surprised that my mom has come home for dinner, honestly. Knowing that her grandbaby is asleep in the hospital just a few miles away makes her appearance at this dinner table seem almost mythic. But my dad had convinced her that she will have a lifetime of memories with Landon, and I don't think there has been a night in my parents' thirty-five-year marriage where my mother has not provided dinner for my father. I used to resent that about her, it was part of my whole hang-up about her becoming a homemaker when she has an entire bachelor's degree and a state teaching credential, but now I find it kind of endearing.

"That's great, Ken," my father says just as my phone chimes on the shelf behind me. I had tried to be respectful and not bring it to the table, but I also didn't want to miss hearing from Jordan as soon as he touched down back in Atlanta. Still, I try to focus my attention on my plate even though I am dying to turn around.

"You can check it, honey," my mom says with a wink.

I don't even respond to her, whipping around quickly and grabbing the device.

Jordan: Landed. Miss you already.

Kenley: Miss you, too.

We've both included a broken heart and the emojis might say one thing, but I know that the smile on my face says something else. I can feel my parents' eyes on me as I turn around and resume my meal.

I still don't know how to discuss this with them. Normally I feel like I can talk to my parents about anything, but my love life has always been the one exception. I mean, they haven't dated anyone new since they were twenty-one. Not only has dating changed drastically in the last thirty-six years, but dating in your thirties is vastly different than meeting the love of your life in a university classroom. I wouldn't know where to begin in talking to them about this.

"Did Jordan land safely?" my mom asks, clearly dying for more details.

I nod and shove a bite into my mouth in hopes of stopping the conversation.

Instead, she sets down her fork, much like she had done on my first night in town when my father had mentioned my gentleman friend for the first time. Who could have known then what this would become.

"Am I being stupid, do you think?" I ask, instead of satisfying her with the kind of juicy gossip after which I know she'd been hinting. To be honest, I feel kind of stupid. Not because I think I'm being hoodwinked or anything, it's just that I am not normally this girl. I am always careful to keep people at a distance and to not let anything distract me from my path. To feel like everything with Jordan is the opposite … it makes me feel foolish.

"I think it's romantic," my mom says.

"Romance and stupidity are often synonymous," I say, vocalizing my thoughts before I have a chance to process them. It is absolutely the wrong thing to say to my mother.

I catch my dad chuckling as he attempts to hide it. He tries not to involve himself in these discussions when he thinks my mother and I might be about to argue.

My mom is a hopeless romantic; maybe that's how she and my dad ended up engaged after their first date. I remember being home sick from school as a child and sitting with her while she watched her afternoon soap operas. When I was in eighth grade, I borrowed one of her romance novels for a book report that became the cause for my only-ever visit to the principal's office, and my mother had assured the school faculty that it was harmless. Jackie Graves lives for romance, and the thought of her own daughter being swept off of her feet so suddenly is the most romantic thing she can imagine. I don't want to argue with her, especially not on a topic so near and dear to her heart, I just don't want to take her advice if her judgment is going to be clouded by romanticism.

"Dad?" I ask.

I can sense my mom shooting daggers at him across the table. My parents don't argue about many things, but with this one, my mom has chosen her hill on which to die.

My dad doesn't respond right away, wanting to carefully choose his words before he responds. I appreciate this about him, and it's where I learned to do it, too. When he does finally speak, I am expecting something profound, and he does not disappoint.

"Kenley, somewhere along the way in life, you decided that taking risks wasn't worth it. I'd say I don't know where you learned that, but I'd be lying because I know it was from me. When you and your sister were young, I was so worried about screwing everything up. I had watched men I knew lose their jobs, get involved in the wrong kinds of things, struggle to provide for their families ... and I loved your mother so much that I was terrified of what would happen if I became like those men. So, I played it safe. I made a plan and I stuck to the plan, and I'd say that my life turned out pretty great. But I regret that I didn't teach you early what it could look like to take risks. I regret that I made you believe that the only way to be successful in life was to be cautious. I am so tremendously proud of you, and that has nothing to do with your accomplishments. I want you to know that I would also be proud of you if you failed completely at life and had to go live in a box on the side of the road. Kenley, I just want you to live life, experience joy and failure and heartbreak and, yes, love. And sometimes taking a risk can make you feel stupid ... but you shouldn't let that feeling stop you from

144

trying," he says.

"Well. Okay," is all I can say in reply.

It's almost like he's reading it out of a book instead of speaking off the cuff. But that's him in a nutshell. My dad is typically a man of few words; he has always chosen to lead by example instead. I have never doubted my father's pride in me, he has made it abundantly clear on more than one occasion in my life even if he hasn't said it outright. But it *is* nice to hear him say it and to issue some advice on the side. I know I am like my dad, and I know I learned so many of my behaviors from him, so to hear him say that he has some regrets is a huge wake-up call for me, and it gives me a lot to think about.

———

For as long as I can remember, my parents have had the same after-dinner routine. They clean up the kitchen together then head into the living room for an exciting night of TV watching. At some point, one or the other of them will get up for a snack, usually a bowl of ice cream, that they bring back for the other. After the first thirty minutes of the ten o'clock news has concluded, they will turn off the TV and head down the hall to their bedroom. I used to wonder how they didn't get bored doing the same thing night after night, but as I have gotten older, I have come to appreciate the predictability of their routine. Especially on a day like today, when so much has happened and I just want to decompress.

"Ken, look what's on," my mom says, making a selection on the channel guide screen. *Sliding Doors*, the Gwyneth Paltrow movie we had just discussed over lunch days ago, illuminates the screen. It has already been playing for some time, and it is a bit difficult to pick up the plot at this stage, but the reminder of the film does enough to trigger my thoughts.

When my mom and I had been having lunch, it was before my date with Jordan, and I had been thinking a lot about the idea of what my life would have been like if I had never left Bloomington. That feels like ages ago instead of days. Jordan had helped me to see that my life here would be different, and while it would probably be a life I enjoyed, it wouldn't be the life I have now. But the feeling of

Sliding Doors still applies in some ways—on one side is the life I had previously: working as a lawyer at a law firm, starting a relationship with Luke, building a nice nest egg for future security. On the other side is the life I am currently heading toward: working in a job that makes me feel fulfilled, getting involved with Jordan, actually doing the things I have always wanted to do. It's interesting to get a chance to see what life is like on the other side of the door.

The vibration of my phone snaps me out of my thoughts. Before I can even look down at the screen, I catch my mom sending me an absolutely deranged-looking smile, as if there is nothing in the world that is more exciting than the prospect of my telephone ringing. "You should answer that," she says with an exaggerated wink and a nudge.

It is Jordan, and I do want to talk to him … I just feel weird about my mom being in my business like this. "Okay, thanks. Good night," I say before I stand and retreat down the hall, waiting to answer until I have reached the safety of my bedroom.

"Hey beautiful," Jordan says as soon as I have closed the door behind me. It feels like days, not hours, have passed since I've last seen him. Is this what long distance is like? Am I always going to feel it's been too long since we last spoke?

"How was your flight?" I ask, laying down on my bed as he answers. It's the very same bed where I had woken up in his arms just this morning, and without him it already feels empty. But I can't allow myself to think that way. I have no idea when the next time I see him will be. Which makes me wonder, too … now that he's gone and back to his real life, has the magic of our own private Bloomington bubble been broken?

"Tell me what you're thinking, Baby. You seem quiet," he says in a freaky intuitive way that makes my heart skip a beat in my chest. He can't possibly be able to read my mind over the phone, can he?

I wish I could picture him in his life, but the truth is that I know so little about it. I can't visualize his condo or imagine the way his skin smells after a shower. With him back in another place, it almost feels like he's not real. Like none of this was ever real in the first place.

"Ken?" he asks. The way he says my name is gentle and feels way more intimate than any pet name he might use.

"I'm just worried that now that you're back home, none of this is real anymore," I say. The other end of the phone is so quiet that I can hear him swallow. I picture his throat bobbing and wish that I could kiss it.

"I was worried about that, too, when I called. That now that I was gone maybe you would have moved on," he admits. "But this is real, Kenley. This is real for me."

I can't help the smile that creeps onto my face. "This is real for me, too," I say.

As we continue our conversation, the small talk and exchanging of pleasantries is weirdly easy with Jordan. It had never been my forte, but I find with him that everything I have always known to be true seems to be the opposite. Like the fact that Jordan had ever had a crush on me in the first place, I will probably mention that on my deathbed someday because I will never be able to wrap my mind around it. That is the very enigma of Jordan to me—I can't fathom him, and yet only he can put me at ease. Our conversation lasts for hours, until neither of us can stay awake a second longer. And with the sounds of Jordan's sweet goodbye echoing in my ear, I sleep like a baby.

24.

The rest of my time in Bloomington passes uneventfully. I spend time with my sister and the baby, get dinner with EJ and Kaylee, where we talk about their future, and I don't spend a single second thinking about the difficult conversation I have to have when I return to Los Angeles.

Honestly, the things I need to say to Luke have nothing to do with Jordan. I think that I have known that it wasn't right and that it wasn't going to work for longer than I let myself admit, but I had a lot of fear that was holding me in place. Fear of confrontation, yes. But also, the fear of losing my friend, and the fear of navigating the world of unemployment on my own. I think, too, that once I lost my job I felt a void, and Luke had quickly slipped into that space. Just because he was there in that moment, though, doesn't mean he has to be there for any others. We've been through a lot together over the years, and I will be sad if we can't be mature enough to maintain a friendship after this, but I just don't know how Luke will ever be okay with that.

I am so lost in my own thoughts that I almost completely miss Jordan standing right in front of me when I deplane in Atlanta. Which is a feat, because he is almost always the tallest man in any room.

"Hey," he says when I finally spot him. He's holding a paper cup of coffee in one hand, which he immediately offers to me, but I don't take it right away because I am too busy processing what is happening.

"I know you have your airport thing, and you want to go sit at your gate to make sure that the plane doesn't leave without you, and I don't want to interrupt that. I just couldn't let you be in my city without seeing you," he says when I still haven't spoken.

"How did you get through security?" I ask. It's a sweet gesture, though I truly hate surprises. Still, all I can think about are the logistics.

"I bought a cheap plane ticket," he says sheepishly. "I'm sorry, maybe I shouldn't have surprised you. It's just ... talking on the phone isn't enough. I wanted to see you. Is that okay?"

It's strange to see this giant, confident man stumbling all over himself in my presence. What he's doing on the outside is exactly what my heart is doing inside my chest at the thought of him being here, but he's right about one thing. I am not going to let the gate for my connecting flight out of my sight.

"It's okay," I say, standing on my tiptoes to place a soft kiss on his lips.

"What about work?" I ask as Jordan picks my bag up and hoists it over his shoulder.

"I took the afternoon off," he says. In a matter of seconds, his fingers find mine, as if there is no other place they belong. As we walk, Jordan tells me that he has already found my next gate and that the correct flight info is displayed, showing that my flight is on time. It's a simple gesture, but it's the exact thing that calms all of my anxieties.

I never thought that I was one for grand gestures. I hate being the center of attention. I have never liked the idea of someone making a spectacle at my expense, and I always thought that a big romantic gesture had to do those things. Somehow Jordan has managed to do something huge while keeping it low key, and it's exactly what I didn't know I needed.

I can't believe he's here. When he got on the plane on Monday, I hadn't had any idea when I would see him again, and I'd been a little down about it. I know we agreed to try the long-distance thing, but I feel like that is always easier in theory. A part of me had wondered if he would forget about everything that happened in Bloomington as soon as he got back to Atlanta. Now I can see, though, that he has been thinking of me as much as I have been thinking of him.

"Thank you for doing this," I say once we've settled into a pair of seats in front of my gate. There is an hour until boarding, but seeing as it's an hour spent with Jordan, it's going to feel like minutes.

For a while, neither of us says anything. We're sitting side by side, his arm around my shoulder and my head rested on his. It's comfortable like this, sitting in our own silent bubble surrounded by the hustle and bustle of the airport. I know it's only been a few days, but I continue to be amazed at how meaningful the nothingness is with Jordan. We don't need activities or even words when we're together, which is honestly the way I like things. The drama that Luke had stirred up in my life has been too much for my nervous system, but the silence that Jordan offers already seems to be undoing so much of that damage.

"Attention passengers on Flight 72 with service to Los Angeles: boarding for this aircraft will begin in about ten minutes," an announcement comes over the terminal intercom. The anxiety in my body reacts before my brain even has a chance, but Jordan squeezes my hand. He doesn't have to say the words for me to know what he's saying. It's the same thing that I have been trying to tell myself with my pep talks all these years. *Take a deep breath. It's going to be okay.*

"I might have a meeting in L.A. in a couple of weeks," Jordan says then.

I look at him with a start.

"I don't want to say for sure yet, I'm still working out the details. But I started working on it as soon as I got back because I suddenly need an excuse to get there as soon as possible," he laughs. "So, I'll let you know once it's finalized. That is ... if you want to see me?"

"Yes. Yes, I want to see you," I say, surprised by the speed with which it comes from my mouth. I am not one to rush into situations, and the fact that I seem to be so willing to do just that with Jordan is baffling. My father's words echo in my ears: "When you know, you know." At the time I had poo-pooed him, saying that I didn't feel like I knew anything ... but maybe I had been wrong.

As soon as the boarding announcement for my flight blasts over the loudspeaker, Jordan stands and pulls me to my feet to follow. To an onlooker, it could appear that he is happy to be done with me, but I know that he is aware of my travel anxiety and that this announcement means that it is time for me to go. Reluctantly, he pulls me into his embrace.

"Call me when you get home," he says into the top of my head, squeezing me tightly in his arms like he's afraid that letting me go this time might really be the end. That's one of my fears, too—it has been since the beginning, but I am trying to no longer be the person who doesn't try something just because they're scared.

I hope that the kiss I give Jordan in reply is enough to put his mind at ease.

I know it works when he says, "Damn, I wish your layover was longer."

The last thing I see before heading down the jetway to my plane is Jordan standing in the terminal and watching me walk away.

———

Part of my airplane anxiety has to do with who I might end up with in the seat beside me. I hate traveling alone because I have no control over what stranger might become my cross-country travel companion. So even when a well-dressed woman who appears to be about my mom's age sits down beside me, I don't let my guard down.

"Hi there, how are you?" she asks, spreading out her belongings and making seat 24E her home away from home. The only thing worse than an unfriendly stranger is a friendly one. I offer her a smile before I turn back to the in-flight magazine I have been browsing during the boarding process in hopes of looking occupied and unapproachable.

"I saw you with your boyfriend in the waiting area, y'all are just the cutest," she continues, not taking the hint. It's interesting that at the thought of Luke being my boyfriend, I cringed, but at the mention that Jordan might be, it doesn't faze me.

"Thank you," I say, rather than arguing the terminology.

"How long have y'all been together?" she asks. I smile, closing the magazine on my hand, because sometimes you just get a talker and there is nothing you can do about it.

"Five days," I tell her. At first she thinks I'm joking, and I watch the realization creep into her expression.

"Well, you could have fooled me. The way you interact and look at each other, I would have thought it was much longer," she says. I smile in acknowledgment and reopen the magazine to the page I had marked with my finger.

The thing is, it feels that way to me, too. It feels almost like I did start dating Jordan in high school and that we have had the last sixteen years together. There is something that I get when I am with him, a feeling of being deeply seen and known, that doesn't usually come with the start of a relationship—that feeling usually comes later, after a lot of time and effort have been invested. But not with Jordan—with him, that has been there since day one.

"So, did you meet him here in Atlanta?" my nosy seat neighbor asks. I sigh and close the magazine for good, placing it back in the seatback pocket in front of me. I hadn't been reading it anyway, just hoping to appear busy to thwart this exact situation.

"I actually met him in high school," I begin. If you can't beat them, join them, as they say. By the time I am done telling my story, we are somewhere over Arizona, and my enraptured audience is hooked.

Although I prefer keeping my private life to myself, something about recounting the story of the last twenty-six days to this woman I have just met feels therapeutic. Until I hear myself give the details out loud, I almost wouldn't have believed that it hadn't even been a month since I was let go from Sullivan and Dunkirk. So much has happened in that short span of time that it feels like I have lived in several iterations of myself. One month ago, I couldn't have imagined what was in store for me. It makes me wonder, though, if so much could have happened in just a month outside of my carefully executed plan, what had I missed out on for the last twenty years?

"I am loving these twists, girl!" says 24E with a chuckle. She tops off her plastic cup of white wine before turning her attention back to me. "Don't forget to add the one about how you met your new landlord on a flight from Atlanta to your story when you tell it. No one will see that one coming."

"I'm sorry?" I ask, confused by what she has just said.

"My brother, God rest his soul, kept a house in Sherman Oaks. He never had any children and when he passed a few years ago, he left it to me. I've been renting it out—it just never felt right to sell it. But my renter just moved out, and I'm on my way to L.A. to see about relisting it. If you're interested, I don't have to list it at all. It has three bedrooms and two bathrooms with a detached garage," she says, polishing off her wine.

When I had planned my trip back to Illinois, I had expected a quiet reprieve from the issues which had plagued me in Los Angeles. I thought I might have some meals with my parents, smile my way through Jessica's shower, and head back to L.A. without much additional insight into what to do about my life. I had sort of been faking it when I told Luke that I was going to have things figured out by the time I got back. I certainly didn't expect to be returning to my flaming dumpster with a fire extinguisher.

"I like you, Honey," 24E says sweetly. "You remind me a lot of myself twenty years ago."

"Was your life falling apart, too?"

"You could say that," she says with a smile. She doesn't provide any additional details before she continues. "I learned that sometimes things have to fall apart so that they can start coming together."

25.

It's okay if you fall apart sometimes. Tacos fall apart and we still love them.

When I show Jordan the wooden sign, which is the only piece of decor that my new landlord has left prominently displayed in the house that she had all but rented me on my flight from Atlanta over video chat, he laughs out loud.

"We can never get rid of that," he exclaims. I had shown it to him because I found it funny, too, a reminder that nothing ever falls apart so badly that it can't be redeemed, but it's his use of the word "we" that sticks with me.

It's a word that we've said dozens of times since we have left Bloomington, and each time it becomes more serious. Each use of the word "we" solidifies a little more the fact that we are really doing this, we're together—a couple, that this is for more than just right now ... which is exactly the thing I said to Luke after our second night together, and it just reminds me that I still need to have that talk with him.

The truth is that I haven't found the time. Between getting back to town and signing a new lease, starting my new job two days ago and doing the long-distance thing with Jordan, sitting down with Luke has been the furthest thing from my mind. And that's because I put it there on purpose so that I didn't have to sit and overthink about how ending our romantic relationship means losing the only friend I have in Los Angeles. But even from the other side of the country,

Jordan makes me feel less alone. We talk pretty much constantly with multiple video chats a day sprinkled in between our nonstop texting sessions. It's kind of like he's with me even when he's not.

"I got that meeting scheduled, the one I've been telling you about out in L.A. How do you feel about having a houseguest?" Jordan asks, snapping me out of my thoughts. It's what I've been waiting for, and I tell him as much, both because what is happening between us has me wanting to be with him as much as possible, and because a part of me is curious if we still work on my own turf. But even as we make plans for his trip, the fact that I have to talk to Luke starts flashing through my mind like a neon sign.

———

The restaurant is crowded and noisy when I arrive, which is exactly perfect for this conversation I've been dreading. Something about being in an intimate setting with Luke feels wrong for so many reasons, the least of which is Jordan. It feels safer to meet with Luke in this loud restaurant where there are a lot of witnesses, which should say everything about how I feel this is going to go. He's already seated at a table when I approach, and he stands up as soon as he spots me, a smile spreading across his face, which breaks my heart instantly.

"Hey!" he says, coming toward me. But as he leans in for a kiss, I turn my head so that his lips land on my cheek.

"Hi, thanks for meeting me!" I say, trying my best to brush off the awkward greeting. He looks so hopeful as we take our seats at the small table and I try to hold onto my resolve. I suddenly wonder why I agreed to dinner, which is just going to inevitably prolong this difficult conversation.

Ever since I got back to L.A., I have been trying to prepare myself for this meeting. Yes, I met someone, but that doesn't have anything to do with why Luke is wrong for me. Being away from him for the last two weeks has helped me to be able to look at our relationship objectively and identify all of the red flags. There are things I didn't even notice, like how I let him slowly cut me off from my other friends, and things that had bothered me before I left town, like how he is trying to plan my life for me. Though I don't see how it is possible, I am open to maintaining our friendship, but I am going to need to put some boundaries on it, and those have never existed in our relationship before.

"So, how was Illinois?" he asks.

It's a simple enough question, but I know what he is hinting at. I had told him that I needed the trip back to see my family to think about us, and what he wants to know now is what I have decided. It's too early in this dinner for that, though.

"It was nice to get back there and not feel rushed," I begin, before telling him about Landon's birth and how I had gotten to spend some time with him that I hadn't anticipated. I have never talked to my sister more than since she became a mother. I have been video chatting with my nephew daily, which at this age just means I've been chatting with my sister, who seems to be thriving in motherhood even though she is constantly exhausted.

I've talked to all of my family more since I left Bloomington. Though I had only been home for a week, it felt like we really got reconnected, and I feel much closer to them now than I did when I had first arrived in town. It's something I am committed to maintaining even though I have returned to my life. I've been talking to EJ about how he and Kaylee can tell my parents about the baby. I've been chatting with my mom about (what else?) Jordan. My dad and I have been keeping each other updated on work. And even when the conversations are light, the feeling of connection is deep, and it's something I didn't realize I had been craving.

"I am glad you had a good time," Luke says. We're interrupted then by our waiter, who comes by to take our order.

"We'll both have the chicken tacos and a Cadillac margarita," Luke starts. It's bold of him to assume but also totally expected. Luke and I used to frequent this restaurant, which is known for their margaritas, a few times a year when we worked at Sullivan and Dunkirk, and every time, Luke had ordered me chicken tacos. No matter how many times I have explained to him that I ate so much chicken growing up that it now triggers my gag reflex, it hasn't stopped him. When the waiter looks at me for confirmation, I shake my head slightly and place my own order.

"May I please have the steak nachos and a Diet Coke?" I ask sweetly. Luke shoots me a deranged look, like this is the first time he has ever heard this order and not the thirtieth. I do love the Cadillac margarita here, at least he had gotten that part right. But I need to keep a clear head for this conversation. Truthfully, I haven't felt much like drinking ever since the night that everything went wrong with Luke in the first place. I've only had alcohol twice since then, both times with Luke, and even if I do love a good margarita, today I have one particular job to do.

"Not feeling the tacos today?" he asks, puzzled, after the waiter walks away.

"I don't actually like the chicken tacos," I reply.

Luke cocks an eyebrow. He clearly doesn't believe me. "You get the chicken tacos every time we eat here. It's your favorite meal," he says.

"It's not my favorite meal. I hate chicken. I can hardly eat it without gagging. It's your favorite meal, and you created fantasies about your dream girl sharing all of your favorite things," I tell him as the waiter returns with my soda. I make myself busy with unwrapping the straw that has been placed on the table beside my glass.

"It's just a little ... overbearing," I say softly, more to myself than to him. I am not here to pick a fight with Luke. We are two friends having dinner.

"I would call it being attentive to your needs, actually," he says. I can hear the disgust in his voice.

I take a deep breath so that what I say next comes out as calmly as possible, because what I want to say is, *Being attentive to my needs would require you to pay attention.* What I say instead is, "You always order what you think I want, and you never even try to remember what I like."

"It's just tacos, Kenley."

"It's not though," I say, taking a long sip of my drink. "It's adding vanilla to my coffee even though you have seen me countless times making my cup with only milk. It's insisting that I want a lemon with my vodka soda even though when I order for myself, I get lime. You want the version of me that you created inside your head," I say.

Someone from the bar comes by with Luke's margarita then and I am grateful for the distraction. I had tried hard not to have expectations for how this conversation was going to go. I had talking points that I rehearsed on the drive over, but I had been careful not to try to imagine his responses ... maybe that had left me unprepared.

"The only version of you that I want is the one I know is real," he says earnestly. "I know you, Kenley."

I sigh, taking a long drink and using it as an opportunity to look around the restaurant. Or at least that's what I pretend I am doing as I try to remember my talking points. I had known that seeing Luke tonight was going to be difficult, but it doesn't help that he isn't even trying to hear me.

"What's my favorite color?" I ask.

All I can think about is that night that Jordan and I laid in my bed in Bloomington, playing twenty questions. This question was the first one, and Jordan had committed the answer to memory, finding little ways to sneak the color green into my life ever since.

"Orange, same as mine," Luke says matter-of-factly, like I have just asked him the easiest question of his life.

"What's my favorite animal?" I ask. There is no use arguing with his answer since he is so certain of his rightness.

"I don't know ... a monkey?" he asks. "Why are you asking me these stupid questions?"

Maybe they are stupid questions, but they hadn't felt that way when Jordan and I had been asking them of each other. In fact, playing twenty questions with Jordan that night had felt intimate and profound, even if the answers might have seemed trivial.

"It's a giraffe. Followed closely by a llama. There's something about long-necked creatures that I find fascinating ... but that's not the point," I say.

Luke sighs, I can tell that this dinner isn't going the way he thought it would, any more than it is going the way I had imagined. "Well then, what is the point, Kenley?" he asks.

"My favorite color is green. I never eat chicken because it makes me gag, except, weirdly, in Indian curries. I hate vanilla in my coffee, and my favorite animal is a giraffe. If you knew me like you say that you do, then you would know all of these things. That is the point."

We sit in silence for a while as my words settle over the table. It's eerily quiet to the point that the server hesitates when he comes by the table with our meals, and we're given a brief reprieve from the tension as we begin to occupy our mouths with something other than this awkward conversation. I don't know what I had expected coming here tonight. I don't know what I thought was going to happen, or why I thought that talking to Luke in person was going to be a good idea.

"You look refreshed and happy," he changes the subject. There is a hint of sadness in his tone, like he's sad that I am happy without him. "It makes me a little worried that you're going to decide to move back after all." That had been his fear on the night he stopped by my apartment to say goodbye, that I would realize that I had missed it so much that I would want to move back. It's funny, thinking about it now, because those thoughts had crossed my mind. Not that I would have moved back to Bloomington, but just wondering what my life might have been like if I had stayed.

"I actually signed a new lease on a place in The Valley," I tell him. I'm not sure what kind of response I am expecting, or why I have even bothered to bring it up in the first place, because I know he's going to have something to say about it. People who grew up south of the Hollywood Hills tend to have a lot of opinions about the San Fernando Valley, often referred to as "The Valley," to their north. But in particular, Luke seems to have something disparaging to say about all of my life choices lately.

"Wow. Congrats," he says dryly. His words say one thing, but his voice is deadpan and I know that he doesn't mean it. I know he's been looking for an apartment, too, in hopes that I might agree to move in, thereby solving my problem for me.

"Are you sure it's wise to do that before you've found a job?" he continues. I haven't told him about that yet, either. It used to be that Luke was the first person to whom I would tell anything, but now it feels painful to give him any detail of my personal life. I can't help feeling like he is just looking for things he can use, ways he can criticize my choices, opportunities to swoop in and be my hero.

"I have a job, I started on Monday. That's why it has taken me so long to get in touch," I say. That and the fact that I have been absolutely dreading this conversation.

"At the nonprofit? Are you sure that's stable enough to sustain a new lease?" he asks.

"Well, it isn't any of your business, but I have more than enough saved for a security deposit, and the rent is well within the range of my salary," I snap back, even though I mean it when I say it's none of his business. I'm so tired of being treated like I am some naive little girl who needs a big strong man to be her savior. Which is also ironic, considering that if Luke and Jordan were to stand side by side, Luke would practically disappear—I have definitely found a big, strong man, and he hasn't once tried to save me.

"Okay, sorry," Luke says, raising his hands in mock surrender.

Thankfully, the waiter returns to check on us and I don't have to answer.

"Where in The Valley?" he asks once the waiter has walked away. I don't like the way his tone is accusatory, as if I am a dimwitted child who needs his superior knowledge of Los Angeles neighborhoods. I take a deep breath in an attempt to calm myself; it only half works.

"Sherman Oaks. It's a quiet, suburban street. I like it a lot," I reply. I am prepared for more questions, as this was one of my planned talking points, and steel myself for the onslaught.

Kenley, you knew he was going to be like this. You were prepared for him to be like this. This is the reason you knew you couldn't be with him in the first place. It's Luke being Luke … it's just something you never noticed about him before, because you were too busy with work and his was a friendship of convenience. But he's always been this way. Just take a deep breath and get through dinner.

For a few moments, as we both pause to dig back into the plates in front of us, it almost feels normal sitting with Luke. When we're too busy eating to talk, it feels a little like we are just friends again, having dinner after work like we had done at this restaurant so many times before. The fact that he ordered tacos is only serving to remind

160

me of this week's mantra: *It's okay if you fall apart sometimes. Tacos fall apart and we still love them.* But as soon as Luke opens his mouth to talk again, I am reminded that this meal is completely different from any other that we have ever had.

"So that's it then," he says.

"What's it?"

"That's everything on your list that you wanted to do before you felt like you were ready for a relationship," he says.

That is technically true, but I have realized that I don't want a relationship with him.

This is the part of the conversation I have been dreading since before I took the trip home to Illinois. It took me a while to recognize that I had been feeling it that long, but it's not normal to feel anxiety about spending time with your supposed best friend. I should have listened to my doubts about the changes in our relationship from the start instead of letting it go on this long.

"Luke, I ..." I start.

"No," he interrupts. I haven't said the words, but I can see in the rage on his face that he already knows. "No."

Rage isn't a reaction I had expected from him. I don't think I've ever seen Luke get angry in the ten years that I've known him. There were times I would hear yelling coming from his mediations, but the raised voice had never been his. Luke is a peacemaker.

I don't say anything. There is nothing that I could say that he would hear right now anyway; he has already proven that with our earlier conversation. Luke had decided before he came here tonight that he was coming to get the girl of his dreams. In his mind, there was no possibility that my asking for time and space to figure things out would ever lead to me not wanting to be with him. Now it's like he has snapped.

I think I broke him.

To my right, two women have stopped their conversation and seem to be tuned into ours, and the last thing I want to do is escalate him further and cause a scene. But I can already tell that Luke will not give me that luxury while he is this angry. He thinks I have wronged him, probably that I have strung him along.

I should have done this sooner, before I gave him hope.

"You said you needed time and space, and I gave you that. No, you don't get to friend-zone me again," he says. His volume is rising with every word.

"I never 'friend-zoned' you. We are friends," I say, trying to keep my voice calm and steady even though I want to crawl under this table and hide.

"Whatever. You've already made up your mind," he replies.

He is right that I have made up my mind, but this idea that I am putting him in the friend-zone as a way to somehow punish him has nothing to do with that. I am not trying to punish him, but maybe only time can teach him that.

"Is there someone else?" he asks.

I hate how guys assume that the only reason you might not want to be with them is because you have found someone else. While I did meet someone, I already knew that everything with Luke felt wrong before Jordan was even in the picture.

"Does it matter?" I ask.

This is clearly the wrong answer. Luke's anger is becoming evident to tables beside us, who are throwing side-glances our way. The two women who were already listening in have set down their utensils and are resting their hands on the table like they're ready to push off and head in our direction.

"So, there is. When did you meet him?"

I take a deep breath. I might as well be honest. "In Illinois. Technically in high school, but we ran into each other when I was home and reconnected."

Luke sits back in his chair like he can't believe I've betrayed him.

I lock eyes with one of the women at the next table and she mouths, "Are you okay?" at me.

I offer her a weak smile and a nod, though I am not convinced that my answer is true. I hate being the center of attention, and Luke is very quickly making us that. I was under no illusion that the conversation tonight would be easy, but the direction it has taken is surprising to me.

"I waited so long for you. Ten years. I waited for you to be ready.

And then when I finally make my move, you decide that you would rather have someone else," he says, finishing his margarita in one big gulp.

I wish that there wasn't any alcohol involved in this conversation, we both know all too well what can happen when alcohol is involved.

"It doesn't have anything to do with him," I say. I know he won't believe me, but it's true and it's worth a shot.

"Lies."

I should have brought cash so that I could slam it down on the table and walk away, but I had overestimated Luke's ability to be mature and I only have my card. Luke is a lawyer who is used to looking at all the facts, and I think that once the emotion clears, he'll be able to see that the reason I kept asking him for time and space was because I knew even before I had left for my trip that this wasn't right. But for now, I am stuck here at this table with a man who is temporarily incapable of seeing anything clearly.

"It doesn't. I have been asking for space to process everything between us for weeks. I tried to express my feelings that night at your birthday dinner. I wanted my trip to Illinois to be a time for me to think and figure things out, and it was that. One of the things I figured out is that there are people who love and support me, and who are genuinely happy for me no matter what choice I make for my own life, instead of trying to advise me on what they think is best for me. I had forgotten about that kind of support, and I feel liberated by it. I had no idea that you had any interest in me beyond friendship until you 'made your move,' as you call it, and when that happened, we were both drunk out of our minds. I don't owe you a relationship with me just because you created a fantasy about me in your head. I will not become your human doll, who is just here for whatever you'd like to do. I'm sorry that you're hurt and that you feel used and betrayed by me. It was not my intention to hurt you, and I am truly sorry for that," I say.

I catch a server's eye over Luke's shoulder and pantomime for the check. I have said everything that I need to say tonight. I can only hope that Luke might come around and our friendship can continue. But I am not dumb enough to expect it.

"I'll cover it," one of the ladies beside me says. "Why don't you wait outside with Nicky?"

I don't have many girlfriends, and the idea of women looking out for one another isn't a familiar concept to me, but at this moment it's exactly what I need. Especially when Luke grows even more irate.

"You brought backup? Like you don't trust me? Unbelievable," he practically shouts just as our waiter returns and asks him to keep his voice down.

All eyes are now on me as I make what must be a walk of shame toward the doors of the restaurant, my nachos only partially eaten on the table. Nicky, I learn, is the woman who had asked me if I was okay, and she links her arms through mine as we make our way through the maze of tables. I'm grateful for her support even though I have never met her before. I've never been one to rely on the kindness of strangers, but lately that track record seems to be changing.

"We should be okay here for a few minutes. Shanna said that the manager has now gotten involved, and your friend won't be leaving any time soon," Nicky says, glancing at her phone.

"Thank you," I say. "This is so humiliating."

Nicky is tall and thin, with mid length brown hair that falls down her back in perfect waves. She's probably around my age and still looks like the quintessential L.A. girl. It's a look that I have never been able to pull off, even as a blonde, and it used to make me wonder if I wasn't cut out for a life here.

"Don't be embarrassed. From what I overheard, it sounds like you tried," she says, giving me a warm smile. It's only another minute before we're joined by her companion, who grabs us both and quickly pulls us around the corner to stand in front of another well-lit restaurant.

I honestly don't know what I would have done if these two women had chosen to have dinner at a different restaurant tonight. Trying to imagine how I would have escaped Luke's anger on my own is impossible, and I don't know what I was thinking, agreeing to meet him like this. I had hoped that being in a public place would force Luke to think before reacting, but I guess I should have known better.

As much as I hate being the center of attention, it should come as no surprise that I try to avoid crying in public at all costs … but this night has already been humiliating enough, why not add one more reason to want to crawl into a hole?

"Oh, Honey!" Nicky says, wrapping me tightly in her arms. I can feel another pair of arms wrap around me, too, as sobs begin to wrack my body. I may not have many girlfriends, but these two strangers are treating me better than any friend ever did.

"I'm sorry, I'm not usually like this," I muster through my tears. If I thought that Luke's explosive reaction inside the restaurant had been humiliating, standing on the street in the arms of strangers crying my eyes out is ten times worse. We stand like that for I don't know how long. It feels like hours but is probably only a few minutes, and they don't push me to stop crying or seem at all eager to be done with me and on their way to continuing their night. I had somewhat been able to understand the idea of women supporting women inside the restaurant but the idea that they're still supporting me even after the drama has ended is beyond anything that I can comprehend.

"Hey, so I don't mean to be rude," Nicky starts. I pull back from her embrace, fully expecting her to announce that I am now a burden and that they need to go.

"But we were eavesdropping on your conversation."

Oh. That wasn't what I had expected, and the contrast from what I had been expecting brings a small smile to my lips. If I had been in their position, it would have been hard not to listen in on the conversation that was happening at the next table, Luke had made sure of that.

"And I was just kind of thinking that if you just signed a new lease, maybe it would be a good idea to go ahead and move in? Or at least sleep there for the time being? I mean … I assume the guy you were with tonight knows where you live now. I wouldn't feel right about letting you go back there alone," she says.

"It's eight o'clock on a Thursday night, how am I supposed to move now?" is all I can ask, because Nicky brings up a very valid point. Luke does know where I live, and I wouldn't put it past him to show up there.

"Well, you have us!" Shanna says. She also looks like the quintessential L.A. girl, except that her hair is red. "And I know a guy with a truck who owes me a favor."

Just like that, I find myself in the back of an Uber with these two women whom I have just met but who have already proven themselves to be way more of a savior than Luke could have ever dreamed to be. It's late in Atlanta but Jordan had told me he would wait up until I was done with my dinner so that he could say goodnight, and when I pull my purse from my bag, I can already see a text waiting from him.

Jordan: How did it go?

Kenley: Bad. It was bad.

Jordan: Are you okay?

Kenley: No? Moving into the new place tonight, it's too long of a story to tell you over text.

No sooner has my text gone through than my phone lights up with a video chat, Jordan's face and bare shoulders illuminating the screen.

"Ay, Chihuahua!" Shanna says over my shoulder at the sight of him.

It makes me giggle because I can't exactly say I disagree. When I accept the call, I try to angle Shanna out of the shot, but she manages to wiggle herself into it anyway.

Jordan looks relaxed. He's lying on his bed, as if he had been waiting to hear from me just to say goodnight. I've gotten used to seeing him this way. It's one of the things I hate the most about this long-distance thing. Once my day is finally winding down and I have the time to talk, he's ready for bed, and I always feel bad to keep him when I know he gets up at six every morning to go to the gym. He never makes me feel like an inconvenience to him, though, always acting like he would rather talk to me than do anything else. And maybe that is how he feels, because I know that I would rather be talking to him than doing just about anything else.

166

"What happened?" he asks before I can say anything.

"It was awful!" I exclaim before launching into the story, Shanna peeking over my shoulder every few sentences to get another look at Jordan. As I recount the story to him, about Luke's behavior at the restaurant and how I should have done this before my trip to Bloomington in the first place, I can't help but feel a little sad. I had thought I'd been prepared for the possibility that my friendship with Luke would not survive, but facing the reality of it is a lot more heartbreaking than I had anticipated. With the end of that friendship, and the insistence of my two saviors that I move out of the place that Luke knows tonight, it is a reminder that the life I had built for myself here is completely gone. Starting tomorrow, every single thing will be new.

"Mm-kay, Jim is in," Shanna says, glancing quickly at her phone.

"I'm sorry, who is Jim?" I ask.

"My friend with the truck. Keep up. He'll be in Silver Lake in an hour," Shanna says. I can't imagine what she has done for him that he owes her a favor of this magnitude, driving his truck across town to help a stranger move in the pitch darkness, but I can't afford to ask questions.

"So you're really doing this tonight?" Jordan asks.

"I wouldn't feel safe letting her stay there any longer," Nicky chimes in from the front seat, and I angle my phone so that Jordan can see her, too.

When I turn the screen back to face me, I catch her mouthing "Damn" and fanning herself. When I had a crush on Jordan back in high school, that reaction is exactly what I had dreamed of eliciting from the other girls in our class. It's nice to know that he still has the same effect on the female population sixteen years later.

"I'm sorry I'm not there, Ken," he says, reminding me that his use of my name is way more erotic than the use of a pet name ever could be. I know I've said it before, but hearing my name on his lips is hot.

"I know, but don't worry about me ... I'll be fine," I say, willing it to be true. I will be fine, eventually.

He laughs through his nose as if I have made a hilarious joke, but before I can get offended that he doesn't think I'll be fine, he says,

"I'm always going to worry about you because I ..." he tapers off before beginning again with a new train of thought, "just be safe, okay? Text me when you're done, no matter how late."

I tell him I will, though what I really want to know is what he was about to say before he stopped himself. I'm always going to worry because I ... what? Because he loves me? It's way too soon for that, and yet I can't stop my heart from saying that that's exactly what he meant.

26.

It's a late night, but as I sink into bed in my brand-new bedroom in the wee hours of the morning, my heart feels full of gratitude. Much like I have never been the type of girl who has a mantra, I've never been the type to reflect on gratitude. That one in particular has always been difficult for me, because I work so hard day in and day out for the things that I have that I always feel like I am the one who deserves my thanks, but this morning feels different.

I don't know what I would have done if those two girls hadn't been at the restaurant last night. I could have very easily not had any place to go except for the apartment Luke knew, which makes me feel even more grateful for my airplane seatmate turned landlord. And she probably wouldn't have noticed me or struck up a conversation if Jordan hadn't surprised me at the airport. I still think he might have almost told me that he loved me last night. The even crazier thing is that if he had, I might have said it back. My whole life has been turned upside down, and all that I am able to feel is gratitude.

The gratitude in my heart is immediately followed by guilt. There is, first, the guilt for feeling grateful after I have broken Luke's heart. That is quickly followed by the guilt I feel about feeling grateful when I haven't done anything to deserve that gratitude.

"I'm a mess!" I exclaim to no one as I reach for my phone and fire off my good morning text to Jordan. It's become our morning routine since I've been back in L.A. I send him a text as soon as I wake up so that he knows when it is safe to start talking to me without waking me up.

While I wait for his reply, which usually comes pretty quickly, I reach for the cardboard box that contains all of the loose items from my nightstand. Inside I know that I will find the journal where I have been listing the one thing every day that makes me happy. Yesterday I had hastily scribbled "new friends to the rescue" before tossing it into the box and applying a haphazard layer of packing tape and throwing it into the back of Shanna's friend's pickup truck. Finding the journal, I add a date to yesterday's line item before adding today's entry: "gratitude." Gratitude might be a new feeling for me, but I'm pretty sure it can make me happy. Right?

I do hate that I feel guilty, though. I mean, I am probably rightfully guilty for hurting Luke. Every time I think about last night, more than his anger (the likes of which I have never seen from him before), I picture his face when he saw me enter the restaurant: the way it lit up, the way he went in for a kiss … the way I ripped all of that hope away from him. I can't help but wonder if I would feel less guilty if I had been honest with him from the start instead of leading him on while I tried to figure out what I wanted. But dwelling on what might have been puts a damper on my gratitude, so I try to push it from my mind.

Another thing to dwell on is the fact that Jordan hasn't responded to my text yet, which is very unlike him. I don't have much time left to dwell, as I am expected to show up to work no matter how late I might have been up moving the night before, but that doesn't stop me from thinking about it. Our routine has been that we exchange texts all day, starting from the moment I get up until I am off work, at which time we talk on the phone until I get home, and we switch to video chat. This has been true even when one of us has a meeting; we'll usually just send a quick note that says "in a meeting" so that the other is aware. To have no contact, even in response to my good morning text, is alarming. I have quickly come to rely on his daily "Morning, Gorgeous" reply to get me through the first part of my day. But more than that, my mind is leaping over flaming hurdles as I jump to all of the conclusions about why Jordan isn't responding.

The most likely scenario is that he deeply regrets that he almost told me that he loves me last night on the phone, because it is obviously too early. It is, I decide, probably easiest for him to ghost me completely rather than to admit his embarrassment. Another possible reason for his silence is that he has been kidnapped and is currently sitting in a warehouse somewhere in Georgia where he has been bound and gagged and no longer has access to his phone. I have also considered that he has come down with acute appendicitis and has rushed himself to the hospital for emergency surgery.

I'm already through my first morning meeting and considering calling the police for a welfare check when my phone finally vibrates next to me on the desk. I have never unlocked my phone so quickly, only to find that after hours of no contact, Jordan has sent me a link to the music video for Miley Cyrus's "Party in the USA." The question mark I send as a response doesn't do enough to convey my confusion.

Jordan: I hopped off the plane at LAX, with a dream and my cardigan ... although it's a little warm and I don't even own a cardigan.

The way I fly up out of my chair as if he is about to come walking through my office door must surely be comical. I immediately find myself hitting the call button on Jordan's contact screen.

"Hey, Baby," he answers after one ring.

"I thought you were dead!" I say. I realize that this is not a normal greeting, but it's the only thing that comes to mind.

"Well, I feel a little bit like it. There weren't any exit row seats available, and I had to cram my body into a regular economy seat that did not have the 'ample leg room' that was advertised," he replies.

"But, why?" I ask. The word is a question in itself, of course, which is good because I can't bring myself to ask the full question as I intend it: Why would you fly across the country for me? He was planning on coming here for a meeting next week, but it doesn't make sense that he would come a week early just for me.

"Kenley, I would do just about anything for you," he says. Hearing my name on his lips once again sends a wave of heat through my core.

"But, your job! And … and your life!" I exclaim.

"I took a sick day, and I can work remotely next week. I needed to be here with you. It was important to me," he says.

I can't remember a time in my life when anyone had prioritized me and my crisis. My parents were always incredible and treated me with dignity and respect, but they were my parents, and I had spent my life questioning their motivations. Perhaps I should question Jordan's motivations, too. It is, like I said, way too soon for any of this to be real, and yet I have absolutely no questions. This feels right.

"I felt so helpless last night when you called and told me you were moving. And I know you're a rockstar and you did it with minimal help, but I still hated that I was on the other side of the country and that you had to do it alone. I was already on my way to the airport by the time you texted me that your move was done," he says. My usual rebuttal about being a strong woman who is more than capable of functioning in the world on my own feels like it is on the tip of my tongue, but the words don't come out.

Proving that he gets me without my having to say a word, Jordan says, "And I know you are fine and you're happy to do it on your own. But just because you can go through it alone doesn't mean that you have to."

People have tried to tell me this for years, but I had never believed them. I have always believed that in order for anything to be done correctly, I needed to be the one to do it. I am perfectly capable of succeeding on my own, and I have done so for more than a decade. These days it is a point of pride to be able to share all that I have accomplished on my own. But maybe if I had listened to everyone who had told me that I didn't have to do it all on my own, my dumpster wouldn't have ignited at such a spectacular rate.

"Thank you for coming," I say instead of arguing. For some reason, I can't find it in myself to argue with Jordan, even when I do already have a typical argumentative answer in my repertoire.

"You're my girl, Kenley. I'll always be here for you," he says then before switching gears and asking me to text him an address so he can call an Uber. And even as we hang up and I send the address for the office, I still can't get that one word out of my head. Always.

27.

Together is a wonderful place to be.

I can't believe Jordan is here. It was one thing starting our relationship in Bloomington, which was neutral ground. It was something else to keep things going long distance. But now, he is here in what is essentially my turf, and it is a completely different feeling. What if our attempt to cohabitate is disastrous? What if he spends three hours a day on the toilet, or can't get past my habit of waiting to take the trash out until there isn't any possible way to shove anything else into the bin?

"I don't have any furniture," I tell him, placing the key into the lock of the door that leads into the kitchen. The house has a detached garage with an entrance to the kitchen off of the driveway, and honestly it could have been thirty-seven stories tall with only one room on each floor and I still would have been happy to have it.

Even though Jordan knows I moved in less than twenty-four hours ago, I am suddenly incredibly worried that he'll pass judgment on my lack of furniture and the fact that moving boxes and black trash bags full of my belongings are strewn throughout the house. The trash bags weren't my first choice for packing, but when Nicky and Shanna had offered to help me move last night, it was the means to an end.

"Kenley, do you not want me here?" Jordan asks then.

"No, it's not that. I'm just ... this is real life. We haven't done real life yet. What if you hate it here?" I panic, unable to turn the knob to let us into the house.

"In real life?"

"In MY life." I'm being ridiculous. I know I'm being ridiculous, but I can't help myself.

Instead of answering with words, Jordan pulls me into his arms and places a sweet kiss on my nose. We've been touching for hours, of course, because that is what we do. Jordan had met me at work, where I had given him a tour of the office and then my boss excused me early to account for his arrival. As soon as we were seated in my car, Jordan's hand found mine. In the grocery store, where I had needed to stop on the way home, he had found a way to touch me the entire time: holding my hand, an arm draped around my shoulder, or his hand pressed against the small of my back. And now, outside of my back door, in his arms.

"Hello?" a lady's voice comes up the driveway. "I'm your new neighbor!"

I don't want to break from Jordan's embrace, but the last thing I want is to be rude to my neighbors. My seatmate had been so generous with this lease, and I would hate for it to somehow get back to her that I am rude or ungrateful. *This is the plight of everyone born to Boomer parents*, I think.

"Hi there!" Jordan says, releasing me and quickly heading down the driveway with his hand extended. *He doesn't even live here* I want to say, but the neighbor is already eating him up with her eyes. As they shake hands, their voices lower to normal volume and I have to physically walk over to where they are in order to participate in their conversation. The only thing worse than an overly friendly airplane seatmate is a nosy neighbor.

"You live in that house there?" he is asking when I reach them.

"Yes, my name is Julie, and my husband is Scott. I'm sure you'll see us around often," she says.

"I'm Jordan, and this is my girlfriend Kenley," he says. Girlfriend. I had been so turned off by Luke's use of the word, but when Jordan says it, it somehow makes me feel at peace.

"Girlfriend?" Julie asks. "You're not married then? Any kids?"

It's none of your business, Julie. I think. But Jordan is, thankfully, more polite than I am. "No ma'am, but we're working on both," he

175

says.

We are? Kenley don't panic. He's just being cordial to the neighbor. It is way too soon for him to be talking like that, he's just putting on a show. Take a deep breath and keep smiling, she'll go back home soon.

"Kenley," Jordan repeats, realizing that I have not heard the last question that was apparently directed at me. "Julie was just asking about your work."

"Oh, I'm sorry, long day of moving and getting everything settled," I lie as I offer her what I hope looks like a sincere smile.

The chat continues for a few more minutes, Jordan's hand tucked behind my back for emotional support. Some people carry around emotional support cups of coffee, have emotional support animals, listen to emotional support music ... I think I might have an emotional support boyfriend. And as we say our goodbyes and head back toward the house to bring in the groceries, I can't get that idea out of my head. I have a boyfriend, and it's Jordan Freaking Thomas. Jordan Thomas, who wants to work on getting married and having kids with me ... his girlfriend.

"Are you okay, Ken?" Jordan asks, unpacking a box of dried pasta that we had decided could be turned into our dinner.

"Yes. I'm just thinking about that conversation with Julie," I say.

"What about it?" he asks.

"You said a lot of words."

"Words?"

"Yeah. Big ones."

Jordan is silent for a moment, digging through one of the cardboard boxes labeled "kitchen" in search of some sort of vessel to cook the pasta. *This is it,* I think, *the moment where he takes back those words.*

"Yeah," he says, finding a saucepan and holding it up triumphantly before turning to face me. "I meant them."

———

In addition to being my boyfriend, Jordan Thomas is a wizard in the kitchen, which is a good thing because I am whatever the opposite of a wizard is. I am surprised that I even owned a pot in which to cook pasta. When I was working at the firm, I ordered dinner to my desk most nights, and on weekends I would eat whatever leftovers I had brought home. Learning to cook had never been on my list of things that I wanted to do; eating already prepared food is more my area of expertise. But Jordan has made us a meal that puts me at risk of revealing my gluttonous side to him too early in this relationship.

"Where'd you learn to cook like this?" I ask.

"Well, remember I told you that I tried everything to fill the hole in my life after my divorce? That list was not comprehensive. I also took cooking classes," he shrugs. "And I learned to knit, but that does not leave this room."

It's hard to try to picture Jordan sitting in front of the TV with his knitting the way that my grandmother used to do, but I appreciate the mental image. I can understand where his desire to try new things to fill the void had come from; it's not unlike how I had launched myself into a life that barely resembled my own from the second I lost my job. Sometimes, in the moment, it felt good to do those things, but those good feelings never lasted.

"The cooking classes led me to the gym, because if I was going to be eating well, I also had to work out more, and working out led me to therapy. So, it was all worth it," he continues, clearing our plates from the small table that had worked well in my tiny apartment but looks completely out of place in this big house.

"And the knitting?" I ask, feigning innocence. He gives me a look, as if I am not supposed to have said it out loud. "What? We're technically still in this room."

"Cute," he says, leaning in to kiss me. "My grandma taught me, said it kept her from having idle hands, and busy hands kept her from having an idle mind. I figured it was worth a shot."

The kitchen is a mess, both from the moving and from the dinner prep, but standing at the sink with Jordan feels the opposite of messy. It's stupid that I feel this way. I met Jordan eighteen days ago, so there is absolutely no reason that I should feel the way that I do about him ... but I either can't help it, or I don't care. When I had talked to Jessica after two weeks of seeing Luke, she told me that I should have a sense of whether it was right or not, and if I had been honest, I would have been able to admit that it was wrong. But now, with Jordan, that same question already reveals a completely different answer.

"What are you thinking about?" he asks.

"My parents got engaged on their first date," I blurt out, unable to stop myself. Jordan laughs as he closes the door of the dishwasher before turning back to me, caging me against the counter with his arms.

"So, you're saying we're behind?" he asks, leaning down to kiss me.

"Just a reminder to myself that it's not too soon to feel this way," I say, snaking my arms up around his neck and pulling back so that I can look into his eyes.

"And how do you feel?" Jordan asks. The atmosphere between us is suddenly thick, but I am afraid of letting go. Maybe that's how Jordan has felt since the minute we connected, unable to let go of me for fear that it might make this feel less real.

"I feel ..." I start, unsure of exactly how to finish that sentence.

"Like the things you said outside sound good," I say.

Jordan smiles that killer smile that he used in high school. "Yeah? The big words?"

I nod emphatically. Our faces are only inches apart and I can feel his breath on mine, but I don't make any moves to pull away. This feels like a moment, like something important is happening between us, like confessions are being made.

"I think I am falling in love with you, Kenley," he says then.

His words instantly warm me from my head to my toes. I should have known that with Jordan I wasn't going to have to try to read between the lines and make sense of his behaviors. From the very second we met in the Atlanta airport, he has been nothing but open and honest with me and has never beaten around the bush about his feelings.

"Last night ..." I start.

"Yeah, last night. I almost fucking said it," he says with a breathy laugh, pulling back from me and hunching his body forward,

178

cradling his head in his hands.

"When I got your text that your talk had gone badly and that you were moving in the middle of the night, I felt like I was choking. I felt so stuck and helpless on the other side of the country. All I could think about was how I finally found you after all this time, and how I'm already pretty sure of where this is going and that I might never get to tell you that. I had to get here."

In the expression of his panic, the hulking man before me looks more like a scared little boy. If he wasn't standing right in front of me, it would be hard for me to picture him this way. Jordan is a looming presence in every room he enters, but at the moment, in my nearly empty kitchen, he seems so small.

"I'm okay," I say, rubbing his back softly.

"But what if you weren't? What if that guy had tried something and you had gotten hurt?" he asks. The anguish in his voice tells me that he has been running this worst-case scenario in his head since last night, imagining over and over again a world where he could do nothing to help me. I have spent large portions of my life imagining worst-case scenarios, but Jordan is so laid back that I know this is brand-new territory for him.

"Hey. Hey," I say, placing my hand on top of one of his that is still clutching his face. "I'm okay. Nothing happened. I'm here with you."

In response, he pulls me to his chest and wraps his arms tightly around my back. I've never been much of a hugger, but I feel safe here, like I am in my own little Jordan cocoon, being made into the best version of myself. Because, the truth is that Jordan is not the only person here who is catching feelings, and I can already tell that I am going to be made better because of them.

"God, I can't take it anymore," he says then, breaking me from the peaceful moment and catching me off guard.

"Can't take what?" I ask. This is the worst-case scenario that has lived in my head, the realization that Jordan doesn't want to be with me after all. It's sudden, but I have prepared myself for this and steel myself to whatever he might have to say next.

"You still being in clothes," he growls, his hand reaching under my shirt and up my ribs until his thumb pokes under the band of my bra and gently caresses the flesh of my breast. The jolt of electricity that runs through my body puts all intrusive thoughts completely out of my head.

The task of getting my clothes off is quick, as I hardly have to do any of the work. Jordan is eager like a kid on Christmas morning. When I am finally naked before him, I don't feel embarrassed or ashamed because he is looking at me like I am a valuable piece of art. No one has ever looked at me this way before, and it makes me feel powerful.

"Holy shit," he whispers, falling to his knees before me and bringing his mouth to my right breast. The way he sucks and nips and teases the nipple with his tongue is exquisite, and I can't quite believe that this is only foreplay.

"The number of times in high school that I got myself off just imagining your tits," he says, his mouth against my skin. Usually I find dirty talk unnecessary, but I think that's because I had never heard those words from Jordan's lips. "My mom had to buy new towels every couple of months, I thought of them so often."

If Jordan can be dirty, I can try, too. "What did you want to do to them?" I ask.

He lets out a breathy laugh, moving to the left and unleashing the same amount of pleasure. "Everything," he says between licks and sucks.

"Do they live up to expectations?" I ask. It's not a dirty question, but I am curious, nonetheless.

"They're better than anything I could have dreamed up, even as a perverted sixteen-year-old," he says. As he speaks, he grabs my butt and pulls my body closer to him and then rubs a finger softly against my core, which is already ready for him. I wiggle a little so that his finger dips inside ever so slightly, and he lets out a laugh before pushing the finger all the way inside.

I haven't been finger fucked since college, but somehow with Jordan it feels right. After all, we're still exploring our high school fantasies about one another, even as we forge forward with this adult relationship. "I used to imagine what it would feel like for you to come on my fingers," he says, as if on cue.

"You dated so many girls," I say then, my breathing labored.

"Yeah, but I only ever thought about you," he says, thrusting his fingers in and out, harder and faster, the pace of his breath matching my own.

"Are you close? I'm about to lose it," he says. I can hear the horror in his voice at the thought that he might come before me. But little does he know that I've never had an orgasm. Sometimes people find that hard to believe, but I've just always figured they weren't meant for me. I'm usually too in my head, thinking about what I am supposed to do with my hands, or if my breath stinks, or if the garlic I ate for lunch is having an impact on the taste and smell of other areas of my body ... There is just so much that goes into sex for me, and like with all things in life, I'd rather keep my head on straight.

"Let me help you," I say, reaching forward to unclasp his jeans.

"I'm not going to make it," he says. His finger is still inside of me, but his thrusting has become erratic as he tries to keep it together. I'm pretty sure that I have never had this kind of effect on a man, which just gives me even more to think about. When I reach inside of his boxer briefs, I am surprised by the sheer size of him as I lower the band, my hand wrapped around him. Touching myself with my other hand to get something slick with which to stroke him causes him to make a sound that is almost animalistic, and it only takes two pumps before I feel the spray of hot liquid across my abdomen and Jordan lets out a wail.

I think we're done, but Jordan is determined that his premature finish is not the end as he starts to move his fingers inside of me again, devouring my breasts like they're his last meal.

"It's okay, I don't need to come," I tell him.

"Yes, you do," he replies, sucking the side of my breast so hard that I know I will have a mark there tomorrow.

"No, really. It's okay. I don't usually ... or ever actually. So, I'll be fine," I continue. He stops abruptly and sits back on his heels. He is still twitching above the elastic band of his underwear, which is a little distracting even though this is a semi-serious conversation.

"Never?"

"Not so far ... and I mean, I'm old enough now that you'd think if it was going to happen, then it would have happened. So, it's fine. We can just take care of you," I say. Jordan tugs my arm, pulling me down onto his lap so that I can feel him pulsing against my bare skin.

"It's going to happen," he says, capturing my lips with his, and I instantly feel him stiffen beneath me.

"I'm still covered in you," I say, matter-of-factly. But Jordan has a solution for that, too, quickly whipping off his t-shirt and using it to clean me up. His bare torso is spectacular. I never thought I would use that word to describe a man's body, but then I never thought that I would see Jordan Thomas shirtless.

"We're in the kitchen," I say then. When I was growing up, my mom had a book on her shelf, which she said had been a gift, that was called *Sex Begins in the Kitchen*, and though I never read it, I am pretty sure that it was not about this.

"Kenley, do you not want me to fuck you?" Jordan asks. "Because if you're not ready, we can stop."

"I just don't want you to be disappointed if I can't … you know …" I say.

"When I played football, Coach always used to tell us that you can't win games if you don't show up for practice," Jordan says then, lifting me with one arm as he slides his pants and underwear off with the other. "And I intend to put in a lot of practice."

"I'm on the pill," I blurt out then, because it seems like important information to share. I had talked to my doctor as soon as I had started hooking up with Luke because I didn't know how long that was going to go on, and it had been hard for me to talk about condoms. "And I'm clean," I add because by the time I had officially gotten the appointment, my sexual relationship with Luke had already ended, and the test she had given me in her office had told me I was in the clear.

"That's great news," Jordan says, tossing his pants into a pile with his discarded t-shirt and lowering me back down on top of him so that he is hovering right at the place between my legs where I most want him to be.

"Practice makes perfect, right?" I ask, lowering myself onto him, which isn't as simple or romantic as it seems. Everything about

Jordan is giant ... EVERYTHING. To distract me, he wraps his arms around my back so that we are sitting together, staring into each other's eyes.

"You okay?" he asks.

Yes, you're okay. This is Jordan we're talking about ... forget your high school fantasies, you've never felt so safe with anyone in your life. This is it, Kenley. This is real. This is what you thought you'd have to earn. And he's right here in front of you ... more than in front of you. INSIDE of you. Breathe into it. Try not to think about it. Just be here with him, like you said you were when he was freaking out.

"I'm okay," I say, shifting slightly to take him completely and eliciting a moan from his perfect mouth. As his hips buck to meet mine, we fall into a steady rhythm, our eyes never leaving one another's in a sort of intense stare down that makes it impossible for me to get lost in my own thoughts. It's like I'm in a tunnel, unable to react to anything except for this feeling of connection with the man beneath me. There is nobody in the whole world except for us.

"Do I make you feel good, Baby?" Jordan exhales, driving into me hard and sending a jolt through my entire body.

"Y-Yes!" I practically scream. I am close, I've never been this close before, and now that I know what it feels like, that fact is abundantly clear. I can't tell if Jordan is just this good or if it is so good for me simply because it's Jordan. The harder and deeper he thrusts inside of me, though, the more I realize that the reason doesn't matter.

I never imagined that when my first orgasm finally happened it would be on the kitchen floor. But at a certain point, as Jordan keeps pounding into me, his gaze locked on mine, I can't take it anymore and I feel myself let go, collapsing onto his chest as he holds me.

"Fuck!" he exclaims, thrusting into me one last time before I feel the heat of his explosion on my insides. And we sit like that for a minute, me on his lap, him still inside of me, just breathing into one another as we come down from the high.

"Touchdown?" I offer once I have regained my wits. It's probably the only time in my life I have ever said that word. I had tried to be into football back in high school, in hopes that Jordan would notice me then, but my lack of interest in the sport had greatly outweighed my commitment to winning his heart.

Jordan's full-bodied laugh catches me off guard, shaking my body right along with his. I realize quickly that it is my favorite sound in the universe, deep and penetrative yet carefree. I could listen to Jordan's laugh on repeat in my earbuds for the rest of my life and I would never get tired of it.

"Yeah, it's official. I am so fucking in love with you," he says.

Correction ... that is my favorite sound in the universe.

28.

The bed is empty when I wake up, which immediately causes me to panic. After our amazing kitchen sex, Jordan and I managed to christen just about every room in the new house before we finally passed out in bed around midnight, and I expected him to still be there when I woke up. Since I lost my job at the firm, I had taken to sleeping in as late as my body felt like it needed to, and after last night's physical exertion on top of the late-night move the night before, my body needed today's sleep especially. But that doesn't mean I'm not freaking out a little bit about the empty spot beside me. Thankfully, when I grab my phone, I see a text from Jordan waiting for me:

Jordan: Got up early to workout. My body is still on Eastern time.

Even though I didn't require an explanation, my shoulders heave a sigh of relief.

Kenley: Last night wasn't enough of a workout for you?

I type out in reply before I chuckle to myself as I set down my phone and wonder how Jordan will respond if he is not, presumably, in the house. But instead of a text, the bedroom door pushes open, and Jordan comes in shirtless and in a pair of loose-fitting sweatpants, carrying a cup of coffee.

"Morning, Baby," he says, setting the cup down on the nightstand beside me before going around to the other side of the bed and sliding under the covers on his side. It doesn't feel the slightest bit weird to think that he has a side in my bed. In fact, it feels completely normal.

He smells faintly of soap, which is my first indication of how long he has been awake since he's already had a chance to shower. The fact that he remembered my need for coffee in the morning honestly means more than any declaration of love could. To me, it's love in action.

"Sorry I slept so long," I say, taking a sip from the cup that has the exact right ratio of milk to coffee. It's weird that he gets me so easily.

"You didn't, it's only eight thirty on a Saturday. But my body thinks it's eleven thirty, I couldn't stay asleep, and I didn't want to wake you," he says, reaching for my free hand and intertwining our fingers. We are both awake in the same location, so naturally our touching should begin.

The bedroom is sparse because of the quick move. Jordan was honestly lucky to find the bed fully assembled with sheets on, because I had known I wasn't going to be able to sleep Thursday night if it was on a bare mattress on the floor. But beyond the bed, the room is virtually empty. Living in a studio for so long meant that I don't have a lot of furniture. My apartment had come with a built-in armoire, so I hadn't needed a dresser, and since my bedroom was also my living room, the only television now lives several rooms away from where I sleep. The lack of things in this room makes the whole thing look industrial and sterile.

"You're thinking again," Jordan says. He's tracing figure eights on the back of my hand with his thumb, but otherwise we've just been sitting in silence. I will never stop loving the way I can do that with him. Silence is something I consider to be one of the greatest treasures in my life, and with Jordan, I never feel like I have to compromise that.

I don't answer him because I don't want to admit that this house is probably too big for me. I am grateful to have it, and if I have to spend thousands of dollars filling these empty rooms and walls, then I will.

"Do you want to go shopping?" he asks, even without my response.

"How did you …?" I begin.

"You're looking around the room frowning, which is adorable but also easily remedied," he answers before I can finish.

I hate shopping. There are too many people around everywhere, and I always feel pressured to support commissioned retail workers. But I do need furniture, so I am afraid I have no choice. At least I'll have Jordan for moral support … he really has become my emotional support boyfriend.

Neither of us moves to get up right away, though. The last time we had woken up together, in my childhood bedroom, we had been hurrying to get up to the hospital, so it's nice to be able to take our time drinking coffee, scrolling our phones, and stealing small kisses in the morning light. It would be foolish of me, as much as I don't want to think about Luke anymore, not to recognize how different things are with Jordan. With Luke, I never felt comfortable, flying out of bed as soon as my eyes opened and hurrying to get dressed and be on my way. With Jordan, there is no sense of urgency. His words back in Bloomington are ringing in my ears: "I know we've got time."

Knowing we've got time is what is on my mind when my phone suddenly starts ringing in my hand, and I see Jessica's face illuminate the screen with a video call. "Oh no!" I exclaim, throwing my phone down and burying my face in Jordan's shoulder. He laughs softly.

"Are you ashamed of me, Baby?" he asks playfully. I shake my head, but I can feel the heat in my cheeks against his bare chest.

"No! But we're clearly in bed, and you look naked," I say quickly.

"It's just Jessica," he says.

"My family has no secrets!" I exclaim. I have been reminded again and again lately how true this is. I had tried to have secrets before my trip home, but EJ and Jessica had both opened their mouths in front of our parents on my very first night in town, proving that my attempt at setting boundaries and maintaining a bit of privacy was, in fact, impossible.

"Answer the phone," he replies. I shake my head against him, but I know exactly what he's doing when he reaches to the spot beside me where I threw my phone.

"Hey Jessica," he says before I can grab the phone out of his hand.

There's silence at first on the other end, which makes me think for a split second that he has been teasing me, but then she speaks. "Oh, hi Jordan. Tanner, look, it's Jordan," she says.

This feels fine, I think to myself, *it's just Jessica and Tanner and they're rooting for us. Try to think of it that way.*

But then: "I thought you were calling your sister," my mom says. I can see her face appear in front of Jessica's as if it wasn't my sister who initiated the call in the first place.

"I did call my sister," Jessica says knowingly.

Oh, dear god, make it end. I want to throw these blankets over my head and hide from the world until my family somehow, hopefully, forgets that this ever happened.

"Oh my gosh, is everyone there?" I squeak, grabbing the phone from Jordan and showing my beet red face on camera for the first time.

"It's just Mom and Dad, the boys, and me," Jessica says, as if this makes it all so much better. This isn't an unusual gathering. Even before the baby arrived, my parents often spent Saturday mornings with Jess and Tanner. What is unusual is that they have decided to video call me while they are all together. We've been talking more frequently since I returned from my trip, but this call is particularly inconvenient.

I can't be upset with Jordan for answering. He had thought it was just my sister, who happens to be married to one of his closest friends. If it had only been Jessica, I might not have been as horrified. The fact that my parents are also there, and staring at a shirtless man in my bed, is not Jordan's fault. I would not have expected my parents to be on the call either since I have only just recently convinced them that texting me is a much better form of communication than a voice call, and they struggle to understand how the camera works on their smartphones.

"Well, hi everyone, I guess," I say. My plans for my parents to live out the rest of their lives believing that I am a virgin are certainly out the window now.

"Kenley, why didn't you tell us that Jordan was visiting this weekend?" my mom asks, offended, pushing her way fully into the camera's orbit. I know she wants to see for herself that Jordan is here with me, and that it isn't some new private joke about my love life that I share with my sister. She wants to be able to ask about it later and feel like the two of us have something private and special to talk about, too. Only, this isn't private at all. It's on display for the whole family to see.

"In her defense, Mrs. Graves, I didn't tell her I was coming," Jordan says, leaning back into the shot. I can see her visibly swooning at the sweetness. If only she knew that it wasn't actually an act of sweetness, but one of panic that brought Jordan to the other side of the country. I guess maybe I do still have some secrets from my family after all.

"Oh Honey, call me Jackie," she says. Jordan is using the same charm on my mother that he used on our teachers in high school, and I am honestly grateful because if he can woo her just a little, maybe that will help turn this phone call into something that doesn't permanently destroy the relationship I have with my family.

I love my family, and yes, they know a lot about my life. But this is a private moment that I would rather not share with them. It was bad enough that my dad was home that morning that Jordan slept over in Bloomington when nothing happened between us. This feels eight hundred times worse. I am trying to hold onto a sliver of hope that maybe, just maybe, they won't be able to tell how we spent all of last night, but the longer this goes on, the harder that is becoming.

"Bro! Nice! Text me!" Tanner says then, appearing over Jessica's shoulder. And … all hope is gone. This is a disaster.

"Tanner! Ew. That is my sister! Jordan, do not text him," Jessica warns. This whole call is dissolving quickly into madness, and I want nothing more than to hang up, but I also don't want to be the one to hang up for a variety of deep-seated reasons that probably indicate that my family needs therapy.

"Was there a reason that you called?" I ask then, trying to get everyone back on track. If I can't be the one to hang up, maybe I can be the one to steer us back to normalcy somehow.

"We were just thinking about you, and Jessica suggested that we call. If you're busy, we can let you go," my dad says then from somewhere off camera. I'm sure he's intentionally not looking at the screen because my mom has already told him what he'll find if he does. I am begging for the rest of the family to get the hint from his words.

"Well Honey, if you're busy why did you answer?" my mom asks.

"She didn't answer, Jordan answered," Jessica says.

"Bro! Nice!" Tanner says again.

"TANNER!" Jessica scolds.

"Okay, I'm going to hang up. Love you!" I say quickly before hitting the end call button and melting into the bed to die of embarrassment. Jordan dives over me with his body so that his head and torso hover over my own, a sheepish expression on his face.

"I hate you," I pout.

"No, you don't," he says, a laugh in his voice. He's right, I don't.

"That was mortifying!" I say. "My parents definitely know we had sex."

I know that Jordan understands this to some extent. He had grown up in an extremely sheltered religious home, which was largely the reason that he hadn't been the ladies' man that his high school reputation made him out to be. Like me, sex wasn't something that was discussed in the home growing up, though in his house it was because sex was considered an all-out sin, while in mine it was just a private topic not meant for conversation outside of the mandatory "birds and bees" talk. Even though we are adults now and our parents at least assume we have had sex at some point in our lives (Jordan was married, for crying out loud), it still feels uncomfortable to talk about it.

"So," Jordan says, breaking the silence. "What are you going to tell them someday when we have a baby?"

Though the question is asked with a good dose of sarcasm, it stirs something inside of me that I haven't felt before. Jordan had told the neighbor yesterday that we were working on marriage and kids, and while he told me he had meant it, it's not something we've ever talked about.

Kenley, this is a good man. It's only been a few weeks, but it already feels right. Talking about kids is not the same as having them. There is no harm in discussing these things to make sure you're both on the same page. That is what couples do, and you and Jordan are a couple. Don't overthink it, he's not asking to knock you up today.

"Well, that will be something to figure out in the future, when that time comes," I say, trying to calm my inner freak-out.

"Hopefully not too far in the future," he says. He is still hovering over me, propped up on one arm while the other hand takes liberties in exploring the bare skin beneath my sleeping shirt. It's tempting to give in to his touch, but this is an important conversation that needs to happen now.

"Not too far, but not too soon either," I say, my voice faltering as he glides his fingertips with a featherlight touch over my nipple. I reach and grab his arm, stopping him in his tracks.

"Jordan, stop. This is important," I say. His eyes lock with mine before he sighs and rolls onto his back beside me. Neither of us speaks for a moment, and I can't help but wonder what just happened.

"I'm sorry. My therapist says I have to stop using sex as a way to avoid difficult conversations," he admits, giving me the answer to the question that I hadn't yet vocalized.

This revelation feels more important than the conversation about our potential future kids. Jordan has been nothing but open about all of the destructive habits he developed after his divorce and how he's in therapy now, but he has never been so forthcoming about what he's been working on in those sessions. I want to know more, but I also want to give him the space he needs to feel like he can talk about these things with me without feeling any pressure. Being in a mature adult relationship is a lot harder than I ever imagined.

Jordan and I are both coming into this relationship from our own unique versions of having lost everything. Between the two of us, there is more than enough baggage to fill all of the empty rooms in this too-big house. I used to think that I couldn't bring any baggage into a relationship, that's why I had worked for so many years to perfect my career before I shifted the focus to my personal life. But even in these few weeks that Jordan and I have been together, I've started to see that it isn't about who brings the least amount of baggage into the relationship but rather how you help one another carry it.

"I'm sorry," Jordan says then. "I started panicking ... again."

I want to ask why he was panicking when it was my family on the other end of the most embarrassing video chat in the history of technology, but when he slides his palm onto mine, interlocking our fingers, I forget all about my question.

"Ever since I left Bloomington, I have been imagining what life with you will look like someday. Marriage, kids, vacations at Disney World, the whole nine yards. But now that it came up in real life, I got scared because we haven't talked about it before, and maybe I am just living in my fantasy world ... and what if you don't even want a family?" he says.

It's interesting to hear a man vocalize thoughts like these. With girlfriends I've had over the years, we've talked about our fantasies and our dreams for the future, and while I've never doubted that men *have* these kinds of thoughts, I have never heard about them. Jordan is being extremely vulnerable with me, and I want to answer him exactly right to put his mind at ease, but the truth is that the idea scares me, too. I have always wanted a family of my own, I just always thought that I still had more time, and now that I have an amazing man beside me the answer doesn't roll off of my tongue quite as easily.

"Talking about the future can be overwhelming, and all of this is still new between us," I admit. "But, if you're asking if I think that I would maybe like to someday have a baby with you, then I think that the answer is probably yes."

It's not a very confident-sounding answer, but Jordan doesn't seem to care as relief floods his whole body. Just as quickly as he had rolled off of me and onto his back, he rolls back, caging me in with his arms before lowering his mouth to mine.

When I laugh and ask him what he is doing, he says, "We're going to need a lot of practice."

He's right, I guess. Practice makes perfect, after all.

29.

The last time I had Saturday night plans, I was at least three years younger than I am today. I know that seems hard to believe, but it's true. I hadn't intended to completely ignore my social life until all of the friends I had managed to make in my adopted hometown gave up on me, but I was also fully aware of where my career was heading, and I only had time for one thing. Of course, the fact that my best friend worked at the same law firm made it so that my work life and my social life had become so enmeshed that I didn't notice the latter had ceased to exist on its own.

But tonight, I have plans. Or rather, we do. I have to keep reminding myself that Jordan and I are a package deal. The idea still feels so bizarre.

If the last time I had plans was three years ago, then the last time I was at a bar in Hollywood was at a point so far in the past that I can no longer remember. I wouldn't even be here tonight if it wasn't for my saviors turned new friends, Nicky and Shanna, who invited me to join them on their outing to see one of Shanna's clients perform with her band.

Thursday night had been a blur of throwing my belongings into suitcases, boxes, and garbage bags and then piling everything into the back of a stranger's pickup truck before unloading it all into my new house. But in between all of that, I had gotten to know my new friends. Shanna, I had learned, is a talent agent representing hopeful actors at a small agency in Century City, which sounds way more impressive to me than my own job, maybe because she also gets to read contracts for a living and she didn't have to go to law school to do it. When I first moved to Los Angeles, I had envisioned myself hobnobbing with Hollywood types at every turn because that was all that I knew about this city. In reality, my contact with the industry, as it is called here, has been extremely limited and I still find the whole thing incredibly fascinating.

"Kenz, over here!" Shanna calls to me as soon as Jordan and I have stepped through the doors of the dimly lit club. It's not lost on me that she has already given me a nickname, something I had been lamenting not having just two weeks ago.

The booth where they are sitting is in the very center of the room, and I am sure that it has been reserved for them specifically by Shanna's client, whoever she is. Both women light up as soon as they see Jordan, as if he is some kind of prize they have been waiting to win, and completely ignore the man sitting with them at the table, though he doesn't seem to care in the slightest. He looks younger and exactly like the kind of guy I would expect to see at a bar in Hollywood on a Saturday night, which is the opposite of me. Ever since we walked in, I have been nervous that I look as out of place as I feel. But Nicky and Shanna don't seem to care, they both run to hug me as soon as we approach their table.

As out of my element as I feel by the location of this meetup, I feel that much more at ease as soon as I am invited to sit on the padded bench of the curved booth. Having Jordan with me helps, but even if he wasn't here, I feel like I can be myself around these girls. I guess it has to do with the circumstances of how we had met and how quickly I had to trust them. We had done a lot of talking during the move on Thursday night, and it made it feel like I have known them for ages. It's exactly what I needed to find right at the exact moment I walked away from my oldest friendship.

"You look quite sated," Shanna teases when she slides back into the booth beside me. My cheeks immediately feel hot as my heart races from embarrassment, and I slide a little more into Jordan on my other side as an act of security. His hand immediately curves around my hip. It's nice having an emotional support boyfriend.

"It was a surprise, he flew out yesterday after … you know, everything," I reply, trying to regulate my heartbeat.

"That is so sweet. You guys are adorable," Shanna says, before turning to glance quickly at her phone on the table, declaring that her client's band is on second.

The noise level in the room is reminding me of exactly why I don't go out to places like this, but supposedly building human connection is important and one cannot spend all of their time alone. I think about this as I watch how easily Jordan has already become friends with the table's other occupant.

"Hey man, I'm Jordan," he says, offering his hand.

"Marco. I'm a friend of Nicky's," the other man replies, shaking Jordan's hand firmly. Shanna uses her hands to indicate that Marco and Nicky are sleeping together, and my face gets hot again. Why is there suddenly so much sex in my life? Are people just out in the world going at it like rabbits all the time? All while I was sitting in my office, working?

The two men enjoy a light conversation and the hand that Jordan had curved around my side never moves, even as a server comes by with our drinks and we raise our glasses to toast the rest of the group. I have never been one for public displays of affection, and yet with Jordan, I somehow can't help it nor does it make me feel embarrassed or ashamed. Like with everything else in our relationship, being close to Jordan in public feels right.

As the music of the first band begins, it becomes harder to hear each other talk, but that doesn't stop Jordan from leaning into my ear and asking questions like "Having fun?" and "Are you good?" in between stealing small kisses and trying to pass off the inability to hear the other members of our party by smiling and nodding. I can't help but chuckle to myself when I think about how just yesterday, I had been worried how he would fit into my real life. Now it seems like such a ridiculous question.

On the break between bands, the conversation picks back up again. "Have you seen this band perform before?" I ask Shanna, trying my best to make small talk.

"No, I've been trying to, but their shows have never lined up with

195

my schedule. My client has been begging me to check them out for months," Shanna says.

"Oh, what's your client's name anyway?" I ask just as the emcee for the evening ascends the stage.

He says, "Ladies and gentlemen, The Smoke Alarms!" right as Shanna says the name, "Lauren Goldstein."

30.

Everything happens for a reason.

It's all I can think about as soon as the words land on my ears. If I hadn't been fired from my job, I never would have hooked up with Luke. If I had never hooked up with Luke, I never would have gone running home to Bloomington. If I hadn't made that trip home for Jessica's shower, I wouldn't have met Jordan. But that isn't the end of the story, I know that for sure.

There is certainly a chance that Luke isn't here. In the time I have known him, he has attended less than a handful of his sister's shows, but I have a sinking suspicion that the streak of good luck I have had as of late is about to run out. If I've been learning anything in this month since I lost my job, it is that my instinct is pretty powerful and that my gut is to be trusted. And that's exactly what scares me, because my instincts are sending up emergency flares all around me.

Kenley, take a deep breath. It's okay. You're allowed to exist in the same world as Luke. You don't owe him anything. Take a deep breath. Luke can't touch you. Jordan is here, and you might joke that he is your emotional support boyfriend but if Luke tries anything, he will become a lot more than that. Just breathe. And again. And again.

"Are you okay?" Jordan asks, immediately noticing the tension in my body. I shake my head rapidly, trying my best to follow my breathing exercises while also scanning the room for the one person I am not ready to see again.

I don't see Luke anywhere, but I can just feel that he is here by the way my body is reacting. Even though my eyes are scanning back and forth across the expanse of the room, it feels like the walls are closing in from the outside, and the longer I spend searching the room, the more I feel like there isn't enough oxygen. I can feel the desire to curl into Jordan's side to seek protection, but my body feels paralyzed, like my limbs simply won't respond to anything my brain is telling them to do.

"It's his sister's band," I manage to say into the space directly in front of my face. Thankfully it's loud enough that both Jordan and Shanna respond, because I don't know what I would do if I had to repeat myself.

"Is he here?" Jordan asks, pulling me into his arms and immediately offering me the relief that my body had craved but been unable to claim for itself. I shrug against his chest, but I want to scream YES, even though I don't know for sure. Everything in my body is telling me that Luke is somewhere in that room, but I am too afraid to find him.

It turns out that I don't have to find him, though, because before I have a chance to look again, our server appears in front of our table, carrying a drink purchased by someone at the bar. It's a vodka soda with lemon.

"Can you take this back, please?" Shanna asks the server without even looking to see my reaction. She already knows, because everything happens for a reason, and if I hadn't met Jordan, things with Luke might not have ended so badly. And if things with Luke hadn't ended so badly, then I wouldn't have needed to be rescued from the restaurant by strangers. And if I hadn't been rescued by Nicky and Shanna, then I wouldn't be sitting in this bar in Hollywood on a Saturday night, having a panic attack.

The server seems bewildered by the request but takes the drink away anyway. Shanna places a hand gently on my knee. She blames herself, even though there is no way this could be considered her fault.

"What are the chances?" she asks aloud. I can't tell if she's asking herself or talking to Jordan and me, but either way, no one responds because her question is the only right one to ask. What are the chances that of all of the people in Los Angeles, the one who rescued me from who knows whatever Luke might have done on Thursday night is his sister's agent? It's honestly comical, and I would laugh if it wasn't happening to me.

The band has started playing and Lauren's voice is quite good, but I can't focus on that because I am too busy waiting on Luke. He's been my best friend for a decade, so I know he is not going to sit by idly and observe, especially not when he feels slighted. He is sitting somewhere, biding his time. And it's worse that he can see me, but I can't see him.

"Do you want to leave?" Jordan asks.

I do, but that isn't the answer. I can't run away from Luke for the rest of my life. Not given our history. I shake my head. What I want is for him to reveal himself so that we can get this over with. But I am not prepared for what that looks like when it happens.

I sense Luke before I see him approaching our table from Shanna's side. He looks tired, like maybe he hasn't slept since Thursday, and he's walking with a kind of stagger that says he's been drinking since then, too. For a split second, I feel guilty. Everything happens for a reason, and I broke his heart and led him to this place. But as soon as he pulls his arm back to swing at Jordan, every ounce of guilt vanishes. Jordan's years as an athlete serve him well, though—he catches Luke's fist midair and lowers it.

The cacophony that blasts my eardrums in the following moments is hard to describe. People who have witnessed the ordeal are screaming about a fight, which startles a server, causing them to drop a tray full of glasses, creating its own kind of chaos. The music of the band continues over the screaming while a bouncer comes through the front door, yelling about security. And then there is me, in the middle of it all, clinging to Jordan with everything I have while trying to plead with Luke through a look. Silent chaos is sometimes worse than the loudest, most raucous noise.

"Luke Randall Goldstein!" Lauren admonishes from the stage. It brings a record scratch silence to the room and someone near the stage says, "Ooo!" in that sing-songy way that kids in school used to do when someone got called to the principal's office.

If I had been watching this scene unfold from across the crowded bar, I would have tried to crawl under the table from secondhand embarrassment. Unfortunately, I am not sitting across the bar. Instead, I am stuck in the terrible position of being the reason that my best friend is attacking my boyfriend in a crowded bar. It's clear that Luke is not sober, and Jordan hasn't had a drink of alcohol in over a year. Between that and the difference in their size, if Jordan was willing to engage in Luke's assault, there would be no contest. To his credit, though, he doesn't move, keeping one arm around me, pulling me close to his side even as Luke attempts to lunge across the table, just as the bouncer reaches us and pulls him back.

"That's enough, pal," the bouncer says, holding Luke's hands behind his back. "The police are on their way."

"No," I say before I can stop myself.

The bouncer looks at me with confusion, but I only speak to Jordan when I continue.

"If you press charges, he could lose his law license," I plead. I feel the squeeze of his hand on my hip in response. Even if it's not what he would want to do on his own, I know he'll do it for me.

"Yeah, man, we're good," Jordan says. The bouncer almost looks disappointed as he loosens his grip on Luke, though he doesn't release him completely, guiding him to the front of the bar where he will be barred re-entry.

In all of the years I have known Luke, I have not known him to be so passionate. There is a time for passion as a lawyer, sure, but it's not anything like what I have experienced the last two times I have seen him. Maybe a more secure woman would say, "Yeah, I did that," but I just can't bring myself to be that girl. I can recognize and accept that I broke Luke's heart, but his behavior is not something in which I take pride.

"I feel like I should talk to him," I say.

Jordan stiffens beside me. He may have been willing to do anything I asked a second ago, but the only experiences he has had with Luke to date have involved violence or the threat of it, so he's ready to draw the line.

"You can come too, I just ... I can't leave it like this," I continue, hoping that my offer to let Jordan stand nearby will help put him at ease.

The bar has regained its original volume by now, with everyone discussing what they think they saw. Shanna is beside the stage, talking to Lauren who, it appears, is apologizing profusely for her brother's behavior, and Nicky and Marco have their tongues so far down each other's throats that I'm not even sure they knew there was a ruckus to begin with. But as we cross the room, I can't help but feel like everyone's eyes are on me. I can't help but feel like they *know* that I am the reason for all of this.

Outside, Luke is sitting on the curb, clutching a bottle of water that the bouncer must have provided. The security guard himself is back at his post in a chair by the door, checking the IDs of a group of girls who don't look old enough to be in this bar and are wearing fewer pieces of clothing between them than they have years. He lets them in anyway just as I sit down on the sidewalk beside my friend.

"Hey," I say. Luke looks up, startled, but doesn't respond.

"So, what are the odds that my friend Shanna is Lauren's agent?" I ask, hoping to break the ice.

It's not cold out by any means, but I feel a chill at Luke's silence, and I wonder if it was a mistake to come out here. The old Kenley wouldn't have come outside at all. She would have done everything in her power to avoid this confrontation, but it's amazing how much I have changed in such a short amount of time. Because even though sitting here on the curb, getting the icy treatment from Luke, feels uncomfortable, I can still trust that this is where I am supposed to be.

"It's different with him," Luke says then, breaking the silence.

"What do you mean?" I ask.

"I was watching you in the bar, and you looked so different with him. You're so at ease, so relaxed … I've been your friend for ten years, and you've never been that way with me," he says.

"It is different with him. I can't explain it, exactly. It's like when I met Jordan again after all these years, everything just clicked," I say. For a split second I feel afraid to utter Jordan's name in Luke's presence for fear of the reaction, but that is something that the old Kenley would have thought about. The new Kenley is learning to sit with the uncomfortable.

"It's fast, Kenley," Luke says then.

It's funny coming from the man whom I slept with for exactly a week before he called me his girlfriend, but I hold my tongue because it's not the time to have that argument.

"Yeah, but when you know, you know, I guess," I say instead.

"And when you don't, you don't, huh?" There is contempt in his voice, but I know that I deserve his anger. I had known that Luke wasn't right for me, but I had been too afraid of ruining our friendship to say anything, and my hesitation had given him hope.

Neither of us speaks for a while, and I know how it must seem to him even before he says the words. "My heart is broken and you're out living your best life. You have a new job, a new house, a new relationship ... The whole thing caught me off guard. All these years, I thought you needed me."

There is a cool breeze that carries the smells of Hollywood on its back as it rolls down the street. The crisp smell of the night air mixes with the wafting aroma of a street vendor grilling bacon-wrapped hot dogs somewhere down the block, and along the way those combine with the scent of car exhaust tinged with urine and the permeating essence of marijuana smoke. It's a unique olfactory experience that I know will forever remind me of this moment, sitting on the curb in front of a bar with Luke. Jordan isn't far away, respectfully giving us distance to talk in private but staying close enough that he can swoop in should Luke try to throw anymore punches.

"There is a difference between needing you and using you," I say. "I have needed your friendship more than you will ever understand. I couldn't have survived life at a corporate law firm without you. But I would never want to use you, and the things you were offering me felt a lot more like I would be using you."

Luke starts to protest, and I know what the argument would be: it wouldn't be using him if he was offering. But it just doesn't feel that way to me. Part of what had felt so wrong about being with Luke was the thought that he wouldn't let me do anything for myself. I never wanted to be beholden to him. I wanted to figure things out for myself.

"You found me a job. You were looking for a new apartment so that we could move in together ... Those were things that I needed to do on my own," I say before he has a chance to speak, and I watch his shoulders fall. I have always hated the expression "his heart was in the right place," because I feel like it gives people a pass, but in Luke's case, I think that I finally understand it. He was doing all of those things because he wanted me to see how badly I needed him, but in the end, they had done the opposite.

"I was right, you know?" he says after a moment.

"About what?"

"I told you that if anyone was capable of doing the things they had always wanted to do, it was you," he says. Luke fumbles with the water bottle in his hands, unable to look me in the eyes, and in his anxiety, I can truly feel his pain.

"I'm sorry, Luke."

"I've been feeling plenty sorry for myself. I don't need your pity, too," he says. I can hear the emotion in his voice, it reminds me a lot of the night in his childhood bedroom when we had a talk that wasn't that unlike this one.

"It's not pity, it's just ..."

"No, I get it," he says, and for the first time since I began thinking about this choice I had to make, I believe him.

"So, he's a good guy then?" he asks, changing the subject.

"He really is."

Luke is silent for a moment that feels like forever. I wonder what he's thinking. We used to be close enough that I could almost read his mind, but already I can tell that a wall has come up between us and I don't know if I will ever be able to take it down.

"The speed seems so unlike you. You're usually so cautious," he says. That is true of the old Kenley; she's making a lot of appearances tonight. She's the girl that Luke always knew.

"Honestly, I am scared to death," I say.

"That the shoe might fit?" he asks.

"What?"

"It's a song. I'll text it to you," he says. Then, "You should probably get back in there. Are we good, though? If all of this means that I lose my friend, then I wouldn't be able to live with myself."

"Yeah, we're good," I say, reaching for his hand and giving it a squeeze.

And when he does finally send the song in the early hours of Sunday morning, the lyrics are perfect.

31.

My latest mantra is all I can think about on Sunday morning as I watch Jordan sitting on my kitchen floor, assembling a newly purchased table and chairs that came in at least three hundred individual pieces. In between the embarrassment of Saturday morning and the disaster of Saturday night, we had managed to make it out of the house to buy a few things to make this place look and feel more like home. And while I did, technically, have a table that moved with me from my apartment, the upgraded version has room for four chairs and makes me feel a lot more like an adult. What makes me feel most like a real grownup, though, is standing here watching this man, who I become more convinced with each passing moment is going to be my future, and I can't stop thinking that *everything happens for a reason*. There have been so many *everythings* over the last month, and I keep looking at my life now and thinking this is the reason, only to find that another reason comes along. Maybe it's just that this is the first time in my life where I have ever done anything remotely close to living.

"I have a confession," Jordan says, snapping me out of my thoughts.

"Okay?" I ask from my perch against the countertop where I have been supervising his work. I set my coffee cup on the counter behind me to give him my full attention. Two months ago, I would have been absolutely beside myself at this sudden mention of a confession. I would have needed lists and pep talks and a good amount of denial to even get me through this conversation, which I would have been convinced was a recipe for disaster. But now, this kind of announcement feels totally casual. Maybe that has something more to do with the deliverer than anything else.

"Remember that meeting I have on Friday? The one I was supposed to be coming to town for next weekend instead of this one? I moved it up to tomorrow since I'm already here, and ..." he says, not looking up from his work. "It's kind of a job interview."

"Kind of?"

"Well, it's sort of a technicality. There is a beverage company out here that has been trying to poach me for years, but I didn't know that I had any reason to want to be in California," he says. "Then I met you again and found out you'd been in L.A. for all this time. So, I called them as soon as I got back to my office and told them that I was ready to talk."

From those very earliest moments with Jordan back in Bloomington, it has been pretty clear that our relationship is going somewhere. I was scared to admit it at first, because I have been used to living by my plan for so long, and everything in my life had felt out of my control. For over a month I have been trying to reconcile with the idea that things don't have to happen according to my plan, and an important caveat of that is to also say that not everything that feels like it is out of my control is bad. Case in point, Jordan's confession.

"So, you'd be moving here?" I ask.

"Only if you're okay with it. I mean, I know this is all happening really fast ... it's only been two weeks. I don't want to freak you out or anything. But I want to make this work with us," he says. I love that he has the same tendency to ramble when he's nervous that I do.

"Yeah, I'm okay with it," I say with a smile. I kind of can't believe that it's true, even as the words leave my mouth. Jordan's right, everything is happening really fast. Frankly, though, what scares me isn't the speed of our relationship but the fact that the speed doesn't scare me at all. It's like Luke said last night, it all seems so unlike me. I am usually so cautious and calculated. And with Jordan, I have been the opposite from the start. With Jordan, it's like I knew immediately that this is where I fit, and it's a comfort to know that he feels the same way, even if it might appear to others that we are moving too fast.

"Why didn't you tell me before?" I ask, sitting down beside him on the cold linoleum.

"I was worried that it would freak you out because it is soon. Then I didn't want to get your hopes up ... or mine," he says. His knee brushes mine like there is a magnetic pull between us that will always find a way for our bodies to touch.

"But you said it's a technicality, right?" I ask. He has gotten my hopes up a little bit.

"More or less. There is still a process to go through, but the job is basically mine," he says. Then, "I wish I had accepted it when they first started offering, I could have been here already and found you sooner."

That's what people in love always say, isn't it? *I wish I had found you sooner so I could have loved you longer.* The truth is that it doesn't work that way. Even if Jordan had taken the job and moved to L.A. years ago, he had no idea I was here until we met in the Atlanta airport. We could have both been living in the nation's second most populous city for years and never crossed paths. I have lived here for a decade already and am yet to have my fantasy meet-cute with any of the celebrities who also call this city home; the odds that Jordan and I could have found each other on our own is slim. The truth is that we needed that chance meeting in Atlanta, which means that we needed Jessica and Tanner's baby shower, which means that I needed to lose my job in order to find the time to go ... because *everything happens for a reason.*

When my life seemed to implode thirty-six days ago, it was hard to imagine what the reason could be. And now I am sitting next to him while he builds furniture on my kitchen floor. It is all happening fast, but some things are meant to.

———

When Jordan had shown up on Friday, I was worried about how

our lives would fit together. We had never existed as a couple in the real world, and I was afraid that the added pinch of reality would leave me with a bad taste in my mouth. That's why I am surprised that life with him is so easy, especially because the days since his arrival have been anything but drama free. Our Sunday is completely ordinary, and it's nice to have this glimpse of what this life could be. But there is a part of myself that I had awakened in those first days and weeks after losing my job that I am starting to miss. I never thought that I would be one to crave adventure and excitement, but completing the items on my short list had stirred something in me, and it's something that I am afraid of losing. Not because I think that Jordan wouldn't encourage me to be adventurous, but because I can already tell how easy it will be to fall into this comfortable routine of a completely ordinary life.

"Will you do something with me today?" I ask. Jordan has just emerged from the shower, still wrapped in a towel, and the sight of him nearly makes me choke on the words in my throat.

"Baby, you could ask me to help you commit murder and I would probably do it," he says. I know that's true, even if it does sound a little like he is joking. Jordan came to Los Angeles with the specific thought that he might need to cause someone bodily harm, so I know he means it.

"When I lost my job, I had a lot of time on my hands, and so I started doing the things I had always said I would like to try but had talked myself out of since I suddenly had nothing but time and was out of excuses. And I don't want to stop just because I have a new job or ... you. So will you do something adventurous with me today?" I ask. As the question leaves my mouth, I am worried that Jordan is uninterested in adventure. One thing I have learned about him already is that he is a bit of a risk-averse homebody, not unlike myself, a thought that had shattered every image I had in my head of him from before. But I have also learned quickly that he is interested in doing practically anything I suggest as long as it means we get to do it together, so I know he's going to agree before the words even leave his mouth.

In the first two weeks after losing my job, I had been so gung-ho about this new life project. I had gotten my tattoo, gone skydiving, and felt like I was ready to take on the world. Then I headed out of town and met Jordan, and everything changed so quickly that I lost my momentum. Now that the thing with Luke is behind me and a whole life with Jordan is in front of me, this is a part of me I want to stay connected to.

"Are you going to tell me where we're going?" Jordan asks, his hand on my thigh, as I merge onto the 405. It's my least favorite freeway in Los Angeles (everyone has a favorite and a least favorite, and if they tell you they don't, then they're lying), and I try to avoid it as often as possible, but today it is necessary to get us to where we need to go. I'm grateful that, since it is still relatively early on a Sunday, the traffic has not yet reached bumper-to-bumper level.

"Parasailing," I say, waving my hand in front of the rear-view mirror as a way of thanking the car that has just allowed me into their lane.

Jordan groans.

"What?" I ask.

"I just ... it would have been better if you had asked me to help you commit a murder," he replies.

"Have you ever been parasailing?" I ask.

"No. Because it involves the ocean. There are sharks in the ocean. Sharks eat people," Jordan says matter-of-factly.

"Okay, a fear of sharks is a totally normal thing. But the odds of being bitten by a shark are like one in three million. Especially when you're parasailing and going from a dock to a boat to the sky and back to the boat," I reply, my eyes glued to the road in front of me. I don't want to force Jordan to do anything he doesn't want to do, but I also want to do this with him today.

"You know the probability of being bitten by a shark off the top of your head?" he asks, and I can't tell if he is impressed or creeped out. I shrug.

"I don't know if I have the number exactly right. But sometimes when I can't sleep at night, I let myself get down a Wikipedia rabbit hole and then tuck away the little tidbits of information that I discover. You can Google it if you don't believe me."

He's already typing on his phone before I finish speaking. "One in three-point-seven million," he says. "That's pretty impressive. You never stop surprising me."

"We don't have to go parasailing if you don't want to, I just ... when I've been to the beach, I've seen the boat go by pulling the parachute behind it, and I've always wanted to try it. I'm trying to embrace this side of me who does the things I've always been afraid to do. But you make me feel brave, and so I thought it was something that we could do together," I say. I know it probably sounds like I am trying to lay it on thick and guilt-trip him into going with me, but I am not. I genuinely want Jordan to be a part of this element of my life, because I want him to be a part of everything in my life.

Jordan doesn't answer right away, and I know that he is thinking about it. I don't want to make him feel any pressure to decide, and I never mind the silence between us, so I don't say anything else.

"No sharks?" he asks again.

"I promise."

"Okay, then let's do it."

———

One thing that I have taken for granted in the decade I've been in Los Angeles is the proximity to the ocean. The Midwesterner in me finds that shocking. When I moved here for law school, I had imagined myself going to the beach every weekend. But then life happened, and the drive to the coast felt so long, even though the distance to the beach had been only twenty miles from my apartment for all those years. It became one of those things that was easy to say, "Well, the beach will always be there when I have more time..." and I just never found the time. Still, as soon as we are in view of the water, my entire body relaxes. It's interesting to me that Jordan's does, too.

"I thought you hated the ocean?" I ask him.

"I love the beach, I just don't like going in the water," he says.

It's a beautiful, sunny day, and I am surprised that the parasailing company is able to accommodate us so quickly. Before I know it, we are fitted into harnesses and life jackets and we're sitting on the high-powered motorboat, waiting our turn to fly. I expect more tension from Jordan, given his apprehension, but he rises to the occasion, just like I have watched him do again and again in the short time we've been together.

The ocean is calm as the boat travels beyond the breakwater of the marina and into the open ocean, heading north toward Santa Monica. There is something that I have always found so grounding about being on the water like this. I think it's the fact that out here, I have absolutely no control. The ocean is a powerful entity capable of destroying entire communities. It makes me feel so small, and being the control freak that I am, that strangely brings me peace. As Jordan and I watch group after group ascend into the air, my soul feels totally calm, especially with Jordan's fingers wrapped tightly around my own.

When it's finally our turn to take to the sky, Jordan's nerves return, and he pulls my hand back into his as soon as we are given the all clear. Once we're attached to the parachute and gaining height, though, I can feel him relax.

"Wow," he says, looking out over the shoreline.

"Thank you for doing this with me," I say, giving his hand a squeeze.

"Thank you for convincing me," he laughs. "This is incredible."

It is pretty incredible, the feeling of flying above the water like this. The serenity of the silence that comes this high up reminds me a bit of skydiving, an adventure I had shared with a stranger. Although parasailing may not seem as adventurous as jumping out of an airplane, I get to share the moment with the love of my life— something which is both too soon to admit and too undeniable to ignore.

"What are you thinking?" Jordan asks, his uncanny ability to read my thoughts coming through again.

"I'm thinking that …" I start. Do I want to say it? Right now, when we're flying in the air five hundred feet behind a boat on the edge of the Pacific? It would be epic to have the first time that I tell Jordan that I love him be while we're doing something like this; a reminder that our whole life together is an adventure. He's already said it, more or less ... and I know what I feel. It's just still so soon ...

"I'm thinking that ..." I begin again, my voice almost at a whisper. "That I love you."

The words come out of me before I can stop them. There's something about being up here like this that has me feeling everything in my body all at once, the biggest of which is how happy I feel to have Jordan by my side, and it's something that I feel like I have to share immediately. I don't have a mountaintop from which to shout it, but being this far above the water will do the trick.

"I LOVE JORDAN!" I scream, kicking my legs under me and causing myself to giggle. To my delight, Jordan lets out his own giggle.

"I LOVE KENLEY!" he shouts in reply. I can't help but wonder what the other parasailers think of our spectacle from the boat below, but I also don't care.

Parasailing is definitely something that I am going to remember for the rest of my life.

32.

The future begins today.

I'm a bundle of nerves all day on Monday, wondering about Jordan's interview. He had said it was more of a technicality than an actual interview, but I still can't wait to hear the results. The problem is that work is busy, and I don't have time to babysit my phone waiting for his update. But even when I do finally get a second to check my device, it is silent.

The last time Jordan had gone silent on me, he had been on his way here to surprise me. That was only three days ago, and it somehow feels like we have lived an entire lifetime since then. This time, though, I know he's not on a plane, so that can only mean that his interview is either going really well or horribly wrong. I sincerely hope it's the former because I have already grown accustomed to waking up next to the man I love.

"Hey Marlena, it's Kenley Graves. I'm sorry I haven't been in touch, how have you been?" I say into the phone. The reason for my call today is twofold. One, I need the distraction from the silence of my cell phone and two, I had not anticipated how much work was going to be waiting for me when I accepted this job, and I had gotten the president of the organization to agree that we needed someone else. I already had someone in mind when I'd brought it up in the staff meeting this morning. Marlena had always been a fantastic lawyer, and I know the kind of work I am doing now is something about which she is passionate.

"Hi Kenley, how are you?" Marlena asks formally. I wonder if it's because I haven't called, or if it's because she's a little older and of the mind that one should always answer the phone formally. I had considered her a friend throughout our time at Sullivan and Dunkirk, so the reception is surprising, but I don't let it put me off of my mission.

"I'm doing well, how are you doing?" I ask. I've always hated these questions since I don't much like small talk, but I am genuinely curious to know what Marlena has been up to over the last month.

"I am getting by. I'm sure I don't have to tell you how hard it is to find work when your resume has been tarnished," she says.

"That's why I am calling," I tell her before launching into my spiel about the job and the work we are doing here.

"The organization was so backlogged coming out of the pandemic that they really need a whole team of lawyers, but I've managed to convince them to hire one more, if you'd be interested in working with me again?" I ask hopefully. Not only would it be nice to have a familiar face around, but I do need the help.

"Wow, I don't know what to say," Marlena says. "Why me? You and Luke were always so close ... you know, I'm surprised that nothing ever happened between you, too."

I let out a sigh that sounds more like a laugh, and it immediately puts Marlena onto me. "Oh my god! Something did happen!" she practically shrieks, pushing aside all of the formality she'd held just a moment ago.

I laugh. *Busted.*

"Um, briefly. Just in the confusion after everything that happened at S and D," I tell her. "But it turns out that we are much better as friends. I just started dating someone else."

"Much better as friends, but not as co-workers?" she asks. She's still wondering why I would call her.

"First of all, Luke is going to go work for his dad. Second of all, he's mostly a divorce lawyer, and what we do here has a lot more to do with fostering and adoption. I think that your background, and your interest in immigration law, could really be an asset to the company. I only brought your name to my boss, Marlena," I tell her honestly.

Truthfully, I had never considered that she might not want the job, and I had sold the idea of hiring her to my boss based on a false sense of confidence that she would accept. I hadn't even thought about whether or not she had gotten another job or if her interests had changed like mine had.

The silence on the other end of the phone is not the comfortable kind that I have grown used to sharing with Jordan; instead, it makes me want to get up and pace around my office. Which I do, placing the phone on speaker so that I can hear her if she ever decides to respond. It's not that I can't do the work without Marlena, but during my time between jobs, I came to appreciate the idea of a work-life balance and if she says no, it will be a little while before I am able to have that again.

"Who am I kidding? It's not like I have other offers on the table, and the work sounds fulfilling. When can I start?" she says, pulling me out of my panic spiral. I run back to the desk, taking the phone off speaker and sharing with her all of the details about the new job. I am excited at the prospect of being able to have a friend at work again.

———

By the time I leave the office, I still have not heard from Jordan, and I don't know how that should make me feel. I am trying to keep myself from going headlong into the idea that I had scared him off with my declaration of love. Jordan is not a commitment-phobe by any means, at least not in my experience with him, but I know he's been through a lot when it comes to relationships, and I refuse to let myself be convinced that this means the end for us. Still, his silence bothers me, so I am relieved when I pull into my driveway and see him moving around in the kitchen through the window. Well, relieved and also a little miffed.

"Jordan?" I call as I step through the door to the kitchen. He's nowhere to be seen, but the evidence of him is clear. The kitchen smells amazing, and my mouth immediately begins to water. To say that he is a good cook doesn't do his ability justice. I can't fully identify what he has prepared, but based on the aroma, I already can't wait to eat it. The sound of soft music floats through the house, and I drop my purse in a basket on the floor near the entrance from the kitchen to the rest of the house as I follow the sound, hoping to find my reward.

Calling what I find a reward would be putting it lightly. The living room is filled with roses and candles. A blanket has been spread on the floor, and the feast Jordan prepared is displayed beautifully on top of it. And in the middle of it all, there he stands, holding a bouquet of roses and a glass of wine. If I had to guess I'd say he's giving me the Evergreen Lake picnic that I never got to have in high school.

"Hi," he says sheepishly, as if he had been so busy planning the aesthetics that he had forgotten to give any thought to what he might say.

"What's all this?" I ask as I approach him, standing on my tiptoes to place a soft kiss on his lips. I still can't believe that I get to do that, that we love each other and can kiss any time we want. I mean, I had sworn for four years back in high school that I was in love with Jordan ... but that was nothing like the real thing, and I truly can't believe this is real.

"I wanted to do something nice for you," he says, handing me the glass of wine so that he can then have a free hand with which to pull me toward him and gently squeeze my rear end.

"I love it," I say, taking a sip of the wine. What I would love to do is to tear into the meal Jordan has prepared. It looks as good as it smells, and I am starving. But he wants to make this special, and I know that dinner will be worth the wait.

The setup of the room and Jordan's nerves are all screaming one thing at me. This looks like a proposal. I know we've already confessed our love to each other, and I fully know that this is the man that I want to be with forever ... and I know my whole philosophy for our relationship has been "when you know, you know"—but even I can admit that it is too early to get engaged. We're still just starting out and getting to know each other, even if it does feel like I have known him forever. But what if this is a proposal and I say no? Would that put an end to our relationship before it has begun? Do I even want to say no? Honestly, if he asked me right now, I would probably say yes … as stupid as that would be, because this is all still so new.

"I wanted to do something special because …" he starts. Oh my gosh. Is this it? Is this really happening?

Beep. Beep. Beep. Beep. comes an electronic timer sound from the other room, cutting him off midthought.

"Fuck. I have to get the oven," he says, handing me the bouquet of roses more hastily than he had probably intended to. I quickly place them off to the side so that they don't get trampled. "I'll be right back, make yourself comfortable."

Making myself comfortable feels impossible. I would be lying if I said I wasn't freaking out a little bit. Is this how it's supposed to feel?

Kenley, I remind myself. *You don't even know what is happening here. Yes, it looks like a proposal. But until you hear those words come out of Jordan's mouth, you can't know for sure. Take a deep breath, enjoy the food he has cooked for you, and just take it one second at a time.*

Unconvinced by my pep talk, I pull my phone out of my back pocket and type out a text to Jessica, because she happens to be married to Jordan's best friend and I can only hope that guys talk about this stuff together the same way girls do.

Kenley: What does it look like is happening here?

I send her a picture of the living room picnic.

Jessica: OMG!!! Ken!!!

Her use of the heart eyes and diamond ring emojis do nothing to calm my nerves. It also doesn't tell me what she knows, but it tells me that I'm not crazy to view the room this way.

Kenley: Has Tanner said anything? I'm freaking out.

I can hear Jordan in the kitchen, and I know I only have a minute before he's back.

Jessica: No, and if it is what I think it is and he knew and didn't tell me, I'll kill him.

Jessica: Keep me posted.

Her second message arrives just as Jordan emerges from the kitchen carrying a platter full of sliced roast beef. I definitely did not own a platter before tonight—he must have bought it when he purchased all of this food.

After setting the platter in the center of our picnic blanket, Jordan sits and invites me to sit beside him. My palms are sweating, and I can only hope that he doesn't reach for them, but I know I'm only kidding myself, because this is Jordan I'm talking about, who can't go more than three seconds without touching me whenever we are together. Still, I do my best to remain composed.

If we have to talk about dream proposals, this would definitely check off all of the boxes on my imaginary list. I certainly wouldn't want a public display, and I don't want to have anyone involved except for me and the person doing the proposing. I could do with or without the flowers and candles, but it certainly paints a beautiful memory.

"As I was saying," Jordan begins again, "I wanted to make this special because ... I got the job."

"Oh my gosh! That's amazing!" I interrupt, kissing him in congratulations. To be honest, the second I had walked out of the kitchen I had completely forgotten about his interview.

"Thanks, Baby," he says, smiling that genuine megawatt smile that I adore. "They want me to start in three weeks. So, I'm here for a few more days and then I have to go back to Atlanta to wrap things up out there—give my notice, list my condo, say goodbye to the few people I care about. And then I'll be back, and I was thinking ..."

Without realizing it, my breath catches in my throat. I didn't expect to be so nervous in this moment, but I can't seem to help it. It feels a little like I am outside of my own body, watching this scene unfold before my eyes. Do I just say yes now and avoid all of the beating around the bush? I can't believe that I am planning to say yes. Who even am I?! I have to remind myself to breathe.

"This is already real, being with you," Jordan continues, "I was just thinking about what the next step is in this relationship and I wanted to ask you ..."

I try to focus on Jordan as he continues, but it is getting to be harder and harder not to shout out my answer as he talks.

Kenley, breathe. Stay in the moment, listen to what Jordan is saying. You already know that you're going to say yes, so don't get ahead of yourself. He has put a lot of thought into this and you owe it to him to let him have this moment, I remind myself.

"... if when I get back to town I can move in here, and then we can do all of this for real, for real," Jordan finishes nervously.

Wait. What?

I can't tell whether what I am feeling now is relief or disappointment or some combination of both. It takes me a second to process the question because it was so far from what I had been thinking about. Meanwhile, Jordan stares at me nervously, which keeps the sensation of the mixed emotions swirling inside of me.

"Um, yeah, of course," I say finally. Honestly, it had never crossed my mind that it would need to be formally decided or agreed upon that Jordan would move in here upon his return. Our relationship has been progressing quickly and it's clear that we both know what we want, so it had seemed obvious to me that we would share a home.

"Are you sure? You seem ... weirded out by the idea," he says.

"It's not that. At all. I would love for you to move in, expected it even," I say.

"Then, what is it?" he asks. High school jock stereotype notwithstanding, I know Jordan to be an intelligent man, so it is hard to believe he could be this dense.

"Just ... all this," I say, waving my arms around the over-the-top romantic display, "looks like you're proposing something else."

Why do I feel embarrassed? Should I feel embarrassed? I was the one who read way more into this situation, I am the one who had it all worked out in my head about how I was about to get engaged. Jordan never mentioned marriage or implied in any way that he was ready for that step. He's only a few years away from his divorce, and I have somehow decided that he is ready without ever talking to him about it.

"Oh," he says softly before chuckling to himself.

"Why are you laughing?" I ask. Yes, I should definitely feel embarrassed.

"Are you disappointed?" he asks.

"What? No!" I say a little too emphatically. "It is way too early for that, but ... I wouldn't have said no."

Jordan smiles to himself as he leans in to kiss me. "That is really good to know," he says.

33.

It's weird to think about my future with Jordan truly beginning. In a way, it had already begun back in Bloomington, but then we had to press pause while we returned to our respective homes. Then when he had shown up in Los Angeles, it was like it started again with a glimpse of what it would be like. Now, he has to go back to Atlanta for a little while, and so it's time to press pause all over again. Recently I've been trying to live by the mantra that *the future begins today*, repeating it to myself every morning as a reminder. But it doesn't feel like the future can really begin until Jordan is in L.A. for good.

Saying goodbye to Jordan gets harder every time I have to do it. The first time felt sad because of the trepidation that things would change once we were out of our hometown bubble. The second time felt sad because Jordan had surprised me at the airport, and our time together was far too brief. The third time feels sad because I realize that I love this man and I just don't want him to go.

"I hope you know that my willingness to drive you to the airport proves that my love is true," I tell him as I merge onto my least-favorite freeway for the second time in a week. It is a commonly known fact in Los Angeles that rides to and from the airport are few and far between. They have Ubers for that. Or taxis. Or buses that will drop you at easier access points in different parts of the city. Or multiple long-term parking lots that run shuttles to the terminals. If a person is desperate, they might rent a car. But we don't give each other rides to the airport except in extenuating circumstances. Like, in this case, the love of my life leaving me again.

"I hate this part," Jordan says.

"Driving to the airport?"

"No, silly. Saying goodbye to you. It doesn't make any sense that I have already had to do it so many times in less than three weeks. It sucks," Jordan says, tracing his thumb over my knee as I drive.

"I hate it, too," I admit.

I want to say that it's the last time, but it's not. I can't imagine going two weeks without seeing him now. The longest we've managed to stay apart to date is eight days, because we have already proven that we can't do long distance, and those eight days were before ... everything. So, I am going to fly out to Atlanta next weekend to be with him there. Which means that we'll have one more round of goodbyes before he makes his move to California official.

"Remember what I told you that first time? That I wasn't going to say goodbye?" he asks, snapping me out of my thoughts. I do remember, I hadn't known what to think of it back then. Somehow that feels like so much longer than three weeks ago.

"What about now?" I ask.

"I'm still not going to say it. Goodbyes are for endings, and what we have here is just another beginning," he says.

"The future begins today," I mutter to myself under my breath, another reminder.

"What was that?"

I sigh. While I had said it out loud, I hadn't meant for him to hear it. I'm not keeping my search for a mantra a secret, necessarily, there just hasn't been any reason to bring it up.

"The future begins today," I say, this time a little louder. "It's a mantra I am trying out."

"That's a good one," Jordan says. "What else have you tried?"

"So many," I laugh. "It's something I started doing when I lost my job. I wished that I had some kind of life motto to cling to in that horrible moment that could serve as a reminder that there were good things to come. So, I've spent the last few months trying different mottos and mantras on for size. I don't think I have landed on one yet."

One thing that I appreciate about Jordan is that he never makes me feel like I need to explain myself. I feel like I have spent my whole life trying to provide answers to questions that haven't yet been asked. But with Jordan, I never feel like he is waiting for further explanation. It's like he understands all of the additional words without my having to say them.

"Do you have one?" I ask.

"I have a favorite quote that I remind myself of, if that counts," he says after a moment. "A person who never made a mistake never tried anything new—Albert Einstein."

It may not sound exactly like a mantra, but it is perfect for Jordan. This man has spent the last few years trying every new thing possible on his quest to happiness, and with those new things came a lot of mistakes. But I've learned from all the time we have spent together that those mistakes do not translate as regrets to him ... they're merely stepping stones.

I smile. "I think that counts."

———

The house is quiet when I finally get back from the airport. I had moved in one week ago tonight, but that was the only night that I had spent here alone, and it certainly hadn't been quiet. Without having someone to share the space with, I am suddenly aware of the size of the place. It's much too big for just me—it's meant for a family to share all of this space, and it's funny to think of how close I feel to having that. At the start of the year, or even as recently as two months ago, having a family wasn't even on my radar. I figured that I still had plenty of time. I still do have plenty of time, but now that I have found Jordan, I suddenly don't feel like I want to wait. I think that is why I had been ready to say yes on Monday when I thought he was proposing.

There is a void in the silence, one that hadn't been in the house when Jordan was here. With him, the silence was never awkward, but now it is deafening. I try turning on background noise on the TV, playing the same episodes of *The Office* that I have seen a hundred times, but even the familiar quips of Dwight Schrute can't drown out the silence.

Kenley: I miss you already. The house is too quiet.

I text to Jordan, who by now is already in the air. So, I am surprised when I receive an almost immediate reply.

Jordan: I miss you too, Baby. Also, my flight has WiFi.

Jordan includes a silly face emoji and as soon as I read his message, the house doesn't feel quite as big as it had just a moment ago.

I try to picture Jordan, sitting in the exit row of the plane for extra leg room. I imagine the thoughts running through his head as he plans his brief return to Atlanta. He has so much to do in a short amount of time, and yet all he could talk about in our last few days together is what we are going to do when he gets back. I'm still lost in thought about him when my phone vibrates again, and I pick it up right away.

Except it's not Jordan this time. It's Luke.

Luke: Hey.

As soon as I see those three letters on my lock screen my heart begins to beat fast, and I can feel my shoulders drawing up to my ears as my body tenses in anticipation. Luke and I had left things in an okay place the other night at the bar, but I don't know if I would say that we're on friendly terms. Luke had been my closest friend for years—it feels weird not to respond to him, but at the same time, although I trust myself, it feels a bit like betraying Jordan to engage with Luke after everything that has happened.

Kenley: Ugh. Luke is texting me. Should I respond?

I ask Jordan, who has quickly earned a spot in my brain trust.

Jordan: What is he saying?

Now I can picture Jordan on the plane again, sitting upright and looking around on heightened alert. He had come to L.A. a week ago because he was prepared to fight this guy, almost had to on Saturday night, and now, as soon as he boards a plane back to Atlanta, Luke turns up. That's why I felt the need to tell him in the first place. I don't want there to be any secrets between us and my talking to Luke without Jordan knowing about it feels a little too much like sneaking around behind his back.

Kenley: Just 'hey.' I haven't responded yet. Not sure if I should.

Jordan: Are you asking for my permission? You don't have to. I trust you.

It's not until I see the words that I realize that's exactly what I had been doing. Jordan was cheated on by his ex-wife, and I don't ever want him to have to question me or my role in our relationship. I want him to trust me completely because I know that he can, and it sounds like from his response he knows that, too.

Even with the conversation with Jordan out of the way, I wait a few minutes before I send Luke a response. I am too curious to leave it alone.

Kenley: I don't know if this is a good idea.

I'm hoping that he'll get right to the point.

Luke: I know I'm the last person that you want to talk to. I just wanted to say that I am sorry. The way I acted last week at dinner, that's not me. I hope that you know that, after all of the years that we've been friends. I was hurt that you didn't choose me, and a little bit jealous that you had gotten your life back on track so quickly. I wanted to be the knight in shining armor, and it clouded all of my judgment. I am truly sorry, and I do hope that we can be friends.

My wish is granted by Luke's quick response. I should have expected it. He must have had it typed in the send box, just waiting for my response.

I love closure. It's one of my favorite things in any situation. One of the things that had bothered me the most about losing my job at Sullivan and Dunkirk was that I never got any closure—they had fired me, and I had to get my things and leave right then. If Luke and Marlena hadn't been terminated at the same time, I wouldn't have even had a chance to say any goodbyes. So, this text from Luke gives me what I need. But it's not a clean break because I owe him an apology, too. I sigh heavily before I open my notes app to organize my thoughts succinctly before replying.

Kenley: I am sorry, too. I realize that I was kind of a bitch to you, coming back and announcing that I was seeing someone after I had told you I was going to take the time away to think about us. I can't imagine how you must have felt in that moment. I'm sure blindsided isn't the right word. I was also a coward. I should have told you the truth as soon as I knew that we weren't going to work out. You deserve better than that and I am sorry.

Once I have read it over and am satisfied, I copy it into the text thread and hit send.

Luke: There is nothing better than you.

He sends back, ruining the mood.

Kenley: Goodbye, Luke.

It's what I have to say because I have spent too long giving him false hope, and if I truly believe that he didn't deserve that, then I need to end this conversation now. I do want to be friends, but I think we both need a full cooling-off period before we decide to try that.

I have to set my phone down for a minute after sending the message. In a way it's a little bit of a heartbreak of my own. Not in the romantic sense, but the relationship I have had with Luke spans years and multiple versions of my life. Jordan is incredible, and every time I think about him, I feel even luckier that I get to be with him, but he will never know what I was like in law school, or that Corporate Law Firm Kenley (I should trademark that term) was a force to be reckoned with. Of the two men, only Luke knows those versions of me, and it is sad to have to say goodbye to someone like that. Even if it is just for now.

Kenley: It's done.

I send to Jordan, with screenshots of the text conversation. Like I said, no secrets.

Jordan: I love you.

Jordan sends a moment later. In those three words, I know I have made the right decision.

34.

By the time my flight touches down in Atlanta, I am ready to run off the plane. Eight days is the longest that Jordan and I have been apart since we reconnected, and we have once again tied that record. I can't imagine how actual long-distance couples do it. We have failed spectacularly, and I don't care. There is a man waiting for me at baggage claim that I haven't seen in eight days, and we only have a weekend together, so I am going to make the most of it.

The last time I stepped off of a plane in Atlanta, he was standing right there, and I am a little disappointed when I emerge from the jetway and I don't immediately see a hulking blond presence lingering over the waiting area. Last time, though, our meeting in the airport was born out of necessity because if Jordan hadn't pulled off that surprise, we wouldn't have had those few extra minutes together. This time, though, we have a whole weekend, and when I make it to the top of the escalator at baggage claim, he barely wastes a second before pulling me into his arms.

"I missed you so much," Jordan says into my neck as he holds me tightly, my feet lifted up off the ground. I normally hate public displays of affection, and it sounds so stupid to say, but it feels like Jordan and I are the only two people in this whole airport.

Kenley, chill out. You're not even kissing. Get it under control, people might see ... but who cares if they see? The only person you know in Atlanta is Jordan, and he's a week away from moving to California to be with you. Let them see.

Even the voice inside my head sounds like a different person these days. These pep talks were always meant to talk some sense into my life; now they're nothing but nonsensical and it doesn't bother me in the slightest. I feel like there might have been a time where I would have found this change in me scary, but it has come on so gradually and so completely that I didn't even notice until it was too late to push back against it with fear.

"I missed you, too," I say, taking in the clean soapy scent of his skin as if it has been a year and not a week since I last smelled him.

When Jordan finally releases me, placing my feet gently back onto the floor, I suddenly understand all of those early moments in Bloomington where he was touching me constantly. I had found it endearing at the time, but now that I have been without his touch again, I can understand the need for it. It's like if I don't hold his hand now, I might actually die. And when I do take his hand, I almost instantly feel my racing heart slow down. Part of me still doesn't know how to feel about that.

"What?" Jordan asks with a laugh, looking back at me.

"I was just thinking that I think I might be going mad," I say sheepishly. Aware that there are other people around, I want to choose my words carefully. I hate to think that my careless use of the words "crazy" or "insane" could be offensive to a passerby.

"Why's that?" Jordan asks, tugging my hand slightly to pull me in the direction of the parking garage.

"I can't explain it. I feel like I am all out of sorts, like I want to be touching you at all times, and I don't care who might see us. It is so unlike me," I manage. Jordan's hearty laugh is not the reply I am expecting.

"Baby, I think that's just called love," he says, pulling me close to him with one quick motion and placing a chaste kiss on my lips.

I've never been in love before. I had always had other priorities and figured love would find me when the time was right. Maybe that's why everything about Jordan has caught me off guard. For all intents and purposes, the timing seemed all wrong, and yet I can't deny that it wasn't until I met Jordan that everything started lining up exactly the way it was supposed to. Maybe there is never a right time, maybe it's more about finding the right person.

"Well, sometimes being in love feels a little like being crazy," I tell him as he pulls me to a stop in front of a dark-colored SUV.

"I know what you mean," Jordan says, opening the hatch and tossing my duffle bag into the back. "All I can think about is how these windows are dark enough that I could easily throw you in the back of this car and have you right now."

No one is around to hear us now, but my cheeks flush anyway. Maybe it's because I am still programmed to shy away from talking about sex, or maybe it's because now that he has said it, it is all that I can think about, too. It's not the first time Jordan has mentioned making love in a back seat, but my reaction is still the same.

"What is it with you and putting me in the backseat?" I ask, trying to laugh through my discomfort.

"It was my ultimate fantasy in high school," Jordan says quickly. "It probably would have been sloppy and unromantic and over in about ten seconds, but none of that bothered me then."

"So, in high school you wanted to have sex with someone in the backseat of a car?"

"Not someone. You. I specifically wanted you in the backseat of my car," Jordan corrects, leading me to the passenger's side door and holding it open for me while I climb inside. As he walks around the front to his door, I can't help but stare into the backseat longingly. Sometimes it's hard not to feel like we found each other too late and have wasted too much time.

"Thinking about it?" Jordan teases, as he slides into the driver's seat.

"I still find it hard to believe that …" I start but Jordan stops me by grabbing my chin and turning my face to his.

"Baby, believe it. You're my dream girl," he says. The kiss he gives me in follow up is the kind that makes me wish that he would make good on his backseat offer.

I know he feels the same way when he pulls back and says, "No. No. We can make it to my place."

———

Jordan's condo is right in the heart of downtown Atlanta, with views overlooking Centennial Olympic Park—at least, that is what I had seen on the internet when he had sent me the link to the sale listing. I couldn't tell you for sure, because as soon as we are inside the front door, Jordan is true to his word. We waited to get from the airport to his place and now we will be rewarded, his hands and lips seem to say.

"What about a tour first?" I ask through kisses.

"Why? I'm moving," he says, not slowing his pace.

"Yeah, but this has been your home for three years. You own it. I want to know what your life is like," I try again.

Jordan stops and pulls back from me, angry.

"None of this furniture is mine. The place has already been staged by my realtor for potential buyers. Mine is all in a shipping container on its way across the country. And honestly, I was kind of miserable here and I am happy to go," he says. This time he doesn't attempt to pick up where he had left off, and I immediately miss his touch.

I guess it was selfish of me, caught up in the bliss of our honeymoon phase, to assume that I was the only reason that Jordan might be willing to move across the country. I knew that his divorce had ended badly, that he was forced to move out of the home he had purchased with his wife, and that the only reason he had stayed in the area at all was because he had a good job that he didn't want to lose. But he had been looking for a way out for a while, that was the reason he had tried so many things to fill the void left in his life by his ex-wife's infidelity. Meeting me and finding out I lived on the other side of the country had presented him with something that he had already been seeking.

"I'm doing it for you, you know," he says, reading my mind.

"Doing what?" I ask, playing dumb.

"Moving. I hate it here, but I didn't leave before. Feeling stuck wasn't enough of a reason. But then I found you, and you became the reason," he says, taking my hand in his again and providing me with the relief of his touch.

Part of the absurdity of love is that even though his words sound smooth, I know that I can believe him. Which is the wild part, because I don't believe anyone the first time, not even myself. For some reason, though, I know that I can believe Jordan. It is pure madness.

"Are you hungry? I made dinner earlier, but there are some leftovers," Jordan says then.

"I have an appetite for something else," I say playfully, wagging my eyebrows at him.

Jordan laughs out loud. "Kenley Graves, are you trying to seduce me?"

———

Waking up in Jordan's arms feels as right now as it did the first time. I had never considered myself a snuggler—I always claimed to love a solitary slumber where I am untouched and unbothered. But Jordan is changing more than one thing about me. Feeling him wrapped around me from behind makes me feel completely safe, and it's a kind of security that I didn't know that I had been lacking before he came into my life. It's the feeling of never wanting to get up, and I wouldn't, except that I need to go to the bathroom.

Men's showers have always been puzzling to me. They're usually an afterthought, like the shower is literally only there out of necessity. I value my shower time and have been known to stand under the hot water for half an hour, scrubbing and soaking and thinking. When I was working long hours at the law firm, it was sometimes the only "me time" I had in a day. But from my dad to my brother to male friends and men I've dated, the shower has never seemed like the hallowed ground I have taken it to be. So, when I step inside the stall in Jordan's bathroom, I am prepared for the worst, and am pleasantly surprised by the magnificence of the unit. I know immediately that I will be standing here for a while.

The nice thing about a long, hot shower is that I have a chance to think about everything and nothing. I am always thinking about something, so to have a moment to completely zone out feels luxurious. That's why I don't notice when Jordan opens the door to the bathroom and pokes his head inside.

"Good morning, coffee's almost ready," he says.

"Thanks. I'll be done soon ... probably. This shower is amazing, and I never want to get out," I admit.

Jordan chuckles to himself, stepping fully into the bathroom.

"If you're never getting out, then I might have to get in," he teases, pulling his t-shirt over his head and discarding it haphazardly on the floor. His chiseled chest is seriously distracting. It is not normal to look that good.

"What do you mean?" I laugh. I know what he means, I'm not stupid, but I somehow never get tired of hearing him tell me exactly what he wants from me.

"Well," he says, opening the door and hitting me with a blast of cold air that causes me to yelp. "I have spent a lot of time in this shower, and I have never experienced the amazingness of which you speak."

"I don't believe that," I say, moving slightly so that he can fit under the rainfall showerhead with me.

"It's true," he says. Widening his stance so that he is a bit shorter, he leans in and takes my lips with his. "I have always viewed the shower as simply a necessity."

His kiss stifles the laugh that threatens to escape from my lips. The amazing shower hadn't been Jordan's doing after all, but that doesn't mean that I love it any less. If it were practical, I would tell him not to sell just so that I could come back to this shower a couple of times a year.

"Dance with me?" he asks, bringing my arms around his neck and lowering his to my hips.

"Here?" I giggle. I've heard of dancing in the rain, but this isn't quite the same thing. Instead of answering, Jordan lowers his mouth to mine, kissing me again. Slowly, I can feel him swaying my hips rhythmically. There is nobody here to watch us and yet I can't help feeling a little silly. I've never been much of a dancer, and I don't know if I am quite ready for Jordan to learn how musically challenged I am—even if he has already learned practically everything else about me.

"There's no music," I point out, thinking that this will put an end to the silliness. But Jordan is determined. He opens his mouth and starts to sing with a shockingly good voice that makes me a little weak in the knees.

I had always imagined dancing with Jordan Thomas. Every school dance season, I would daydream about him asking me to be his date. I would fantasize about the dress I would buy, the corsage he would affix to my wrist, how handsome he would look in his rented tuxedo, and most of all how it would feel to spend the night dancing in his arms with the eyes of the school on us. Of course, it never happened. I didn't go to prom my senior year at all because I couldn't bear the thought of watching him dance with Sarah Morgan after they had been named prom royalty. Jordan had been so popular in high school, and he always had girls lined up, waiting for him to take them to the dance. I truly never thought that I would ever get this dance, and I especially never thought that we'd be naked in the shower when it happened.

"You sound great," I say. "Let me guess, you took voice lessons, too?"

Jordan laughs. "No. But I was in the youth praise and worship band at my mom's church," he smiles.

"How did you manage to keep that quiet in high school?"

"Well, for one thing, it wasn't the kind of church that any of us liked to brag about attending. And for another, the kids that I knew from church weren't really the type to churn the rumor mill at school," he says.

We haven't talked much about how he was raised in such a religious environment. Even though I had known him back then, the person he was at school didn't match up in any way with the idea of that conservative upbringing, and I genuinely had no idea. It's not something Jordan talks much about, and it's something that makes me incredibly curious because I want to know everything about him.

"Why did you stop believing in all of that?" I ask him. We're still dancing, swaying back and forth as the water cascades over our heads. I'm worried that the question might take the intimacy out of the moment, but Jordan doesn't stop moving.

"A lot of reasons," he says solemnly. "By the time I graduated high school, I was pretty much done with all of it. I had tried to believe in it for a long time, but I never found the connection. Like, I remember my mom would always say that if I really wanted something that I should pray about it, and that if something was meant for me, God would answer my prayers. Every single night for four years, I prayed for two things: a football scholarship and a date with Kenley Graves. I didn't get either, and by the time I left for college, I had pretty much decided that God didn't care about me, so I didn't need to bother caring about him either."

This isn't the first time that Jordan has told me about how I have factored into his prayers. I still don't know how to feel about it, since I have never been very religious myself. I don't like the idea of a whimsical deity playing puppet master with our lives, but it sounds like that is the exact reason that Jordan chose to leave it behind in the first place.

"You never asked. I was there the whole time, waiting," I say, lifting my hand to stroke the wet hair at the base of his skull.

"I know. I was young and stupid ... and an asshole," he says with a smile. "But it was easy to blame it on my prayers. Once I got down here and only went to church when I made it back to Bloomington, I decided that I liked living life my way, and that the way I was raised wasn't really for me."

"And what about now?" I ask. He looks at me, puzzled. "You said that before you left for the baby shower, you prayed about how to get unstuck, and then you ran into me. So, what do you think now?"

He laughs. "My mom always used to tell me that the answers to prayers came in three ways: yes, no, and not right now. If I had dated you in high school, as much as I wanted to, it wouldn't have lasted. It would have been memorable and fun, with a lot of car-fucking because I was a boy obsessed. Then we would have graduated and gone our separate ways. You had your ambitions, and you weren't going to let me stand in the way of that. But now, we found each other again at exactly the right time in our lives. And it's already so much better than my childish fantasies from high school."

Neither of us says anything for a few minutes, still swaying underneath the stream of water that has started to run cold. Standing here with Jordan like this feels more connected and intimate than anything else we could do or have done. This feels like one of the moments that I will remember forever.

"Do you think you'll ever go back to it someday?" I ask finally. I guess maybe I love to ruin a moment, because I don't know what my response will be if the answer is yes.

"Maybe in a much more relaxed capacity, with our kids, but nothing like how I was raised," he says so nonchalantly that I almost miss it.

"Our kids, huh?" I ask.

"Yeah. It's happening," he says before he leans down to kiss me again, stopping our dance. It's the kind of kiss that sends me into a daze, almost forgetting that the shower water is no longer hot and is causing me to shiver.

"You're right, this is a damn great shower," Jordan says when we finally pull apart.

35.

The only thing that you can expect in life is the unexpected.

My trip to Atlanta is over far too soon, and even though Jordan is less than a week away from being mine, saying goodbye is still hard. At the time I had booked my ticket, taking a late flight out seemed like a good idea since I could maximize our time together and gain three hours back on my return, but between the late night and a turbulent landing, I am practically a shell of myself by the time I make it into work on Monday.

"Wow, Kenley, are you okay?" Marlena asks when she sees me. Thankfully we've been friends for a while, so I know not to take it personally, especially when her greeting matches how I feel.

"Not really," I reply, taking a sip of my coffee. I know that coffee is not the best thing for an upset stomach, but I had been more afraid of what my day might be like if I didn't have my sacred caffeine fix.

"Are you hungover?" she asks. In all of the years I have known Marlena, I have never once shown up to work hungover, so this question *is* mildly offensive.

"The last time I was hungover was the morning after our last day at Sullivan and Dunkirk and I made very bad drunk decisions. I do not intend to be hungover ever again," I defend.

Thinking back to that morning, waking up in Luke's bed before finding out that my car had been towed, I can't help but think about how far my life has come in such a short amount of time. I wish that I could go back in time and tell myself that everything was going to be okay, but I don't think that I would have believed me. I remember how I felt that morning, in addition to physically feeling unwell, I felt like nothing was ever going to be right again and I don't think anyone, even myself from the future, could have convinced me otherwise. Another big difference between that day and now is that that morning, coffee had been my savior, but today, it's just not doing the trick.

"Well, are you pregnant?" Marlena asks.

I nearly drop the coffee tumbler in my hand. "Um, no," I respond quickly. The last thing I need is for rumors to start at my still fairly new job. "I got in late last night and my flight was really bumpy."

"So bumpy that you're still nauseous almost twelve hours later?" Marlena asks.

Shit. She's right. Not about me being pregnant, there is no way that I am pregnant ... I mean, I guess there is a way that I could be pregnant, I do understand how pregnancy works. But it's not possible. Things have been happening fast in my relationship with Jordan, just not that fast. It doesn't make sense, though, that I would still be nauseous from my flight when I've been on the ground for this long.

"I'm not pregnant, I'm on birth control," I say, more to convince myself than her.

"So was I when I got pregnant with my son," Marlena says, sitting down in the chair across from my desk.

Kenley, breathe. It's just an idea, it's not like she knows something that you don't know. Yes, she's had two children, but that doesn't make her an expert on pregnancy or your body. You know your body and you know that you are not pregnant. Right? ... You're totally not pregnant.

I wish my internal pep talks were more effective like they used to be; that's one thing I miss about my life before. I might have been living in a blissfully ignorant world, but I could always rely on my internal dialogue to talk me down from whatever stress ledge onto which I had climbed. These days, they just serve to further feed my anxiety.

"Look, it's not a bad thing. A child is a blessing," Marlena says, making me regret the day I thought it would be a good idea to work with her again. But I smile at her anyway because that is what I do in situations in which I am uncomfortable.

"Sure, one could be ... if I were pregnant, which I am not," I say, still trying to convince myself.

I haven't been on the pill long, but I am one of those annoying people who reads the literature that accompanies any prescription from cover to cover, so I know that it starts working immediately if you start taking it during your period, which of course I had done because those are the rules. I had started my period on the day I left Bloomington, and I had taken the first pill when I got home that night. I thought I had been diligent about taking it at the same time every day, but when Jordan arrived in L.A. my schedule had changed suddenly, so there's a chance I may have forgotten. That is, if Marlena is to be believed.

"What are you doing?" she asks. I am sure that I must look like a space cadet, staring off into the distance with my own thoughts.

"Math," I admit. If I'm counting right, it might have happened on the day of our parasailing adventure. The day that we had flown over the Pacific and declared our love for one another had already been memorable enough, but this could cement that day as one for the record books.

Could I be pregnant? Kenley, breathe. You don't know anything yet. And besides, how many times has Jordan brought up having kids? He wants this. It's not like you're a teenager anymore, you have the means for this. You have a good job and a man who loves you and won't stop talking about having babies with you. This would be a surprise, but not the worst thing in the world.

"I'm going to run to the drugstore and buy you a test. I hated being alone when I took them," Marlena says warmly. I guess if there is any friend that I would want by my side for this, it is her.

With Marlena off on her errand, I can't focus. There is work to do, but my anxiety is spiraling too much to allow me to be productive. When I woke up this morning, still feeling unwell, the thought of pregnancy hadn't even crossed my mind, and now it's all I can think about. I'll feel better once I take the test and see that it is negative.

But in the meantime, what do I do? I can't call Jordan yet. I know I said no secrets, but there might not even be anything to tell. Besides, he is busy today with preparing for his move which is happening in two days. Surely, I can wait two days; he'll be there by the time I get home from work on Wednesday.

"Ready?" Marlena asks, poking her head around the corner of my office and dangling a paper drugstore bag in front of her face.

That was fast. I thought that I would have more time to mentally prepare, but it seems that my colleague has developed superhuman speed when it comes to this matter. She's asking the wrong question, too. Of course I am not ready, that's the whole point. I am not ready to take this test, and I am certainly not ready for the impact that the results could have on my entire future. But I also can't confirm it's negative if I don't take it, either.

"No?" I ask in reply, forcing myself to stand and walk with her toward the bathroom.

———

Neither Marlena nor I have been at this job long enough to afford being able to spend a Monday afternoon sitting in a sticky booth at a national chain restaurant picking at cold French fries instead of diving into the pile of backlogged legal documents at the office. But after my morning pregnancy test adventure, it was clear to both of us that we wouldn't be getting any work done.

"When are you going to tell him?" Marlena asks, twirling the straw in her glass absent-mindedly.

Honestly, when I had seen the second line start to appear in the test window, the last thing on my mind was telling Jordan. The number of times in our short relationship that he has mentioned children to me is staggering. I know that he wants a baby, which is comforting, because it's one less thing that I have to worry about in the midst of all of this.

I feel a mixture of everything all at once. Just a month ago I had nearly had a breakdown at Jessica's baby shower as I thought about my sister and brother both expanding their families and wondering if I had put all of my eggs in the wrong basket. I have always thought that I would eventually become a mother, just on my own terms. In a way, this is still on my own terms. I love Jordan and I already know that I want to spend the rest of my life with him, so in that sense, this isn't such a bad thing. It's just a surprise, and I really don't like surprises.

"I want to do it in person. He has too much on his plate with his move right now," I reply. Ever since we sat down at this table, I've had a hand resting on my lower abdomen, as if I might be able to feel something happening in there. According to the app that Marlena had helped me download, my baby is currently the size of a poppyseed, so even with all of the major things happening inside, there's nothing much to feel.

I am grateful to have Marlena here while I sit with the shock of this blessed event. Although her children are grown now, she can still relate to so many of these feelings, and I appreciate not having to be alone.

"I remember how scared I was when I found out that my Madi was coming. I was eighteen, fresh out of high school with big plans for my life. I was so afraid of what having a baby meant for my future," she says then.

That's not what I am scared about exactly, but I don't tell her this because I appreciate her sharing this vulnerable part of her life with me. It's hard to explain exactly what I am afraid of or why this anxiety is rising up in me so intensely. It doesn't have anything to do with having a baby or my ability to do so or how it might impact my future. That part of this I feel surprisingly calm about. I have always dreamed about this, and with Jordan I know that everything will work out. What this is stirring up in me is a lot of feeling about my fear of failure.

Yes, my birth control had failed, even after I tried to make sure that I used it properly. But it's not even that. For so much of my life I had a plan that I was following, doing the next right thing and then the next and then the next ... and pregnancy is, like, the number one recognized "after" list item in Western culture. There are things that were supposed to have happened first that obviously didn't, and for that I feel like a failure. It's stupid, I know.

241

"Are you okay?" Marlena asks finally, placing her hand on top of mine across the table.

"Yeah, I'm okay," I tell her with a weak smile. "I'm in shock, but I guess the only thing you can expect in life is the unexpected."

I think this mantra might be the one.

36.

Not telling Jordan that I'm pregnant before Wednesday is one of the hardest things I've ever done. Every time we talked, I felt myself ready to blurt out the announcement and had to bite my tongue. At the same time, it has been nice to sit with this news on my own for a few extra days. It has been an emotional roller coaster that has taken me in every possible direction over the last two days, from surprise to excitement to grief to fear to joy, and it's one that I have been happy to go through by myself because by the time I do finally tell Jordan, I will be less emotional.

It's been a while since I've made a list, which in itself would tell someone who knows me well everything about how my life is going these days. I haven't felt the need to write everything down and weigh the pros and cons of every little decision in weeks. But suddenly finding myself pregnant feels like exactly the kind of thing that merits a list for the first time in a while. My usual notebook has begun to collect dust by the time I reach for it on Tuesday night, but before I have a chance to turn to a crisp, new page, the book falls open to my "Steps to Happiness" list that I had started back when it felt like my life was falling apart.

1. Find something in every day that makes me happy
2. Do some of the things I never thought I'd do
   2a. Get a tattoo
   2b. Go skydiving
3. Find a job that makes me FEEL FULFILLED

4. Find "the one"
5. BE HAPPY

As I read, I take my pen and strike through every single item on the list.

Have I done it? Have I finally found happiness for myself after all these years? It's funny, because my life is far from perfect—I mean, I am accidentally pregnant for Pete's sake, but I do think that I am happier than I have been in a long time. There are a lot of factors contributing to that, of course, but the most important one seems to be that I started living my life instead of just living by my plan. Everything else fell right into place after that.

That thought makes me feel quite a bit better about the list I am about to write. No longer do I feel like I have to solve everything about this pregnancy and the future, and that is a relief. Still, making lists has always been a calming activity for me, even as a child, and so I set my pen to paper and begin to write.

1. Think of a cute way to tell Jordan
2. Make an appointment with my doctor
3. Start a baby registry

It's not much, but it does help to get the wheels in my head turning about the best way to share the news with the father-to-be.

Although I've had two days to sit with the revelation, I am a nervous wreck by the time I get off work on Wednesday and make my way home. It's not so much that I am worried how Jordan is going to take the news as I am about how this changes our future. We've spent so little time together, really, and this period of Jordan moving to Los Angeles and moving into this house was meant to be a chance to make sure this is right. The baby will expedite that process times a million, and it makes everything different. Still, though, I know I have to tell him, and together we can figure out what comes next.

Originally, Jordan had considered making the drive across the country, but it was going to take multiple days on sometimes desolate highways, and the thought of his being alone through all of that wasn't appealing to either one of us. So, he had found a flight from Atlanta and hired a company to bring his car across the country while a moving pod of his belongings was due to be delivered to our driveway on Saturday. It was easier that way, though it still feels strange to say our driveway.

From the very start with Jordan, saying "we" and "our" just felt natural. We were always meant to be an us, just like my sixteen-year-old self believed back in high school. But having that be true after all of these years still feels so surreal. That girl who had believed so fully that Jordan Thomas was meant to be hers wouldn't be able to fathom this life.

I know Jordan is home when I pull into the driveway because there are lights on in the house. I pat the gift bag on the passenger's seat beside me softly, making sure it has remained secure. I decided to wrap up the positive pregnancy test and the three others I had taken upon my return from work on Monday night and present them as a housewarming gift. I still can't decide if the idea is stupid, but there is no going back now. I take a deep breath before I turn off the car and head toward the house.

"Hello? I'm home!" I call out as I close and lock the kitchen door behind me. Part of me had expected Jordan to be cooking, but there are no signs of him.

"Hey roomie!" Jordan says playfully, poking his head around the corner of the kitchen. I think I will never not be bowled over by the sight of him.

"How was your flight?" I ask, setting my purse down in the basket by the door as he crosses the room and slips a hand behind my back. Already touching, of course.

"It was worth it," he replies, lowering his lips to mine. It's so easy to get lost in this feeling of his hands and his lips on mine, so easy to forget the very important task at hand that I must complete. I grip the paper straps of the gift bag a little tighter.

"What's in the bag?" he asks.

"I got you something," I say, still wondering if presenting it as a gift is a bad idea.

"I got you something, too," he says.

"Can I give you mine first?" I ask. I'm worried that if I wait another second, I might lose the nerve. Jordan nods, accepting the gift bag

I have held out to him. I had wrapped each pregnancy test in tissue paper and buried them under a mound of more tissue paper, and the bag weighs virtually nothing. I can't imagine what he must be thinking as he digs through it.

I hold my breath as he finds the first wrapped stick and begins to unwrap; try to read his face as he stares at what he's holding in his hand; feel the intense need to offer an explanation.

"Um, so, something happened. I thought that I could trust my birth control, but I must not have taken it at the right time or … I don't know. But, um, yeah … surprise!" I ramble softly, still unable to gauge his reaction.

"You're pregnant?" he asks. His voice is monotone and void of any emotion. I know he wants kids, but maybe this is too sudden. Maybe he's not as happy as I thought he'd be. Maybe we're not as happy as I thought we were.

"I think so. There are three other tests in there that all say the same thing," I say. "I'm sorry, I should have been more careful. I …"

"Why are you apologizing?" he asks, cutting me off. He still hasn't reacted, so what else am I supposed to do?

What I should say is that I am apologizing because it's obviously my fault that I have gotten pregnant. I am apologizing because he moved here with a different idea for what our lives were going to look like and now, I have ruined everything. I am apologizing because I didn't mean for this to happen. Instead, I say, "I … don't know."

"Pregnant," he says again to no one in particular. And then he does something that surprises me: he lets out a whoop and lifts me into his arms, spinning us both around in a circle.

"I found out on Monday, but I needed a few days to adjust to the idea," I tell him once he has returned me to the earth. "I know it's sudden and it's soon … but I think we can do it."

"We can definitely do it," he says, a smile spreading across his face. It's the same gorgeous smile that I had been enamored of in high school, the one that lights up his whole face, the one that still has the ability to make my heart do backflips inside of my chest.

"Are you happy?" I ask.

"Yes," he laughs like I am silly for even having to ask. "I love you so much, Kenley."

"I love you, too," I reply.

I let Jordan stand there for a minute, turning the pregnancy tests over and over in his hand, marveling at the idea. I had expected that he would be happy, but it still makes me feel unexpectedly relieved. He's right, we can definitely do this.

"I love my gift," he says then, giving me a kiss. "I don't know how you'll top it."

We both laugh at this because I have, indeed, set the bar high for gift-giving.

"I really love it. And it's going to go super well with the gift I have for you," he says, getting down on one knee.

Epilogue

Six Years Later

Welcome to the Bloomington High School 20th Reunion! reads the giant banner over the entrance to the hotel ballroom. It's not a mantra, but it certainly brings the same sense of foreboding that all of those others did when I was testing them out years ago. It feels like that was a lifetime ago.

"Ken?" Jordan calls from the end of my hand where our fingers have very nearly come apart as a result of my feet refusing to move forward.

"Maybe it wasn't a good idea for me to come," I say, my voice shaky. "You can go in, see all of your friends. I'll call an Uber and pick up the kids."

Jordan tugs gently on my arms and pulls me into his embrace. It makes me feel comforted but doesn't do much to change my mind. I had acquiesced to attending this reunion because I knew it was important to my husband, but the closer we have gotten to walking through those doors, the more unsure of myself I have become. It's my reunion, too, yet it feels like I am only here to support him because I am fairly certain that there is nothing inside of that room for me.

"I think you underestimate how horrible high school was for me," I say softly into his chest.

"And I think you underestimate how much people liked you," he whispers. We've been having this argument, if you can even call it that, for months; ever since the reunion was announced. He's never dismissed my feelings but has tried to help me see myself back then from his perspective. It's been hard to rewire my brain to think that way.

"But what if your mom can't handle bedtime?" I ask him, making a last-ditch effort at an excuse.

"They'll survive," Jordan says. I can hear the smile in his voice even though I can't see his face. Usually when we came back to Bloomington, we stayed with the kids the whole time, or my parents kept them and their cousins for one big sleepover. But Jordan's mom has been asking us for years to let her babysit, and since tonight's outing is only a couple of hours we had finally agreed.

"I love you, Kenley," he says.

"I love you, too," I reply. After all, if it wasn't for that, I wouldn't be here tonight at all.

Though I am still not quite ready to enter the ballroom, our private moment is soon interrupted by someone calling our names. As I prepare myself for the long night of taking a backseat to the man I married, I am surprised to turn and find that the voice belongs to one of the few friends I'd had in high school, Katie Baker. The surprise must read on my face because Jordan leans in and whispers, "Told you."

"Oh my god, you two look exactly the same. Except you're finally together," Katie says. She had been one of the few people outside of my family to know about the massive crush I'd had on Jordan back then. Katie looks relatively the same, too. In some ways twenty years is a long time, and in others it is no time at all.

"Kenley, I haven't seen you since college! What have you been up to?" she asks, genuinely curious. We had both gone to Illinois State, so we had seen each other some, but the relationship we had shared in high school had fizzled out. Katie had taken the more fun college route of pledging a sorority and thriving socially, while I had poured my heart and soul into my pre-law degree, and our plans for weekly hangouts had quickly fallen by the wayside.

"Oh, um, not much I guess," I say. Because I had been so sure that this night would be all about Jordan, I'd been unprepared for small talk, but he knows me well and squeezes my hand in reassurance.

"Kenley's being modest," he says. "She's a lawyer at her own firm in Los Angeles, working with kids in the foster system. She's won the Excellence in Family Law award from the California Law Association three times."

"That's amazing! That was always your goal. I'm so proud of you!" Katie says.

When Jordan talks about me, it is like having an out-of-body experience. The woman that he describes so passionately surely must be someone else. He makes my accomplishments sound far more impressive than they are. The accolades are nice, but I am most proud of the number of families I have been able to help, reuniting some kids with their biological families and helping others build new families through adoption.

I hadn't ever considered starting my own firm until Luke reached out about three years ago and floated the idea. Somehow we had managed to remain friends through everything that happened, and starting a firm together just made sense. It's been great to work with him again; we still work as well together as we ever did. And having his friendship in my life again is an added bonus. It helps that in a turn of events more shocking than those which transpired six years ago, Luke is now married to my friend Shanna, and their son spends all of his free time with my kids.

A crowd has begun to gather around us as we talk, which makes me want to crawl under a table, even though I am here with the most popular boy in our class. Jordan leans in and places a kiss on my temple. "I don't know any of these people, they're not here for me," he whispers.

"What else is new? Any kids?" Katie asks. Jordan immediately whips out his phone to show pictures of our pair of wildlings. After Emma, short for Emmaline for the same grandmother from whom I'd gotten my own name, was born, we had decided that since adoption was so important to me that it made sense for us to go that route, and that is how we had gotten Finn two years later. They're five and three now, and our life is constantly busy and chaotic, but it's also everything I thought I'd never get to have, and I love every minute of it.

"How about you? What have you been up to?" I ask.

"Well, I am living here in Bloomington with my husband and our four kids. My oldest is a freshman at Bloomington High, which is so wild! It seems like just yesterday we were there, and now I'm the mom!" Katie laughs. We are thirty-eight years old, and I cannot even fathom having a child in high school. I still feel like a baby myself. And I know Katie doesn't even have the oldest child among our former classmates.

"Remember how you used to wonder what life would be like if you had stayed?" Jordan whispers into my ear. He's right, I had spent so much time wondering if things would have been easier for me if I had never left Bloomington, and the answer is now staring me right in the face. I would be like Katie, who from the looks of it considers herself blessed and loves her life. I am sure that I would love my life, too, if I had been Katie. But it's hard to imagine a life different from the one I have.

As we make our way into the ballroom, I am struck not only by the number of people I recognize but by the number of people who recognize me. My memories of high school painted me as the studious wallflower who was more focused on getting out of high school than participating in it. I guess the perspective of a grown-up can change a lot of things.

"You're the prettiest girl in this room," Jordan says, lowering his mouth to my ear so that his words are just for me. This is something that he says to me in every room. It started at the wedding chapel in Las Vegas where we eloped the week after getting engaged, but in this room, it feels especially important, because back when we were in school with all of the other women who are here tonight, I felt like an absolute nothing.

People start to notice Jordan then, and by people I mean the ones who I was particularly not looking forward to seeing tonight. Most of them look much older than thirty-eight, and it makes me feel pretty good about the way that Jordan and I have kept up with ourselves.

Maybe it's the fact that we just now have young children, or maybe we have good genes. Maybe it's the California lifestyle or maybe it's sheer luck. As those who I considered to be the popular crowd in high school greet my husband after all these years, I am surprised when they acknowledge me as well, as if we'd been close back then, too.

"Kenley, I love your dress!" says Sarah Morgan, prom queen and one of Jordan's high school flames. She's pretty, just like she was back then, but she seems less outgoing now, like the sands of time have weathered her spirit. Her name tag says her name is Sarah Sanchez now, but she'll always be Sarah Morgan in my heart.

"Oh, thank you," I say sweetly, the first words I have probably ever spoken to this woman.

"Please tell me that you're a lawyer now," she says then. "I would be so disappointed if I found out that you didn't get everything you dreamed of."

It's interesting the way Jordan doesn't gloat when he's right. Apparently, I had been incredibly well liked in the halls of Bloomington High School. People had known about my dreams, and they had wanted for me to succeed. I guess it's a good thing that I didn't know about it back then, it would have put too much pressure on me. It's better to find out about it twenty years later when I have, in fact, gotten everything I ever wanted—including the man on my arm who refuses to let go even as he makes small talk with his old buddies.

Yes, *everything happens for a reason* and seeing all of these old faces tonight is a great reminder that *the only thing you can expect in life is the unexpected.* I guess I never really needed a mantra after all.

~~~~~~

Have you been wondering what Luke was thinking that night in the bar? Curious about what was going through Jordan's head when he saw Kenley in the Atlanta airport that first time? Find out in *The Difference Between Right and Wrong: Bonus Chapters.*

Sign up for my mailing list at the link below and receive these exclusive bonus chapters as a reward!

https://dl.bookfunnel.com/48y7if2bfk

$\mathcal{P.S.}$

The song that Luke sends to Kenley after their heart to heart on the curb in front of the bar is "Beyond" by Leon Bridges.

Acknowledgements

Here I find myself again, in the acknowledgments section that you're probably tapping through quickly so that this book shows 100% completed in your Kindle Library. I get it, I have done it too. But if you are reading this, THANK YOU!

I dedicated this book to my 8th grade journalism teacher who said he absolutely believed that someday I would be a novelist. Now that this is my second, I guess I can say that's true. So thank you, Mr. Slocum. You probably don't remember me at all or realize the impact your belief in me had. I'm sorry that our class got you fired.

I started the first draft of Kenley's story during Nationl Novel Writing Month in 2015. It looked vastly different then, but a decade later, I couldn't get her out of my head. Coincidentally, that is also the month that I met my husband. I wonder sometimes if the story was able to evolve the way it has because of him. Just like Kenley found with Jordan, it can be easy to change when you have the right person (or people) in your life.

That's not always exclusive to romance. I write romance, so there is an emphasis on finding love (it would kind of be a terrible romance without it), but I would be nothing without my other people and without whom this book would not be possible:
- Claire, you're my alpha reader, my beta reader, probably my omega

reader, and everything in between. You're my true soulmate and my ride or die. Thank you for supporting this book from the beginning.

- Sam, you smiled so politely back in 2015 when I sat across from you in the Santa Monica library and told you about the crazy idea I had for the first draft of this story. I cherish your feedback almost as much as your friendship. Thank you for not picturing me during THAT scene in the kitchen...

- Cheese Biscuit (Bre), can you imagine what life would be like if I hadn't inserted myself into your conversation during summer school PE? Thank you for your support and love on this writing journey.

- The president of the #TeamLuke fan-club, I mean Mom, thank you for always thinking everything I do is amazing even when it's not.

- My beta reader, Mackenzie, you responded to a call from a random author on Instagram and ended up giving me some of the best feedback on this book that I got from anyone. You may be a stranger to me, but I am forever in your debt.

To my editor Val Valentine, thank you, thank you, thank you! You were such a joy to work with and I am so happy that you actually liked the book. It was you who encouraged me to query it, and although no one in the world agreed with you, I still really appreciate the vote of confidence.

Finally, to Anna. I said it last time and I'll say it again. Everything I do is for you. You are my favorite person in the world. You are smart and sweet and funny and I can't believe I made you. I love you so much.

Thank you reader, I hope you enjoyed Kenley's story. Stay tuned for part 2!

All my love,
Lindsey Brunette

About The Author

Lindsey Brunette

Lindsey Brunette is the Los Angeles based author of Everything Old. After making the courageous choice over a decade ago to walk away from the life she had created, Lindsey is proud to have discovered the beautiful life that was waiting for her and is inspired to tell the stories of women doing the same. She lives with her husband, daughter, and menagerie of pets - including a Boston Terrier, poison dart frog, flock of backyard chickens, and a tank of fresh water shrimp. You can visit her online at LindseyBrunette.com

Books By This Author

Everything Old